EXTINCTION POINT

Also by PAUL ANTONY JONES:

TOWARD YESTERDAY

DANGEROUS PLACES (short-story compilation)

EXTINCTION POINT

PAUL ANTONY JONES

47N●RTH

Text copyright © 2012 Paul Antony Jones
All rights reserved.

Printed in the United States of America.

Published by 47North
P.O. Box 400818
Las Vegas, NV 89140

ISBN-13: 9781611097993
ISBN-10: 1611097991
Library of Congress Control Number: 2012948734

"Wild dark times are rumbling toward us."
∼ HEINRICH HEINE

"Red rain is coming down
Red Rain
Red Rain is pouring down
Pouring down all over me"
∼ PETER GABRIEL

"Who died and made you
king of anything?"
∼ SARA BAREILLES

TOMORROW

CHAPTER ONE

The waiting room was small and cramped.

Emily hated it. The drab off-white-colored walls, lined with cheap folding chairs, only added to her sense of claustrophobia. At the opposite end of the room, a bored-looking receptionist tapped at a keyboard with a single, neatly manicured finger. Her jaw worked a piece of gum; it appeared occasionally between the young woman's lips as a pink bubble before popping noisily and disappearing again.

A gray-haired man and a teenage boy sat waiting for their turn to see the doctor. The kid was absorbed in a cell phone, his thumbs flying over the tiny keyboard, while the man flipped through the pages of a tattered magazine, pausing now and then to raise a hand to his mouth to cover a dry, rasping cough.

Emily glanced at the magazine in the man's hands: *Dog Grooming Monthly,* the title read.

Why do these offices always have such weird tastes in magazines? Emily wondered as she made her way over to the receptionist's desk. *Was there some obscure magazine subscription plan especially designed for doctors', dentists', and accountants' waiting rooms?*

The receptionist was too engrossed in whatever was going on with her computer to notice Emily as she patiently waited in front of her desk. After a half minute of standing there with not even a glance from the woman, Emily cleared her throat loudly. "Hi! I'm Emily Baxter from the *Tribune*. I have an eleven o'clock appointment with Doctor Evans," she announced.

The receptionist, stopping her constant chewing momentarily so she could push the gum to one brightly rouged cheek, glanced up from her computer, which Emily could now see had some kind of game running.

"I'm sorry," said the woman, "what did you say your name was?" The bubble gum put in another brief appearance, flashing a glimpse of pink against the woman's white teeth.

"Emily…Baxter," the young reporter repeated slowly, just to make sure the receptionist got it right. "I'm from the *New York Tribune* and I'm here to interview your boss about the clinical trial he's working on."

The receptionist made an obvious pretense of checking her computer before picking up the cheap phone sitting on her desk and punching in a pair of numbers.

"Doctor Evans, I have an Amelia Bexter here for you. Yes, she *says* she's a reporter…okay." Emily matched the woman's disingenuous smile at the obvious mangling of her name. "His office is just down there," the receptionist continued, gesturing toward a corridor behind her desk. "Third door on the left."

"Thank you," said Emily as she moved in the direction the woman had indicated, but the receptionist's attention had already returned to the pressing issues of her computer game.

"Bitch!" Emily muttered under her breath before she knocked on the office door.

■ ■ ■

Forty-five minutes later, Emily allowed the door to the doctor's office to swing shut behind her. She let out a small sigh of contentment as the sounds and smells of New York City washed over her. Emily loved this city. She'd grown up in Denison, Iowa, a small backwater farm town that was as unremarkable as the hundreds of other towns surrounding it. Looking back, it seemed like she had spent most of her youth just waiting for the moment when she could get out of town and move somewhere, anywhere, as long as there were people—lots of people.

She had never *meant* to be a reporter; in fact, she had fallen into it by luck rather than design. Like many small towns, hers had an even smaller local paper. It published an issue once a week covering everything from the county sheriff's arrest record to the usual small-town politics. They had been looking for an entry-level reporter to cover the local town board meetings, and Emily had, on a whim, decided to apply for the position. Hal, the editor, had interviewed her. He was a grizzled old man who looked eighty but could well have been one hundred for all she could tell. He had been in the newspaper business since the Second World War when he had served with the US Marines' Combat Correspondent Corps. He'd told her he would try her out and pay her as a stringer for a couple of weeks. "If you fit in, we'll see about something permanent, young lady," he had told her.

Emily had taken to the job in a way she never imagined possible. Within a month, Emily had secured her place as a staff writer for the little paper. Two years later, Emily found herself promoted to lead writer. "Comfortable as a tick on a dog's ass," Hal had eloquently described her success. She stayed with the paper for another five years before she felt she had enough experience to take on the challenges of working for a bigger publication. She'd been pleasantly surprised by the number of requests for interviews she received, but had finally decided to accept an offer from the *New York Tribune* that was just too good to pass up. It was her ticket out of the small town she had longed to leave for so long.

She'd been working the metro desk at the *Tribune* for six years now and loved every minute of it. The job would never make her rich but it paid enough that she got by without having to worry about when the next paycheck was coming. She lived alone, so she didn't have a lot of the overhead other reporters had, like a family to take care of.

Emily never learned to drive; there never seemed to be a need for it. Back in Denison, she could hop on a bike and be anywhere she needed to be in less than ten minutes. In New York City, she would have spent more time stuck in traffic jams than she could afford, so she stuck with her trusty bike. For longer jaunts, she would usually take the subway.

Of course, no matter how much she loved the job and the city, there would always be days like today. It was sweltering hot, ninety-two degrees with 65 percent humidity. When you coupled the coma-inducing humidity and heat with the idiot receptionist and her equally annoying boss, you had the makings of a less than perfect day. But Emily didn't mind too much; it was almost noon and she had her first story for the day in the bag, which meant she was already ahead of the game.

She had a choice now: head back to the newsroom or grab a bite to eat at a local café and then write up her article. Emily pulled her smartphone from its holder on her belt and checked her itinerary for the day. She had another three hours before her next appointment, so the choice was hers.

There was a small Internet café a couple of blocks away that she knew also did an astoundingly good BLT sandwich. At the thought of it, her stomach gave a little grumble. Well, that decided it, then. Emily unlocked the chain securing her bike to a no-parking sign, slung her backpack over her shoulder, and set off in the direction of lunch.

■ ■ ■

Emily brought her bike to a stop in front of the café. She chained the bike to the security rack the store had courteously installed just outside and walked into the café.

As she entered the air-conditioned interior of the café, Emily felt the sweat under her armpits chill uncomfortably enough to give her a little shiver. The mellow sound of smooth jazz and the smells of roasted coffee and fresh baked bread immediately grabbed her attention. Her stomach grumbled in anticipation.

In complete contrast to her reception at the doctor's office, a warm and honest smile from the café's owner greeted Emily as she walked to the counter. "Good afternoon, young lady. What can I get for you today?" he asked, a slight accent betraying his Italian origins.

"I'll take a cappuccino," Emily said after looking over the chalkboard list of coffees, "and a BLT for here, please."

The café was deserted—the lunchtime rush was still an hour away—so she had her pick of tables. She chose a four-seater near the window where she could keep an eye on her bike while she ate. Emily pulled her laptop from the backpack and hit the power button. It only took a minute for the computer to boot up and locate the café's wireless Internet signal. Emily clicked on her e-mail client and waited for it to load any e-mails she'd received since going incommunicado over the past couple of hours. There was a message from her editor at the paper reminding her to get her stories in before deadline, along with the usual collection of spam promising to increase her penis size and offering cheap prescription medication imported directly from China. Nothing important.

She pulled up her web browser and checked CNN. There was the usual potpourri of stories on the news website's front page: conflicts still raged across some godforsaken third-world country, a politician had been caught with his pants down *again*, reports of some weird weather throughout Europe, and some thoroughly uninspiring stock market numbers that meant her 401(k) was going to be worth even less than it was yesterday.

Emily clicked on the weather article and began reading.

The Associated Press was reporting a strange phenomenon throughout most parts of Europe, the article said. Local government agencies were reporting an "unknown red precipitation" with no apparent meteorological cause. The first case had been reported in Smolensk, Russia, over twelve hours ago. Similar reports of what the news agencies had conveniently, if somewhat unoriginally, labeled "red rain" were coming in from Finland, Sweden, Poland, Germany, the UK, and Spain as the day had progressed.

"Anything interesting going on in the world?" the café owner asked as he placed the plate with her sandwich next to her steaming cup of coffee.

Emily looked up and smiled. "Not unless you want to talk about the weather," she said. Apparently, that didn't appeal to the café owner as he fired another smile her way before walking back to his counter. Emily took a large bite from her sandwich—it was absolutely delicious. Being careful not to let any crumbs fall on her keyboard, she continued reading the news report.

CNN had decided to eschew the European press's "red rain" nomenclature and had instead labeled the phenomenon "blood rain." *Right,* her reporter's brain thought. *Good move. Give an arbitrary weather phenomenon a scary-sounding name and it makes the whole nonevent sound that much more frightening and threatening. It virtually guarantees a front-page article and probably gives the writer a chance at a couple of follow-up stories too. Lucky bastard!*

The news piece also had a selection of quotes from eyewitnesses to the blood rain epidemic sweeping across Europe. The witnesses reported that the rain had begun falling at around 12:30 p.m., seemingly from nowhere. "It smelled funny and when I licked it, it tasted like sour milk," one witness in Smolensk had said.

Why the hell would you stick that stuff in your mouth? Emily wondered. The level of some people's intelligence never failed to amaze her. *Who knows where it came from?*

There was no denying it was an interesting story, she had to admit, but the probability was that some unknown chemical plant in an equally unknown part of Russia had gone all Chernobyl and was spilling this toxic red shit into the atmosphere. And, knowing the former Soviet Union's track record for reporting these kinds of accidents, well, it would probably be months or even years before the offending chemical plant was located. Even then the Russians would maintain their "lie, lie until you die" policy of nonadmission. Some things just never changed.

Emily took another large bite from her sandwich and glanced at the clock on the wall behind the counter: the digital display showed 12:28. *Time to get my ass into gear.* She began the process of shutting down her computer and packing it away for the bike ride back to the paper.

Outside the café's window, she could see the daily bustle of life in New York City continuing as it had for countless years. The people changed, the buildings got dirtier and taller, but it all really just boiled down to folks getting on with their lives, doing the best they could to stay in the rat race.

Emily loved it.

"That'll be $8.75," the Italian man behind the counter said. Emily swiped her debit card and typed in her PIN, pocketing the receipt in a small pouch she carried with her. Come tax season every little bit would help.

"Have a great…" He stopped midsentence, his eyes looking over her left shoulder, out to the street behind her. "Whaddya think's going on out there?" he asked almost to himself. Emily noticed a slightly confused look cross the man's face as she twisted around to see what he was talking about.

Through the window, she could see heat shimmer playing off the sidewalk and the asphalt-covered road. Instead of the usual hustle and bustle she had noticed just a few minutes earlier, she saw that many of the pedestrians were now simply standing still. Most were shading their eyes against the bright sun as they looked skyward.

"What the…?" exclaimed Emily, taking a step closer to the window.

From the cloudless New York sky, a crimson rain had begun to fall with the force of a light summer shower. The drops pattered onto the scorching sidewalk, and began collecting into small bloody red puddles.

A thick glob of the red liquid splashed against the store window. Emily watched it slide slowly down the glass; it seemed far more viscous than normal rain and she suddenly had an inkling of how appropriate the label "blood rain" was. In the space of a few seconds, the light drizzle increased to a heavy shower. Red rain pummeled the sidewalks, roads, and buildings beyond the sanctuary of the café. It clung to the glass of the window like mud, or, more appropriately, like blood splatter at a murder scene. Gravity slowly pushed it down the windowpane, leaving a bloodlike trail of the viscous liquid behind. More drops hit the window; these were larger and hit with enough force that she could hear the thump of the impact against the glass. It was almost as loud as hail.

Pedestrians, who had until moments before stood staring in confused fascination at the bizarre spectacle, scattered and ran for shelter. Some held briefcases or clutch bags over their heads as they sprinted under awnings or into doorways and stores. Within seconds, everyone caught outside looked like victims from a slasher movie, their thin summer shirts stained carmine and any exposed area dripping with the blood rain, which seemed capable of adhering to anything it came into contact with.

This is unbelievable!

Emily strained her neck to try to get a better view. It was hard to see clearly because the buildings were so tall, but she could just make out a patch of clear blue high above the rooftops. There were no clouds that she could see and no sign of any aircraft that could have been dumping this stuff—just a pincushion of red dots dropping from an empty sky. So much was falling now that large pools of the gunk had formed on the pavements, fed by the overflowing gutters of the buildings that spewed bloody waterfalls onto the streets below like severed arteries. Streams of the rain ran into the street's gutters and along the sidewalks.

A sudden thud caused Emily to give a yell of surprise and leap back from the window. Something large had hit it and fallen flapping to the pavement just outside. It was a pigeon, covered in the red rain; the half-blinded bird had flown straight into the café's storefront. The bird, with one wing obviously broken, flapped and convulsed in a circle for a few seconds, twitched twice, and then lay motionless on the sidewalk.

As Emily stood mesmerized by the pigeon's final moments, she heard the storeowner exhale a single heavily accented expletive. "*Merda*," he hissed under his breath, reverting to his native Italian in disbelief.

Emily looked up from the dead pigeon in time to see more birds dropping from the sky. They spiraled down like autumn leaves, bouncing off car roofs or hitting the sides of buildings, then falling into the road where some were promptly crushed beyond recognition under the wheels of the few cars still moving. Emily wasn't sure, but she thought she saw crows mixed in with the dying pigeons. Something even larger—was that a seagull?—crashed into the windshield of a parked car across the street, setting off the antitheft alarm, which whooped and wailed in protest.

And then, just as suddenly as it had all begun, the deluge began to slow. The harsh patter faded away to nothing, leaving behind congealing pools of the strange red liquid clinging and dripping from every exposed surface, and eight million utterly perplexed New Yorkers.

■ ■ ■

Within minutes of the red rain stopping, people began to abandon their shelter, tentatively edging out from wherever they had managed to take cover. Some, in typical New Yorker fashion, seemed totally unfazed by the event, interested only in continuing on with whatever they had been doing before the interruption to their day, apparently unconcerned with the unprecedented phenomenon they had just witnessed. Others, in complete contrast, decided to bide their time, choosing to stay exactly where they were rather than risk being caught in another downpour of blood. Emily could see their wide eyes peeking out from under awnings, while others had their faces pressed to windows staring up at the sky, their mouths agape or relaying back what they could see to those who had sought shelter with them.

Emily's heart rate slowly began to return to its normal level as she continued to watch, choosing to stay behind the safety of the café's front door, unwilling to leave the shelter it offered. Those of a more inquisitive nature had begun examining the remnants of the bloody storm—which, from what Emily could see of the puddles outside the café, appeared to be slowly evaporating into the early afternoon heat.

"Jesus!" Emily exclaimed, her natural reporter's inquisitiveness finally getting the better of her as she cautiously opened the door of the café and stepped out onto the sidewalk.

Dead birds lay everywhere, hundreds of them, their bodies littering the road, sidewalks, and parked vehicles. Each tiny body was silhouetted by a halo of the slowly dissipating red goop. It took another couple of minutes for Emily to realize she was missing a perfect opportunity for a story. She unslung her backpack, pulled her Nikon from its case, and began shooting a panoramic HD video of the scene. After she'd recorded enough footage she switched the camera to regular photo mode and began firing off close-ups of the dead birds, the pale shocked faces of bewildered locals, and, most importantly of all, the now fast disappearing remnants of red rain. A few globules of the red stuff still hung from the handlebars of her bike, and she took photos of it as it dripped obscenely into a small puddle around her front tire.

Through the macroscopic zoom of the camera Emily could see that the rain, or whatever the hell it actually was, was not simply evaporating or being absorbed into the pavement like normal liquid. Instead, the red goop looked as though it was breaking apart into smaller pieces. As Emily continued to shoot footage of the puddle she saw one piece simply disintegrate into hundreds of tiny red particles that flipped and somersaulted on the street's warm currents of air like an aerosol spray, before spiraling away like the dandelion seeds she used to love to watch float on an evening breeze as a kid.

"What do you think that was?" asked a young man, startling her from her observation. The kid had been sheltering under the awning of a bookstore next to the café. Streaks of red stained his white business shirt, and Emily could see droplets of the rain still clinging to his hair. "I mean, where did it come from? There were no clouds at all."

Emily considered his question for a moment before replying, "I have no fucking clue, no clue at all."

CHAPTER TWO

Emily stepped back into the café.

"So, whaddya think it is?" the owner asked. He had chosen to stay safely behind his counter and Emily couldn't say she blamed him.

"Your guess is as good as mine," she answered. The old Italian seemed to take her reply in stride, nodding as if she had confirmed something he'd already known.

"Is not natural," he said to no one in particular.

Emily had been meticulous about avoiding the remainder of the red rain, carefully stepping around the puddles on the sidewalk and avoiding any kind of skin contact with the crap. But there was still a splatter of the stuff on her bike's handlebars and she wasn't going to risk touching it if she could help it.

"Can I grab a couple of these?" she asked the Italian, pointing at a container of disinfecting wipes on the side counter.

"Sure, sure," said the old man. "Help yourself."

Emily pulled five of the wipes from the plastic dispenser and walked back out to her bike. She carefully wiped down the handlebars, leather seat, and the crossbar and frame, making sure to toss the used sheets into the trashcan outside the café.

Satisfied with the cleanup, Emily climbed onto the saddle of her bike, gave the café owner an A-OK thumbs-up accompanied by her brightest smile, and then began pedaling back in the direction of the *Tribune*'s offices.

Already the daily routine of New York City had begun to swing back toward normal, as though the downpour of red rain from the afternoon's empty blue sky was an everyday occurrence and not something that should stop the city dead in its tracks. On the streets, the usual sluggish flow of vehicles continued much as it did every day. Horns sounded in outrage as pedestrians chanced their luck at jaywalking and drivers' tempers began to fray. Tourists wandered aimlessly, staring in store windows and snapping pictures with expensive-looking cameras, apparently oblivious to the dead birds littering the sidewalks, while the occasional kamikaze cyclist tempted fate hurtling between vehicles.

But, here and there, Emily spotted remnants of the red rain: in puddles on the sidewalk, on stained clothing, and on the occasional worried face of a passerby. And, she noted, the air now seemed full of barely visible particles of red dust, floating on the warm eddies wafting past her like pollen.

While the majority of the city seemed to have already shrugged off the event, Emily sensed this was no normal day. She knew, with a concrete certainty that sank deep to the bottom of her stomach, the world would remember this day, and those that followed it, for as long as there was still a human race.

■ ■ ■

There are few things more disconcerting to a career reporter than to walk into a paper's newsroom and find it silent. It's where the stories are made, put together, and researched. On any normal day, no matter what time you walked in, the room should be a controlled commotion of reporters running back and forth, consulting in corners, or answering ringing phones; the newsroom is the beating heart of any newspaper.

And as Emily pushed through the double doors into what should have been a room full of chaos and noise—especially given the incredible meteorological events she had just witnessed—what greeted her instead was the sonic equivalent of a library reading room.

Pausing for a moment, she scanned the room. While the day shift of thirty-plus journalists and editorial staff all seemed present and correct, instead of being at their workstations eagerly putting together that evening's edition, they had gathered in groups around the five 50-inch TV screens mounted on the walls of the room. On a normal day, each TV would be tuned to a different major national or international news channel, ready to catch any breaking stories that may have escaped the paper's ever-watchful staff. Right now, every screen showed CNN. The reporting staff, all the way up to the senior editor himself, stood silently watching as others reported on a developing story that, on any other day, they would be tirelessly pursuing.

No one noticed Emily as she entered the newsroom. There was none of the usual banter or greetings from her friends and comrades; in fact, not one pair of eyes shifted from the TV screens to Emily as she moved to her cubicle and dropped her backpack on the desk.

There were only a couple of possible reasons for the paper to come to a grinding halt, especially this close to a deadline. The first was that no one had witnessed the event that had happened less than an hour ago. Emily instantly dismissed this theory, as it was obvious everyone must be aware of what had just happened. She could see from the crimson stains on her workmates' clothing that some, like her, had been away from the office when the red rain struck.

The second reason, and Emily found this *very* hard to believe, was that a news event even more earthshaking had supplanted the one Emily thought would be the biggest event to demand a paper's headlines since the 9/11 attacks…and that idea frightened Emily very much.

"Emily? Where have you been? You okay?" The barrage of questions from Sven Konkoly, one of the paper's assistant editors, broke her introspection.

"Yes. Out. Fine," she fired back before taking a deep breath to calm nerves she hadn't even realized were frazzled. "What's going on? Did you see what just happened?" she asked, her hand fluttering toward the window.

Sven ignored her question. "Come on over here," he demanded. "You need to take a look at this, right now." Not waiting for Emily to comply, Sven grabbed her by her elbow and guided her to the group crowded around the nearest TV. On screen, a female CNN news anchor was talking to a young man via a laptop videophone connection. His frightened face filled a box in the top right corner of the screen, giving the appearance he was talking over the news anchor's shoulder. A caption under the image of the man read, "Francois Reveillion." Emily estimated that he was no more than twenty-six, maybe twenty-eight, tops. His eyes were bloodshot and betrayed a barely restrained panic that belied the calmly delivered answers he was giving to the news anchor's questions.

"—exactly is going on there? Can you describe what you're seeing?"

When the young man spoke it was with heavily accented English. Emily guessed he was either French or maybe Belgian.

"Everyone is very, very sick," Francois said, his face so close to the lens of the camera Emily could see the pale, almost translucent quality of his skin. Red veins stood out on his forehead and a spider's web of tiny broken blood vessels seemed to be spreading from his left temple to his cheek, terminating just above the man's blond mustache. Emily could see beads of sweat pooling on his forehead and beginning to drip slowly down his face. When he turned his head and looked away from the camera for a second she saw more of the ruptured blood vessels on his neck. His eyes were striated with thick lines of red, and deep pockets of blood had collected in the corner of each eye until little of the normal white remained. He looked like a boxer who'd just taken a twelve-round pummeling.

"People are dying here," he said. "Many people. They are becoming sick and then they just die. I see them on the streets, in their cars. There are many, many dead here."

"When you say that there are many deaths, how many? Can you tell us?"

The man paused for a second before replying, "Everyone," he said. "Everyone is dead." His voice stuttered slightly as the terror everyone knew he felt momentarily flashed across his face.

"Look, I will show you," he continued. The screen wobbled as he picked up the laptop and carried it a short distance before turning the lens to face out through a second-story set of bay windows. It was dark wherever Francois was broadcasting from, but light from several street lamps cast enough illumination for those gathered around the TV to be able to make out a tree-lined street with rows of two-story houses on either side. The houses, nothing but dark square-shaped silhouettes, looked European in design, like some of the pictures Emily had once seen of villages in Provence. There seemed to be several cars randomly parked in the road. A white compact was resting half on the sidewalk, its rear end straddling the curb of the road, a telltale plume of exhaust fumes floating up from the vehicle's still-running engine.

"What are those?" a reporter next to Emily asked, pointing to several dark, almost indistinguishable shapes scattered randomly on the sidewalk and in the road. One of the shapes seemed to be slumped against a streetlight.

"Are those bodies? Fuck! Those are bodies!" The panic in the young reporter's voice made his words rise in pitch as he uttered each expletive.

Emily quickly counted at least fifteen unmoving shapes lying in the street. It was impossible to distinguish their sex from this distance, but she could see one that definitely looked small enough to be that of a child. Next to the child a larger form lay spread-eagled on the pavement, one arm seemingly reaching out to the motionless body of the child.

This was bad, she realized. This was probably *very* bad.

The view on the screen switched from the street back to the face of the young man and a gasp of astonishment mixed with horror escaped from many of those watching. In the few seconds the camera was focused on the unfolding disaster outside, the striations in the man's eyes had spread until no white could be seen at all; his eyes looked like two pools of congealed blood. The network of veins Emily had noticed earlier had doubled in thickness and now extended across his entire face. A delicate web of veins appeared suddenly on his cheeks and a steady stream of thick bloody mucous began flowing from both of his nostrils.

Perhaps it was just her own fear reflected back at her but, despite the obliteration of his eyes, which were now nothing but black pits, Emily thought she could still see the terror he was experiencing captured in them. As the group continued to watch in morbid fascination, Francois's mouth opened and closed once as though trying to speak. Instead of words a thick gush of red liquid exploded from his mouth. Droplets splattered against the camera lens and he dropped from view, replaced by the image of a chair leg as the laptop computer toppled from his hands and fell to the floor. A low, gurgling moan filtered through the TV speakers but it was quickly silenced as the newsfeed cut back to the CNN presenter.

The female presenter was visibly shaking, her skin so pale even the layer of makeup she wore could not hide it. She pulled herself together and continued her narration. "If…if you're just joining us…" Her words were lost to Emily as a petite blonde standing next to her suddenly began to sob and grabbed for Emily's hand.

"Oh, no! Oh, no!" the woman, whom Emily did not recognize, gasped repeatedly. The pretty young girl's voice was tinged with a growing tone of panic, and Emily felt the woman's grasp on her hand tighten as tears began to stream down her face. "Is that going to happen to me?" she bleated, her voice barely audible as she clutched at her own crimson-stained blouse with her free hand. "Am I going to *die?*"

Emily squeezed the woman's hand back as firmly as she could. "No, of course not," she said, although she could hear the lack of conviction in her own voice. "We're going to be just fine," Emily reassured her, mustering as much faith to her voice as she was able and reinforcing her weak words with a forced smile.

Sven pulled Emily aside. "Do you believe this shit? Jesus Christ!"

"What about the other news outlets? What are they saying?" Emily asked.

"The same: first the red rain comes and then people die. There's been no news from anywhere east of Germany for hours. It looks like the whole of Europe's fucking *dead*."

■ ■ ■

"So, just what are we supposed to do exactly?" asked Frank Embry, one of the crime-beat reporters. Embry was in his late sixties and looked as though he had been plucked right out of the pages of a Raymond Chandler novel. His hair was always slicked back and he would never be found without his gray raincoat—Frank insisted on calling it a mack—that he wore in winter and slung over his arm in summer. He'd always carry a rolled-up copy of the previous day's *Tribune* in his free hand. "It adds to the mystique," he would tell anyone who asked why he chose to dress like that. Most every other reporter thought he was a little nuts, but Emily thought it was quite charming.

The full staff of the *Tribune* crammed into the lower-floor meeting room. Senior editorial management had decided to call a conference and pulled everyone in twenty minutes after Emily arrived back at the office. A feeling of dread permeated the little meeting room, not helped by the overbearing smell of sweat as too many people crowded into too small a space. Senior staff members were already seated around the eight-person conference table when Emily joined the meeting. The rest of the paper's employees were either standing or leaning against the walls.

"It's really up to you guys," said Konkoly. "On any other day, I'd say we stay at our posts. I mean, shit, everyone remembers

9/11; we didn't leave for three days. But this? This is a whole other bucket of fish."

Under other circumstances, Emily—along with the majority of the staff—would have laughed aloud at Konkoly's unintentional slip of the tongue. He had a habit of mangling idioms when he was nervous, which was endearing and often hilarious, but his mistake went unnoticed today.

"I've spoken with both the senior editor and the publisher," Konkoly continued, "and, while they would obviously like to see today's paper go out, they're watching the TV too. They told me to tell you it was your choice whether we stay or we go."

"You got that right," a voice piped up from the far side of the room.

Konkoly looked around the room at the grim faces staring back at him. "I'm pretty sure I know what the result will be already, but let's see a show of hands for those who want to call it a day and get out of here." All except Frank raised their hands. He continued to lean against the wall, his hands folded in front of him. He'd left his mack at his desk.

"Frank?" The assistant editor's voice was tinged with concern for the eccentric crime reporter.

"I'm staying," Frank replied stubbornly. "I've been with this paper for almost thirty years and I'll be damned if I'm leaving now."

"Jesus, Frank, were you watching the TV? You saw what's happening in Europe. What do you think this town's going to be like if that happens here?" Emily couldn't see who had spoken, but judging by the thick Brooklyn accent it was probably Janice, one of the paper's legion of proofreaders. "You have to go home. Who knows how long this is going to last? It could be days before everything gets back to normal."

"This *is* my home," replied Frank. "Besides, there's no one for me to go home to. At least if I'm here I can do some good. Don't worry about me. I'll be fine. And when this all blows over, I'll be the first to tell you 'I told ya so.'" He added a halfhearted smile to his last statement that seemed to convince everyone he was resolute about staying put.

"All right, people. It's decided: this paper is officially closed until this all blows over. I'll see you all then. Keep your cell phones close; we'll call you when we need you. In the meantime...don't you all have homes to go to?"

The paper's staff began filing out of the meeting; what little conversation there was continued in hushed, subdued voices. Emily stopped at her cubicle and waited, pretending to check through her mail while the rest of the staff grabbed their belongings and headed toward the exit. Finally, when only Frank and Sven were left, she walked over to them. Frank's back was to Emily as he talked with Sven. She pulled the elbow of his tweed jacket to get his attention.

"Emily, my dear," he said, turning to look at her. "I thought I saw your beautiful face in the meeting room. What a day, eh? What a day."

"It truly sucks, Frank. Listen, why don't you come home and stay with me? I've got the room. There's no need to stay here alone."

Frank smiled at her, his gray eyes twinkling, "While I appreciate the offer, I'm going to man my post. Besides, I won't be alone; Mr. Konkoly here has decided to keep me company, haven't you?"

Konkoly just nodded, and while his mouth smiled, his eyes were unconvinced. "Yeah, someone's got to make sure this old coot doesn't run off with the computers."

"You're sure? The both of you are more than welcome to stay with me."

"While the offer is tempting," said Frank, "we're staying. You'll find us right here when you come back. Don't worry."

Konkoly simply smiled and shrugged. Both men looked at her reassuringly and she knew they wouldn't budge.

"Take care, you two," she said over her shoulder as she turned and walked back to collect her belongings from her desk. "You know where I am if you change your mind. Just give me a call and let me know you're on your way if you change your mind. Okay?"

She smiled as she caught Frank's whispered words to Sven, "Oh, if only I were thirty years younger, I might just take her up on that offer. Life is just so damn unfair."

■ ■ ■

Emily pushed through the *Tribune*'s revolving doors and stepped out onto the street. The day seemed just like any other, the streets filled with people and vehicles intent on getting wherever it was they were headed. She couldn't detect any hint of panic or even an undercurrent of unease as she stood for a moment watching. It looked like the news of the deaths in Europe had not yet reached the majority of the city's occupants. Everything looked and sounded so normal. Down the street, near the intersection, Emily heard the screech of brakes followed by a burst of profanity. While the world was falling apart around them, the people of New York continued with their day, either oblivious or uncaring of what was happening across the ocean in Europe.

Occasionally, some would pass her with a look of worry fixed to their faces, cell phones pushed firmly against their ears as they spoke in low concerned tones to those on the other end of the line, maneuvering their way through the crowd and on to some unknown destination. Emily thought she was probably witnessing the slow dissemination of the news as it gradually filtered down to the city's inhabitants.

At some point the spread of information would reach a tipping point among the city's inhabitants, a critical mass that Emily knew would turn this city inside out and upside down. As news of the deaths across the Atlantic became common knowledge, people *would* panic, and then New York would become a very dangerous place to be caught out in the open. It was imperative she got home as quickly as possible. She needed to prepare for whatever was heading her way. Emily had seen enough disaster movies in her time to know whatever came next was not going to be pretty.

She moved out into the crowd, cutting diagonally against the flow of pedestrians so she could reach the bike. She released the lock and unthreaded the chain from between the bike's wheels, stowed the chain in her backpack, checked there were no taxis using the bike lane as a shortcut, and, when she saw it was clear, began pedaling toward home.

■ ■ ■

Forty minutes after leaving the *Tribune* offices, Emily pulled up outside her apartment block. She locked her bike to the security stand out front and headed inside.

The lobby was busier than it should have been at this time of day—a sure sign, she thought, that news of the deaths sweeping across Europe had finally begun to filter onto the general populace's radar. A group of five people waited nervously in front of the elevator. They looked scared, more scared than she had seen anyone since leaving the *Tribune*'s newsroom. She wondered how much information had actually trickled down in the time it had taken her to get home.

Emily recognized a couple of the tenants waiting in front of the elevator and almost said hello, but she noticed stains from the red rain on their clothes and thought better of it, choosing instead to simply nod, smile, and keep what was hopefully a safe distance between them and her. She had managed to keep herself free of any contact with the red rain so far. She did not know if that would matter in the long run, but it was probably better not to take any chances and to remain as far away as possible from those who had been caught in the deluge.

She had no way to tell how the agent—or pathogen or whatever this red rain turned out to be—had killed those people in Europe, or how it was spread. For all she knew, it could be airborne and simply breathing the same air or touching a doorknob used by an infected person could mean the difference between living and dying. In fact, it was probably a good idea to avoid enclosed spaces like the cabin of the elevator, and avoid any con tact with possibly contaminated people, period.

"Jesus!" she said aloud, surprised at how little time it had taken her survival instincts to label everyone a potential threat to her life. She felt shitty for thinking that way, but how else was she *supposed* to think? Less than two hours ago, she had witnessed a man die horribly, live on TV. And if that was what lay in store for the people of New York, well, she was sure as hell going to do whatever it took to guarantee it didn't happen to her.

With that thought still burning brightly in her mind, Emily opened the door to the emergency stairwell and began climbing the stairs up to her apartment.

CHAPTER THREE

Emily knew how lucky she was to have snagged her apartment. Perfectly placed on the Upper West Side of Manhattan, it was just a stone's throw from the Hudson River and some of the most amazing restaurants in the area. It was also handy for the Sixty-Sixth Street and Lincoln Center subway station, if she needed it. It was rare, but sometimes her stories took her outside of her comfortable biking range.

The kind of rent her apartment usually went for was well outside what Emily would normally be able to afford on a journalist's salary, but she'd landed it for an unbelievable price after she'd written a flattering piece for the owner of the complex. Her article had helped him fill vacant units and he'd been very happy with her. To show his appreciation he had given her a sweet discount; that's how it worked out sometimes, just one of the perks of the job. Who was she to complain?

The apartment was a one-bedroom, one-bath studio on the seventeenth of twenty-five floors. She knew a couple of the other tenants on her floor; most were single professionals, but there was a married couple in one of the apartments and a single mom with a eight-month-old little boy—his name was Ben and he was just so adorable—a few apartments down from Emily's. While the majority of her neighbors were friendly, she knew them on nodding terms only; everyone kept to themselves for the most part, which was fine by her.

The complex had its own gym in the basement area and a covered community pool on the roof. Not that Emily ever had the time to use either, of course, but it was nice to know they were there if she ever decided to take advantage. One day, maybe when she retired, she'd get to use them, but until that day she was just too busy and far too committed to her job to be bothered with minor distractions like staying healthy. Besides, her daily bicycle commute was more exercise than the majority of people got in a month.

Emily grabbed a diet soda from the fridge and walked into the living room. The far wall was framed by a large bay window that looked out over the nearby rooftops toward the Hudson River and beyond. She was secretly in love with whoever had designed the apartments because they were smart enough to include a seat beneath the window where she could sit and watch the world pass by. Emily called the little area her roost. It was just a wooden bench with a thick layer of padding and a pastel-blue microfiber cover, but it was one of her favorite places to sit and unwind from the many and varied stresses her job threw at her on a daily basis.

Emily kicked off her shoes and sat down on the bench. Pulling her legs up to her chin, she took a long pull of her soda and stared out over the city. While most of her view was blocked by a row of equally tall buildings positioned between her apartment block and the Hudson, she could still see the tree-lined shore of West New York in the distance.

Until today, Emily had always thought of the sprawling metropolis of New York as a microcosm of the US, a multicultural machine with very different parts that, despite their differences, worked together for the common good of all. It was loud, it was brash, and it was unapologetic. It had always seemed too unstoppable in its continual forward movement. That all changed today. Not since the dark days of 9/11 had she seen so much fear on people's faces.

Emily looked down at the street. The buildings were mainly older office blocks, but sprinkled here and there was the occasional small store. Within walking distance, a hungry office worker could find a coffee shop and a florist, and just across the street from her place, a small corner convenience store that kept a stock of canned goods, newspapers, and candy.

As Emily's eyes roamed the buildings, she saw a flurry of motion in the street. A group of about twenty people had gathered outside the convenience store. At this distance, there was no way she could hear what the group was saying, but their body language was unmistakable; they were pissed. Fingers were being pointed, fists clenched, and people were being pushed. Most of the anger seemed to be directed at a single man; he stood in the doorway of the store, his hands raised to the side of his head, palms out, as though trying to tell the angry crowd to stay back. The crowd, which seemed one wrong word away from being reclassified to mob status by Emily, apparently wasn't having any of it.

Emily thought she saw a fist connect with the man's face and then he disappeared in a mass of flailing arms and bodies as the crowd pushed their way forward, surging through the narrow doorway and into the little store. Seconds later, she watched as people began running from the store, their hands full of the shop's stock. She watched a man trip and fall, the cans and bottles of water he carried spilling from his hands as he sprawled into the road, narrowly avoiding a speeding SUV that barely managed to swerve around him. The vehicle didn't even try to brake, Emily noted. By the time the man raised himself to his feet and dusted himself off, others had already grabbed everything he'd stolen. He stood dazed in the middle of the road for a moment, then took off running up the street, quickly disappearing from Emily's view.

Emily had seen plenty of disturbing incidents during her time at the paper, but there was something uniquely upsetting about the scene she had just watched play out beneath her window. She felt... impotent. It was like watching someone she loved dearly succumb to madness, and there was no one and nothing that could help.

The sound of someone knocking at her apartment door dragged Emily from her thoughts. She wasn't expecting company so it could only be Konkoly and Frank. They must have changed their minds and decided to take her up on her offer to stay with her. But if that was true, why hadn't they called ahead to let her know they were on their way?

"Coming," she called and walked to the front door.

The owner of the building was big on security, so every apartment was equipped with a peephole that gave the occupant a fisheye view of the corridor directly outside. When Emily placed her eye to the viewer it wasn't her colleagues from the paper; instead, she saw a police officer standing outside her door.

■ ■ ■

Emily unlatched the security chain and opened the front door. The cop was a good six-two, with sandy brown hair cut so short most of it was concealed beneath his cap. A nametag over the left breast pocket of his uniform jacket read MEADOWS.

"Nathan? Thank God you're here," she said, giving him a kiss on the cheek. "Have you heard what's going on? Do you know anything?"

The cop didn't answer; instead, he pushed past Emily into the apartment entrance and then turned to face her.

"Shut the door," he said brusquely, his usually calm voice laced with an edge of panic she had never heard before.

"Jesus, Nathan. Not even a hello?" she replied, allowing anger to creep into her voice, more to cover her own uneasiness than because she was truly annoyed at him.

"I'm sorry, Em," he said. He leaned in to kiss her firmly on the mouth. When he finally released her, she took a single step back and stared up into the face of her boyfriend.

"I thought you were on duty today."

"I'm supposed to be," he answered as he walked toward the kitchen, "but, Em, it's crazy out there. I couldn't even get within ten miles of the precinct. Everyone's leaving Manhattan and heading out of the city. The roads are jammed, people are going crazy." He stepped around the counter to the sink, took a glass from the cupboard, and filled it from the faucet.

"I tried calling the captain," he continued, as he sipped at the water, "but the lines are all busy. I thought I'd check on you and hole up here for a couple of hours until the roads clear, and then I'd head in."

They took a few minutes to talk about what they knew. Nathan had seen the same newscast as Emily and had no more information than she had.

"How bad do you think it will be?" Emily asked eventually, trying to keep her voice from betraying the panic she could feel in the pit of her stomach.

"Honestly, I don't know, Em. But shit, did you *see* the red rain? I was on my way out the door when it came and there wasn't a cloud in the sky. You're the reporter; how do you explain that?"

She couldn't, of course. She'd seen the same phenomenon and had no idea how the rain had fallen from a clear sky. "I can't," she finally said, and moved around the counter to join him. "All I know is that I'm glad you're here." She reached out and took hold of the lapels of his jacket, pulled him to her, and kissed him again.

As she released him, Emily felt something wet beneath her fingers. She glanced down at her hand and gasped, feeling the world shrink until the only thing that existed were the tips of her fingers...and the dapple of red covering them.

"Oh!" she said in disbelief, and, as realization of what she was looking at sank in, added a sharp: "*Shit!*" She turned and ran to the kitchen. Throwing open the cabinet beneath the sink, she grabbed the bottle of Clorox bleach.

"Shit! Shit! Shit!" she whispered through panic-stretched lips. She rammed the plug into the drain, then emptied the entire liter container of bleach into the sink, tossed the empty bottle onto the counter, and plunged her hands into the bleach. She counted the seconds off in her head: *one-one-thousand...two-one-thousand... three-one-thousand...*

Only after she was sure her hands had been submerged for at least thirty seconds did she pull them out, just long enough to grab a scouring pad from the counter and begin rubbing furiously at the remaining red stains on her hands.

This cannot be happening, she thought. After all the precautions, after managing to avoid contact with that fucking rain all day and everyone who might have come into contact with it, she'd been tripped up by something as simple as wanting to kiss her boyfriend?

How fucking fair was that?

Emily began to sob quietly to herself as the full weight of the day finally broke through the crack of her consciousness, delivering an emotional sledgehammer blow against her chest.

"Jesus, Em. Are you okay?" Nathan was at her side, a hand resting gently on her shoulder.

She spun around and knocked his hand away. "Why didn't you tell me you had that shit on you?" she yelled, spittle flying from her lips. Nathan flinched and took a step back. While they'd had their arguments since being together, he'd never seen her as upset or as angry as she felt now. "You should have told me, goddamn it. Why didn't you tell me?"

"I…I'm sorry, Em," he stuttered. "I didn't even think…"

Emily looked up at Nathan's horrified face, his concern for her was so obvious and his reaction to her fear so like him. It was a big reason why she loved him.

They had met just over two years earlier at the scene of a multiple-car pileup. The accident claimed the lives of a young family of three along with two other drivers. The guy that had caused the crash—smashed out of his gourd, of course—had walked away with just a couple of scratches.

"How romantic is *that!*" she would usually tell people who asked how two seemingly polar opposites had got together. But the truth was, Nathan was the only cop Emily had met in all her years on the job who was still moved by the arbitrary nature of destruction, loss of innocent life, and the pain he witnessed on a daily basis. Unlike other cops, Officer Nathan Meadows still knew how to *feel*, he retained a human heart, and he wasn't afraid to show it. And in the often-dark world both she and Nathan inhabited, well, that was a trait she found very attractive.

Oh, yeah, and he had no problem with her use of "language," as her mother would call Emily's ability to swear like a proverbial sailor. Dating was hard enough in this town; finding someone to put up with her inordinate knowledge of cuss words was even harder.

Emily felt the anger leave her. She stepped in close to Nathan and threw her arms around his waist, sinking her head onto his chest, aware that she was probably opening herself to more contamination with this simple act of intimate contact, but not caring anymore. She knew she had deluded herself into a false sense of security from the moment she set foot outside the safety of the café after the red rain had fallen.

How did that happen exactly? she wondered.

The world was literally falling to pieces and she was trying to act as though it was all okay, as though she was somehow outside of it. When had she become so unnerved? At what point in the day had her subconscious started to delude her into ignoring the obvious, terrifying probability that the world was about to suffer through a catastrophe unlike any in modern history? How *did* that happen? *I mean, this could be as bad as the Spanish flu, it could kill millions across the globe,* she thought. *Maybe even more.*

Fuck, her mind shouted at the thought of all the suffering this could bring. She buried her face deeper into Nathan's chest, smelling the musk of his sweat through the layers of his uniform, fighting the urge to cry. Dark waves of fear smashed through her body. Weakened by the panic that held her firmly within its grasp, Emily felt her legs turn into so much jelly. She just couldn't hold back anymore; hot tears welled up and began to trickle down her cheeks.

Nathan let her lean against him, resting his cheek against the top of her head until her sobbing gradually began to subside.

■ ■ ■

Emily could not think of any other time in her life when she had been quite as scared as she felt right now. Her fear was a gnawing uncertainty whittling away at the lining of her stomach. It seized every bone, nerve, and muscle in its ice-cold grasp, demanding that she stop, right now, and curl up into a ball until everything was back the way it should be.

She had never been one to simply give in to fear, and she certainly wasn't going to start now, she told herself, despite what had just happened—but her body was in the grip of an ancient, primal survival instinct and she found it very hard to resist.

Nathan had finally managed to connect with the precinct and had spent the last ten minutes stalking back and forth through the apartment while he spoke in a hushed voice to whoever was on the other end of the line. When he was finished, he snapped his phone shut, slipped it back in his pocket, and joined Emily in the living room.

"They're pulling everyone's leave," Nathan said, sitting next to her on the couch. "They aren't telling us much other than the city's going into full lockdown."

"Is that just here or throughout the state?" she asked, blowing her nose into a tissue Nathan handed her from a supply he kept in his jacket pocket.

Nathan considered her question for a second. She knew him well enough to know when he was pondering whether he should divulge some piece of private info.

"Christ, Nathan. It's not like I'm going to run off to the paper and publish your every word. You can't hold out on me with this. Not now. Not today," she said, unhappy with the whiny tone her voice had taken on.

"It's not that I don't want to tell you," he said. "It's just that I don't want to scare you any more than you already are. Besides, the intelligence we have isn't much more use to you than what you're seeing on the TV. The captain told me the word is they're prepping for massive casualties. The CDC has absolutely no idea what to do. They can't even fathom what the red shit is, let alone what it's going to do to us, so there's no chance of a vaccine. They don't know how it's communicated or why it does what it does, Em."

"So what are we supposed to do while these guys sit on their thumbs? Just wait and hope for the best? Shit!" Emily jumped up and began searching for the TV remote. She found it sitting on the kitchen counter and pressed the power button.

The TV was tuned to a movie channel from the night before. It was playing some fifties science fiction flick, so she quickly tapped in the number for the local news station. Unsurprisingly, the presenters were talking about the red rain: "...seems to be confirmation that the news out of most of Europe is as devastating as we have heard. The president issued a statement just a short time ago stating, and I quote, 'While there is no reason to expect the same problems here in the US, I recommend that you practice an abundance of caution and avoid anyone who has come into contact with the red rain until the Centers for Disease Control and Prevention has had time to analyze samples and can determine exactly what we are dealing with.' The president went on to say that he thought it best if all citizens return to their homes and remain inside for the next twelve hours. Reports are also reaching us that National Guard units across the country have been mobilized to help deal with any unrest and to ensure the security of major population centers. Going back to our main story, all contact with Europe and the Russian Federation appears to have ceased approximately eight hours after the first reports of the so-called blood rain. However, news agencies across the US have received numerous videos and messages apparently depicting mass casualties from countries including Britain and France.

"Similar incidents of the red rain phenomenon have been reported across the continental US, Canada, and South America. Again, if you're just joining us, the president of the United States has announced that—"

Nathan turned the TV off. "I'm not reporting for duty," he said. "Fuck 'em. I think it's better if we just ride it out here."

"They'll fire you, Nathan," Emily said, surprised that he would be willing to risk losing his job.

Nathan thought about what she said before answering. "I don't care," he said finally. "Besides, I don't know if there's even going to be a job to go back to."

■ ■ ■

"How much food do you have, Em?"

Nathan's question left Emily stumped for a moment because she hadn't even given her supply of food a thought. Her job wasn't your standard nine-to-five, so most days she would eat lunch at her desk or at the nearest café, as she had today. When she got home, she would usually grab something light like a salad or a sandwich. She didn't exactly keep a well-stocked pantry.

She checked the shelves, inventorying what food she did have: a six-pack of instant soup, two six-packs of V8 juice, a couple of cans of fruit, a can of peas, and a can of mixed vegetables. There was a half a loaf of eight-grain bread in the breadbasket on the counter. The fridge held the remains of a quart of skimmed milk, an almost-full bottle of orange juice, half a pack of honey-roast ham, enough fresh vegetables to make a couple of decent salads, some leftover vegetable lasagna from two nights earlier, and four cans of Bud Light beer. It wasn't what anyone could call a stockpile, but it would be enough to last them a couple of days until this all blew over.

It couldn't take any longer than that, right?

Nathan apparently didn't agree with her assessment because when he saw how much food was left, Emily had to stop him from leaving and heading out to the store to pick up more supplies.

"You can't," she said. "It's not worth the risk. We have to minimize our exposure, and you traipsing off to the store is only going to heighten our chances of getting sick. We can survive for a couple of days on what we have; we'll just have to be careful." She paused for a second then added with a coy smile, "We'll just have to find ways to take our mind off the lack of food."

Nathan seemed on the verge of going anyway. Emily reached out and took his hand in hers. She could see the frustration written across his face; he was a man used to acting in situations, to being in control, a solution-finder who was now faced with an insolvable problem. "It's okay," she said, squeezing his hand. She saw the look of resignation on his face now, but that quickly transformed into a smile. He leaned in and kissed her gently on the lips, then placed both hands on her shoulders and held her at arm's length, looking deep into her eyes. "I love you, Emily Baxter," he said.

She thought about it for only a second. "I love you too," she said, and then pulled him close and kissed him again.

■ ■ ■

There was little real news on any of the TV channels. Most of what was being broadcast was just speculation or reruns of video and audio collected from webcams and phone messages recorded at the time the effects of the red rain hit Europe. And, of course, there was sensationalism, lots of it. Depending on whom a reporter was interviewing, it was variously the Rapture, a Chinese-backed attempt to exert a stranglehold over the world, or just a big hoax to try to frighten the American people into paying more taxes for health care. No one actually *knew* what was going on. It was all just so much speculation, but mainly it was depressing and incredibly frightening. So, after an hour of staring at the same talking heads, Emily switched channels and searched for anything that would take their minds off what was going on outside the apartment. She settled for a rerun of an old black-and-white movie.

Emily and Nathan sat next to each other on the sofa and allowed themselves to be soothed into a sense of normalcy, her head resting against his shoulder, his hand resting in her lap. Her eyelids became heavy and, rather than struggle against it, she allowed the gentleness of the moment to sweep over her. Within minutes, her eyes closed and she was asleep.

■ ■ ■

Emily awoke with a start, unsure of where she was. It took her a moment to realize she was stretched out on her sofa. Nathan's jacket was lying over her chest, but he was no longer sitting next to her. For a brief moment, she thought he had decided to chance a trip out to the stores for supplies but, as she sat up, she heard his voice from behind her.

"Hey there, sleepyhead. How you feeling?" She turned in her seat to face him. He was standing in the kitchen working on a cup of coffee.

"Want a cup?" he asked.

"No. Thanks," she replied, then stretched and stood up, placing his police jacket on the arm of the sofa. She glanced at the stove's digital clock: she'd been asleep for almost two hours.

At some point during her impromptu nap, Nathan had switched the TV back to CNN. He had lowered the volume to just above a whisper.

The news anchor spoke in an urgent rapid tone, but he didn't have anything new to add and was just repeating the same news she had already heard. Emily was reaching for the remote to switch the TV off, still tired of feeling terrified, when she noticed something odd. The anchor was bleeding from his nose; it started with just a few drops splashing onto the pile of loose paper he held in front of him then quickly turned into a rapid drip. It took him a couple of seconds before he realized he was bleeding. He dabbed at his nose with his right hand, a look of surprise and embarrassment crossing his face as it came back bloody. He began to apologize for the unscripted interruption but stopped midsentence as the blood suddenly streamed from both nostrils. His hand fluttered up to his face to staunch the bleeding, but the blood was flowing so quickly it ran straight over the back of his hand and between his fingers.

"Ladies and gentlemen, I…I'm terribly sorry about this…" He began to cough, pulling in huge gulps of air, then to choke, his face turning as white as the blood-splattered sheet of paper he still clutched in his free hand. Emily could see the fear in his eyes as he and probably several million people across the country realized what they were witnessing. With a sudden spasm, the man's head flew back, exposing his throat and the thick bright-red engorged veins pulsing beneath the skin. A violent muscle spasm snapped his upper body forward, and his face and chest smashed into the desk, sending a spray of blood flying across the room. One globule hit the camera and slid slowly down the lens, leaving a pink translucent smear behind. The man convulsed again, his body flying back into the upright position; his eyes stared directly into the camera as a slow wet gurgling escaped from his throat.

The man's microphone picked up screams of terror from the studio staff but they were barely audible above the sound of the TV anchor as he slowly drowned in his own blood, his body gripped by violent convulsions as though he was in the midst of a grand mal seizure. A thick red stream of blood exploded from his mouth, sloshing across the news desk. He continued to shake violently for a few seconds and then abruptly stopped. His jaw fell open and he exhaled a long sigh as his head slumped forward until his chin came to rest against the lapel of his bloodstained shirt.

The screams the microphone picked up as the anchorman died had been replaced by the sounds of faint gurgles and cries.

Emily realized she was shaking. "Oh my God," she cried, through hands clasped tightly to her mouth. "Shit! Shit! Shit! Nathan? Are you watching this? Dear God Almighty, it's here."

Emily turned to look back at Nathan. Her boyfriend was still standing in the kitchen, his face pale with shock, bloodshot eyes locked on hers as a stream of red gore exploded from his mouth, flooded onto his shirt, and began to form a crimson pool on the carpet.

CHAPTER FOUR

Nathan was dead on the kitchen floor.

His body lay slumped against the wall next to the refrigerator, a large pool of blood slowly congealing next to him and on his gore-covered uniform.

Emily wasn't sure how long she had stared at Nathan's lifeless body. It must have been awhile, because the screams and cries of the dying she heard filtering through her walls from surrounding apartments had finally, mercifully, stopped.

She had registered the suffering of her fellow residents only in passing, her attention caught completely by Nathan as he collapsed and began to convulse, his left foot banging spastically against the refrigerator. Each time his shoe struck the refrigerator door the cuff of his jeans inched up a little, revealing the almost translucent skin of his leg. Bulging veins pushed against the skin; engorged with blood, they looked ready to burst out of his body.

The blood-splattered walls of her kitchen told the story of the violence of Nathan's final seconds on earth. *There was so much blood*, she thought. It looked like someone had gone to work on him with a knife. Streaks of blood covered the counter, the cabinets, and the floor. But there were no wounds on Nathan's body, just his open mouth from which a slowing stream of blood still dripped. His wide-open eyes, black with hematoma, stared off into nothingness. Clots of blood collected in the corner of each eye, dark droplets trickling down his cheeks like tears.

Emily noted all of this with a dispassionate eye as she waited for her turn to die.

Death was coming for her. She knew and waited. It would be just a matter of seconds before she joined Nathan and the millions of victims across the world who had already succumbed to this violent, insidious, red plague. What was strange, though, was with the inevitability of her death came a serenity of sorts, a calmness within her mind as everything complicated in her life ceased to matter. Now her only responsibility was to wait.

The cold honesty of her situation, the simplicity of it all, was a welcome relief.

So she waited.

The clock on the stove showed the minutes ticking away: first one, then five, then twenty. Each time she managed to rouse herself from the almost hypnotic state that had overcome her, she would catch another glimpse of the clock and see that time was still passing and she was still breathing. Her hand periodically drifted to her nose to check for the telltale nosebleed that would herald her coming death. The first time her hand came back bloody, she began to sob quietly. She absentmindedly wiped the blood away with the sleeve of her blouse, waiting for the pain to grip her.

When next she checked, there was nothing but dried blood on her skin, and somewhere in the back of her mind she began to realize it wasn't *her* blood; it was Nathan's, splattered across her face in his final seconds as the convulsions seized control of his body and he slumped lifeless to the floor.

Her next coherent thought was that she had done nothing to help him.

But what could she have done, she asked herself. It was all over in seconds, not even enough time to have picked up the phone and dialed 911, and certainly too fast for him to have been saved by paramedics who would have been thirty minutes out, at least, if they even showed up at all. So she had stood there paralyzed and watched the man she loved die.

She was certain some of the screams she had heard echoing through the apartment had been hers, but she could not be sure; the event was already becoming a blur as her mind struggled to grasp the unreal nature of what had just happened. Everything seemed so dreamlike, so distant to her, she couldn't even be sure who she was anymore, whether this was reality or just some terrible, terrible nightmare from which she was unable to wake herself.

Apart from the laconic whir of the apartment's ceiling fan and her ragged breathing, there was nothing but silence now. The constant background noise that city dwellers become so accustomed to became conspicuous by its very absence. The stomping feet of the couple above her apartment, the distant grinding metallic whoosh and whir of the elevators as they moved from floor to floor, the constant roar of rolling tires on macadam outside the apartment had all ceased. As the city's inhabitants died, its essence had died with them; all that remained was this crushing silence.

It was so very strange, thought Emily, as she realized this was the first time she could remember ever hearing her own breathing, or the noise of the icemaker in the refrigerator as it pushed neatly frozen cubes into the dispenser. Even on those rare sleepless nights when she found herself awake at 2:00 a.m., the city still seemed alive. She had still been able to hear the traffic outside the apartment, or the sound of TVs drifting to her ears from other apartments.

Now there was nothing.

New York, the city that never slept, had been silenced forever.

CHAPTER FIVE

An hour had passed since Nathan died. Emily's feeling of calm began to evaporate as she slowly began to surface from her mind's self-imposed fugue state.

She was alive!

Emily tried to stand but her legs cramped and she flopped back down on to the floor, pain spiking up the calves of her legs. She felt as though all her energy had been sucked right out of her.

She crawled over to the coffee table and picked up her cell phone, trying to ignore the cramps in her legs that felt like a dog nipping at her ass.

Flipping the phone open, she punched in 911. "Come on," she whispered. "Please. Come on. Somebody pick up."

The phone rang and rang. No one answered.

She hung up and immediately dialed the number for the front desk of the *Tribune*. It rang four times before a woman's recorded voice answered and said, "If you know your party's extension, please enter it now."

No one had picked up at the front desk, which was okay. She hadn't expected anyone to be operating the reception area; everyone except for Konkoly and Frank had left, after all, so the system had defaulted to after-hours mode. She entered Konkoly's extension number. It rang twice before she heard his voice in her ear. "Hi, you've reached the desk of Sven Konkoly. If you'd like to leave a message—" Emily hit the pound key on her phone and the system returned her to the main menu. "If you know your party's extens—" The recording cut off when she tapped in the two-digit number for Frank Embry's extension.

It went to message too.

Emily carefully worked her way through every extension number she could remember. Each time the voice of her friends and colleagues greeted her and asked her to leave them a message, that they would get back to her when they could. Emily had a feeling that wasn't going to happen anytime soon. She stared at the phone in her hand, willing it to ring, for somebody, anybody to call her back.

The pain in her legs and bottom had turned into tingling pins and needles. She flexed her legs a couple of times hoping to get the blood to flow a little faster. It helped a little but they were still twitchy after so much time spent in one position. She tried to stand again, and found her legs were once again willing to obey her. She raised herself to her feet and moved over to the window. She couldn't see Nathan from there, his body blocked by the counter and the sofa.

There was one more call she needed to make. Slowly she dialed the number for her parents' home.

Mom and Dad had retired ten years earlier. After selling the farm, they had packed up and moved to Orlando, Florida. "Gonna get while the getting's good," her dad told her in his best

John Wayne drawl during one of her annual trips back home. "We're craving some sun and sea," he had gone on to say. "After sixty years of living here, I think we both deserve it, don't you?"

Emily had agreed. It was the best move they could make, but she still felt a pang of sadness at the loss of the home she had grown up in, and, despite her childhood desire to leave Denison as soon as she was physically able, the idea of never going back there had been painful.

Listening to the phone's distant ringing, she remembered how happy her parents seemed the last time she had seen them. They each sported a deep tan from too many days on the beach. They were like a couple of teenagers, holding hands, cuddling up on the sofa together as they talked with their one and only child. When Emily heard the answering machine click on, she let out a deep sigh, fighting back a rush of tears at the sound of her father's voice: "Hi, you've reached Bob and Jane. We can't get to the phone right now but if you'd like to leave a message we'll get back to you as soon as possible."

At the beep, Emily spoke softly into the phone: "Mom? Dad? If you get this message, I'm okay. I'm alive. I think…I think everyone else here might be dead. I love you. *Please* call me." She left her cell phone number on the machine before hanging up. As she flipped her phone closed, she was left with the disconcerting feeling she had not left a message for her parents but rather a good-bye note.

■ ■ ■

Emily stepped into the corridor outside her apartment. She had left her keys sitting on the countertop in the kitchen. The idea she might accidentally lock herself out made her nervous, so she stood in the doorway with her right foot resting against the bottom rail of the door to keep it from closing.

"Hello?" Emily called, her voice echoing along the empty corridor. "Can anyone hear me?" There was no answer, just the gentle hiss of the air-conditioning and an annoyingly familiar sound from farther along the corridor she could not quite identify.

From somewhere on the floors above her, Emily thought she caught the sound of music playing but she couldn't be sure. She had already tried flicking through the local TV channels but found nothing but empty desks and preprogrammed shows. At least the TV was still on the air, she reasoned.

"Hello?" she yelled again—louder this time, but still no one answered her.

Emily stepped back inside the apartment and started toward the kitchen. She grabbed her keys and placed them safely in the pockets of her jeans. Then she turned and retraced her steps back to the front door, opened it, and stepped outside.

The click of the lock engaging as the door closed made her heart pound a little faster as panic gave her system a little tweak. She shrugged it off and started down the corridor toward the elevator.

There were forty apartments on each floor of her building. Emily made her way to her nearest neighbor. She knocked loudly and rang the apartment's doorbell.

"Hi?" she called out. "Is there anybody in there? Can you hear me?" Placing her ear against the cold wood of the door, Emily listened for some kind of an answer, something that would tell her she was not alone. But there was no reply, not even the warning yap of one of the Chihuahuas or shih tzus she knew some of her neighbors kept as pets.

Emily moved on to the next apartment and repeated the process. After the sixth door remained closed, she stopped knocking.

Hiss. Clang. Thump. There was that sound again, so damn familiar, but Emily just couldn't identify it. The sound grew louder the farther she moved toward the center of the corridor.

Hiss. Clang. Thump.

Set back in an alcove off the main corridor, the waiting area for the elevator remained hidden from view until Emily rounded the final corner, following the sound.

Hiss. Clang. Thump.

The body of the dead woman lay half in and half out of the elevator doorway. Every few seconds the automatic doors would try to close and then spring back open as they thumped loudly against the unmoving woman. This was the source of the sound she had been hearing.

Hiss. Clang. Thump.

Each time the doors collided with the dead woman, her body would give a little twitch that Emily found incredibly unnerving.

The corpse lay facedown, her head and upper torso resting on the linoleum floor of the corridor. A halo of congealed blood spread out around her head while the woman's lower body remained in the elevator compartment. Two brown paper bags of spilled groceries lay at her feet. The contents—mostly canned peaches and plastic gallon bottles of water—had escaped from the bag when the woman died and now lay scattered over the floor of the elevator. The dead woman was dressed in an expensive-looking gray business suit. The jacket and white shirt beneath it had ridden up around her middle, exposing the small of her back and the myriad of tiny engorged veins creating an ugly latticework across her pale skin.

One of the dead woman's hands lay outstretched in front of her, her fingers cupped as though she had died while trying to drag herself out of the compartment. Her other arm was pinned beneath her body.

Emily had seen her share of dead bodies in her time in New York; it went with the territory of being a reporter. Most had been the result of accidents, suicides, or the occasional murder. She thought herself inured to the dead, but there was something incredibly disturbing about this corpse's involuntary movements every time the door banged against it that reminded Emily of the zombie movies she used to love to watch. There was that, and the fact that the continuous *hiss, clang,* and *thump* of the elevator doors' opening and closing was headachingly loud in the confines of the elevator alcove.

No way was she going to leave the poor woman just lying there. It was just too disturbing. Emily stood over the body for a few moments before deciding what she needed to do. She placed the heel of her right foot against the corpse's shoulder and pushed. The body moved a few inches, leaving a red smear of blood, but then stopped as the friction of the escalator's rubber-lined floor made it impossible to push her any farther. There was only one way this was going to happen and that was for Emily to pull the corpse into the elevator by its legs.

She stepped gingerly over the body, carefully avoiding the congealed pool of blood and avoiding the doors as they once again tried to close and then sprung back open. Emily half expected the woman to suddenly reach out and grab her foot. She had a mental image of herself being dragged kicking and screaming into the compartment and the elevator doors sliding silently shut, her screams slowly fading down the empty hallway as the elevator moved on to pick up more undead riders to feast on her flesh.

The dead woman didn't grab for her. She just remained where Emily had pushed her. Emily grabbed the woman's legs by her blue pumps—Christian Louboutin, if she was not mistaken; whoever this woman was, she had taste *and* money—and pulled. The body made a disturbing slurping sound as she dragged it feet-first the remaining distance into the elevator compartment.

Emily was surprised at how much flexion there was in the corpse. Wasn't rigor mortis supposed to have set in by now? She lifted the cuff of the woman's trouser and pushed it back, exposing the woman's ankles and a few inches of the calf of her leg. Although the skin was certainly pale, it did not have the gray cast she had seen in other dead bodies. Also, there didn't seem to be any noticeable lividity either, the natural pooling of blood to the lowest point in the body that leaves corpses looking bruised and battered.

Strange.

She was no doctor, but she was sure that was part of the normal course of decomposition. Apparently, she was wrong. Or the rules had changed.

She was so involved in her thoughts that she failed to notice the corpse was now completely clear of the elevator doors, which promptly began to close again. She thrust her hand between them just in time to stop from being trapped in the traveling metal coffin with the dead woman. As the doors opened again, Emily leaped from the elevator cab to the safety of the alcove. Free of their obstruction and with the woman's body curled fetal-like in the corner of the cab, the elevator doors closed, this time all the way. Emily watched the glowing LED numbers on the floor indicator rise through eighteen and then nineteen, before finally stopping at floor twenty-one to pick up a passenger Emily was certain would never take the ride.

■ ■ ■

The door to apartment thirty-two was ajar.

Emily's heart began to beat faster as she approached. Maybe there was someone alive in there.

Not wanting to walk into the apartment unannounced, Emily leaned toward the crack of the door and called out, "Hello? It's Emily. I live in apartment number six. Is there anyone home?" As she leaned in, her shoulder nudged the door open farther and the sudden squeak of its unoiled hinges caught her momentarily off guard, setting her heart racing even more. It took her a second to gather herself before she pushed the door wider and stepped into the apartment.

The hallway lights were on and from where she stood Emily could see the curtains pulled closed in the living room at the opposite end of the corridor, shrouding it in darkness. The apartment was tastefully furnished, an expensive-looking vase resting on a sofa back table in the hallway with a fresh bunch of oriental lilies. Beneath the scent of the lilies was another, not so pleasant smell. Emily recognized the unmistakable odor of vomit mixed with the metallic, heavy tang of spilled blood. It wasn't strong at this end of the apartment, but the open door allowed the air-conditioned corridor to pull the scent toward her.

Emily moved farther into the apartment's hallway, not bothering to announce herself again, as she already knew what she would find. Where the corridor opened into the living room area Emily saw a small shape spread-eagled on the floor: it was a child, no more than four or five, a little boy. His dead, blood-black eyes stared at the ceiling and a tiny fist gripped at the blood-soaked T-shirt he wore. In the dead child's other hand was a small brown teddy bear. An oval pool of flakey blood, leaking from his nose and his mouth, had dried around the boy's head. His mouth hung loosely open, forever locked in a state of shock and terror.

Emily stifled a cry of horror. Trying to avoid looking at the little boy, she stepped around him, keeping her eyes fixed instead on a painting hanging on the far wall as she moved into the living room.

The bodies of two adults lay nearby. The man was still sitting upright on the living room sofa, his arms hung loosely at his side and his head drooped toward his left shoulder. A stream of dried blood and congealed vomit cascaded from his mouth down the front of his business suit, forming a black pool in his lap. The dead man's eyes stared sightlessly at the equally black flat-screen TV fixed to the far wall of the apartment.

A woman—Emily assumed it was the boy's mother—lay crumpled on the floor in front of the man. When she collapsed, she had fallen through a glass coffee table, smashing it into a thousand pieces. Shards of broken glass were everywhere, covering the floor in front of the sofa and jutting from between the threads of a beautiful oriental rug the table had sat on. One large fragment had penetrated the woman's left arm. *It must have severed an artery*, Emily thought, because the lake of blood around the woman was much larger than the ones she had seen from the other victims of the red rain.

Curled up in the corner of the room, she saw another small shape motionless on the expensive carpet. Not a child this time; the family cat, Emily guessed. It too was dead, dark red clots of blood congealing at every orifice. This sickness, this red plague, did not seem to discriminate between species, and Emily was pretty sure that was a *very* bad thing. Viruses were not supposed to transfer between species. It was supposed to take time or bad luck for it to mutate into a form where it would be able to jump across, but this one seemed more than capable of killing any-thing it came into contact with. She remembered the dead birds she had witnessed falling from the sky when the red rain first came.

This was bad, Emily realized. It probably meant the situation was far worse than she had first thought. If the rain was able to kill across species, then where would it stop? Would it mean every creature on earth was affected or just those that had come into contact with the red rain? The idea was terrifying.

It was also something she simply was not willing to contem-plate right now. For all she knew this was a localized event and help was already on its way. If it was, then she wouldn't have to worry about what kind of a threat the rain was. She could leave it to the experts to figure out, not her; she was just a journalist. Emily knew her line of reasoning was tenuous at best, but it was all she had, and she was going to hang onto it at all costs.

There was nothing more for her here. Emily began backtrack-ing toward the front door, careful to avoid looking at the bodies of the family who had once lived here.

Outside, as the cool of the air-conditioning washed over her, Emily considered moving her search to the other floors of the apartment building. She got as far as the elevator and almost pressed the call button before she caught herself from summon-ing the dead woman back to her floor.

She already knew what she would probably find if she left the safety of her floor. If the footage she had seen of the devastation in Europe had been anything to go by, Emily's survival was an anomaly. Everyone else was most likely dead, both here in the apartment building and throughout the city, probably even across the country, and maybe—as hard as it was to allow herself to even contemplate—the world.

And if there were survivors in her building, surely she would have heard *something* from them by now. Someone would have been moving around, looking for others as she was. There was no way she was going to put herself through the pain of finding more bodies like those of the elevator woman and the poor family she had just left.

It was all just too...sad. Yes, that was exactly the word to describe this situation. It was all just too goddamn sad.

Emily stood in front of the door leading into the emergency stairwell. She pulled open the door and yelled into the open cavity, "Is there *anybody* there? Can you hear me?" She waited a few seconds for an answer—none came, just the hollow sound of her own voice echoing back to her and the metallic clang of the door as she let it close behind her.

There has to be another way to get the attention of anyone left alive, she thought as she walked back toward her apartment.

Strategically placed at key points on each floor of the apartment building were four bright-red pull-station activators for the complex's fire alarm system. Emily had passed two of them before she grasped that she had the perfect solution. She stopped at the one nearest her apartment.

Emblazoned with the word "FIRE" in large white letters on each case, the alarm could be triggered by simply pulling down on a small plastic handle. If there was anyone left alive in the building, or even nearby for that matter, this would be the way to let them know there were other survivors—or at least flush them from their apartment.

Still, Emily was reluctant to activate the alarm system. It wasn't like she was yelling fire in a crowded cinema, she told herself; this *was* an emergency and the only way of guaranteeing she would get the undivided attention of any survivors left in the building.

Emily gripped the handle with her fingers and pulled it down.

Instantly, a white strobe light set high up on the wall began flashing. It was accompanied by an ear-splitting alarm so loud it forced Emily to throw her hands to her ears in pain.

"Ouch!" she exclaimed while simultaneously allowing herself a weak smile of triumph. If *this* didn't get someone's attention she didn't know what would.

With her hands still firmly over her ears, Emily sprinted back to the entrance of the emergency stairwell. She opened the door and positioned herself partly in the doorway where she could see anyone who came down the stairs while still having a clear view of the elevator floor display. If the lights of the display changed it would mean someone was using the elevators to head to the ground floor.

The piercing electronic wail of the alarm quickly induced a throbbing headache in the front of Emily's skull, but she waited almost fifteen minutes in the stairwell, hoping someone might appear. But the illuminated floor number above the closed elevator doors did not waver and no one met her on the stairs. Still, she gave it another five minutes before allowing herself to let go of the hope of others being alive within her building.

Fighting back a steadily growing surge of despair, Emily allowed the door to close behind her as she walked back to the refuge of her own apartment.

CHAPTER SIX

Emily unlocked her apartment and stepped inside, made her way to the kitchen for a glass of water, and froze when she saw Nathan's body lying there.

It was as though she had completely forgotten about him the second she had left the apartment. It was the trauma of the whole event, she knew, but this was just too much for one person to be able to handle. How was she supposed to cope with this? There was no one to help her. So what was she supposed to do now? She had the dead body of her boyfriend in her kitchen, a bad enough scenario on any other day, but today it was simply a nightmare.

The sound of the fire alarm was squelched somewhat by the walls of her apartment but it was still loud enough to be a constant distraction, especially as the headache was blossoming into a face-numbing migraine. She knew now she hadn't thought through the whole activate-the-fire-alarm plan quite as well as she should have, blinded by the hope of finding somebody else alive. Sure, it was loud enough to attract attention, but how the hell was she supposed to turn it off? The incessant screech was beginning to drive her just a little insane.

It was all just too much for her overwrought emotions to deal with and she felt her consciousness begin to spiral back down toward that nice, safe place deep inside the recesses of her mind. It was *so* tempting to just let go of reality, to allow herself to regress and forget about the whole god-awful mess she found herself in. But Emily knew that if she allowed herself the luxury of skipping out on reality, the chances were she would never come back. She could feel herself standing on the very brink of madness. All it would take was a single mental step off that precipice and it would all be over for her.

And, oh God, it was so very, very tempting.

"No," she said through teeth gritted so firmly she could feel the pressure waves rolling up through her jaw. "That's not going to happen."

She dismissed any thought of giving up from her mind. She was a survivor. She had *always* been a survivor, and she sure as shit wasn't going to change now just because it looked like the world was ending.

Emily started purposefully toward the bedroom, doing her best to push the sound of the alarm from her mind and concentrate on what she had to do next. Opening the linen cabinet, she pulled out a spare pair of bedsheets. She tossed the top sheet back in the cabinet, choosing the elastic-edged fitted sheet instead. Thankfully, it was a queen size; anything smaller probably wouldn't have worked for what she had in mind.

She took the sheet back to Nathan's body and considered exactly how she was going to do what she needed to do. He was sitting upright, which would help, but he weighed close to one-eighty and she wasn't sure she was strong enough to carry that kind of weight—dead weight, her mind cackled at her, but she ignored it—if this didn't go as planned.

Emily allowed most of the sheet to drop to the floor while keeping the top hem stretched between both her hands. She looped the edge over Nathan's head and forced it down between his shoulders and the refrigerator his body leaned against. She had to press her right knee against his chest so he wouldn't keel over, not just yet. Emily pulled the elastic edge of the sheet first over Nathan's left shoulder and then the right, being sure to push it down as far as she could until both the right and left edges met. She tucked the side edges of the sheet underneath his elbows and pulled the remainder of the sheet down over the feet. With the sheet securely in place, Emily moved off to the side of Nathan's body, grasped the edges of the sheet together as tightly as she could, and then pushed against his shoulder.

Nathan's body slowly slid sideways down the refrigerator until he lay flat against the floor. Emily had to give the edge of the sheet a couple of tugs to pull the right side free so it met the opposite side. She grabbed his legs at the ankles and straightened them out, then moved back to his shoulders, still holding the edge of the sheet together, and pushed.

Nathan's body rolled over to rest facedown on the kitchen floor, completely encased within the fitted sheet like some modern-day mummy.

Emily had already figured out exactly where she was going to have to take him. She had considered the elevator but she just couldn't bring herself to do that. Instead, she decided to take Nathan's body to the apartment where she had found the dead family. It was farther but it also seemed more fitting somehow.

There was a roll of twine in the kitchen utility drawer and Emily cut several four-foot lengths of it. She slid the first piece under the sheet near Nathan's head and wiggled it down until it was parallel with his wrists and then tied the two loose ends together, securing his arms to his sides within the shroud. She repeated the procedure again to secure his arms at his shoulders and to lock his ankles together.

When she was finished, Emily scrunched together a handful of the fabric near his feet until she had enough to give her a secure handgrip. She tied that off with a shorter piece of the twine. She gave the shroud a couple of careful tugs just to make sure Nathan's body was secure within the sheet. Satisfied with her work, she took hold of the handgrip with both hands and began to pull the corpse of her boyfriend toward the front door.

It was relatively easy to slide Nathan along the smooth tiled kitchen floor, but when she hit the carpeted area of the hallway the friction of the cotton sheet against the carpet made moving his body much more difficult. By the time she pulled his body through the front door and out into the seventeeth-floor corridor, she was sweating hard and breathing even harder. She dropped Nathan's feet to the floor and took a minute to get her breath. The alarm, so much louder out here, beat Emily's head like it was a tribal drum. She could feel a vein begin pulsing in her forehead as the pain banged against the front of her skull.

When she reached the halfway mark near the elevator, her head felt as though it would explode, and the muscles in her arms, back, and neck were burning. Her fingers ached in every joint where she had gripped the fabric so tightly to avoid it slipping from her grasp. Emily was half-tempted to leave the body there for the night but the idea of facing this first thing in the morning was unthinkable. She interlocked the fingers of both her hands and flexed them until her knuckle joints popped, and then reached down and began hauling her grisly load toward the waiting door of apartment thirty-two.

▪ ▪ ▪

Emily bumped the door of the apartment open with her butt. She pulled Nathan's body down as far into the entrance corridor as she could before her hands finally told her they could take no more and she had to let go. His sheet-covered feet clumped to the carpet and Emily slumped down right after them, her back resting against the wall as she fought to catch her breath. Her blonde hair had matted to her forehead and she pushed it back out of her stinging sweat-filled eyes. Her head was thumping with the mother of all headaches, her vision was swimming, and her heart pounded in her ears. She had never felt so exhausted in her life. It took all her willpower not to close her eyes and sleep right there. Instead, she raised herself to her feet, ignoring the pain in her back and the objections of her knees, and hobbled out of the apartment.

At the door she paused momentarily and stared at the shrouded form of Nathan. "Bye, baby," she whispered and pulled the door shut until she heard the click of the lock engage.

She had taken two steps toward her apartment when the wailing of the fire alarm suddenly stopped. There was a second or two pause and then Emily heard three short, sharp beeps as the system had either shut itself down or reset.

"Thank you, God," said Emily; she staggered the remainder of the distance home.

▪ ▪ ▪

She was utterly spent.

The pain in her head eventually began to fade but only after she washed down a couple of painkillers with one of the remaining cans of beer from the fridge. Neither the beer nor the painkillers did much to help her back, which spasmed and shuddered every time she moved. And no amount of alcohol or pills was ever going to ease her numbness over the death of Nathan.

She sat facing the window of her apartment, sipping the remainder of the Bud Light while she stared out at her little slice of the city, watching dusk slowly descend over the buildings. Emily had never experienced such a profound silence before, both outside the apartment and within her heart.

Who knew such absolute stillness existed.

The streets were free of cars and people, and the sky, usually buzzing with aircraft and birds, was vacant and clear. It was quite beautiful. A light brown haze of smog still swirled high above the rooftops, the only reminder of the millions of lives that had traversed the streets and alleys below, just hours before.

As dusk gradually edged toward night, she watched the streetlights begin to flicker silently on, casting long shadows that stretched and grew before being swallowed up in the descending darkness.

The silence quickly became intolerable, and Emily abandoned her spot at the window for the couch instead. She switched on the TV, mostly for the comfort gained from filling the room with any sound other than her own breathing. She felt as though her head had been stuffed full of cotton balls. It wasn't a bad feeling, not really, kind of like a shot of Novocain for her spirit, buffering her against the pain of the reality of her situation.

On the TV screen the image of the dead news presenter stared back at her, his eyes as black and blank as she was sure hers were. She returned his stare for several minutes, then switched off the TV and dragged her sorry excuse for a body to the bedroom.

As she passed through the kitchen, Emily glimpsed the bloodstained pool where Nathan's body had lain and the splatter on the counter. She was just too tired to take care of it right now; it would have to wait until the morning. She trudged into her bedroom and collapsed on top of the comforter.

Within minutes, she was asleep. Mercifully, she did not dream.

DAY TWO

CHAPTER SEVEN

Emily woke an hour before dawn and watched the birth of the day from the same window she had watched its death, this time with a cup of black coffee in her hand instead of a beer.

Her body still complained to her for the abuse she had put it through the previous evening, but it wasn't so bad this morning, just the dull ache of stretched muscles unused to having to work. Her head still ached though. She wasn't sure whether that was the stress of the previous day's events, the fire alarm-induced migraine, the beer, or, more likely, a combination of all of them. She still had the strange head-full-of-cotton-balls feeling, but there just wasn't so much of it this morning.

Her eyes had opened right on time for her to get up and get ready for work. She felt a subtle sense of relief as the vague memory of what was surely just a terrible nightmare fluttered from the dark cave of her unconscious mind. But as those first few groggy seconds between sleep and full wakefulness fell away it erased the cobwebs shrouding her mind and the previous day's events cleared into terrifyingly sharp focus.

Reality had chased Emily from her bed and she had all but run to the living room window. *Just in case*, she had told herself. *Just in case it was all a dream.* As she passed by the kitchen, she glanced down at where, in her nightmare, Nathan's body had lain and where the bloodstain should be…it wasn't there. It was gone. Not a trace left.

Just a dream, she thought and raced to her roost at the window. Throwing back the drapes, she pressed herself against the cold glass and stared out at the still empty streets and sky.

Emily stood at the window, watching what should have been—even at this early an hour—a bustling city filled with office workers, joggers, dog walkers, and everything that made New York the only place in the world she would ever want to live. She glanced back over her shoulder at the kitchen and the spot where the bloodstain should be—the blood was definitely gone. Not a trace remained. Was it possible she had dreamed Nathan's death, maybe even his visit, altogether?

That just wasn't a possibility. His police-issue bomber jacket lay on the sofa where she had left it yesterday, and his cap sat on the kitchen table. He *had* been here. He *had* died here. But that didn't explain why his blood had disappeared from the floor.

Emily examined the floor and the walls in the kitchen where she thought the bloodstain had been. There was no trace. It was as though it had never existed, as though not a drop was spilled.

She was sure she hadn't cleaned it up, but, maybe in her stress-induced fugue state, she had left her bed in the middle of the night and removed it. Possible? After what had happened yesterday, she supposed anything was possible. Was it likely? She didn't think so. It certainly hadn't cleaned itself up and she was a little old to believe the elves had done the job for her during the night.

Coffee, that was what she needed.

She opened the cover on the coffeemaker, pulled out the old filter and tossed it in the trash, then replaced it with a fresh one. She spooned in a couple of scoops of ground beans, and filled the carafe with enough water to give her four cups of coffee— she was going to need at least three to get her going—and emptied the water into the reservoir. A few minutes after flipping the machine's on switch, the smell of fresh-brewed coffee began wafting enticingly around the apartment. Emily filled a mug with the steaming coffee before the machine had dripped even half of its precious liquid into the carafe. She walked to her perch at the window, sipping the delightfully strong brew.

Outside the window, the dawn sky was a fiery red above the city's rooftops. With each passing minute morning sunlight pushed back the shadows that had claimed the streets, but there was little consolation for Emily. The streets were still empty.

With caffeine finally beginning to flow through her veins, Emily began to feel the last of the cobwebs clear from her foggy brain. She needed a plan, she decided, some kind of strategy for figuring how to get in touch with authorities and let them know she was alive. There had to be other survivors out there; it was just a case of finding them or leaving enough clues to help them find her.

She walked back to the kitchen and placed the coffee cup down on the counter, found her backpack nearby, and pulled a steno pad and pen from within. For the next hour Emily worked on compiling a comprehensive to-do list. Telephone numbers, e-mail addresses, physical addresses, social media sites—anything she could think of that would help her reach out and locate other survivors. She would need to stick to a strict timetable of calling the numbers on the steno pad every few hours. She could use the time in between to check news portals and social-media websites. If she stuck to that plan it would only be a matter of time until she found *somebody* who could help her, she was sure.

There was no way to tell how long it would take for the cavalry to come riding over the horizon, so she'd need to find some supplies to get her through the next couple of days. She toyed with the idea of checking out some of the apartments on other floors, but she thought the chances were high she would only have the same result as she had on her own floor yesterday. Empty, locked apartments with nothing but the dead inside. If there was anyone alive in the building, the fire alarm would have surely brought all but a deaf person running.

She wished she had been clearheaded enough yesterday to grab what supplies she could from the dead family's apartment. That was not an option now, as she had clearly heard the door lock behind her when she closed it after dropping off Nathan's body. She was going to have to take a trip outside and grab what provisions she could. It would waste time she would rather spend running through her contact list, but it should only take a half hour or so, if she was fast. Besides, she could use some sunshine. That would have to be later though. Right now she needed to make a few calls.

Emily had compiled a list of numbers to try and listed them in order of priority of their likelihood to answer. She picked up her cell phone and dialed the first number on her list, listening as the phone at the other end of the line rang three times before picking up.

"You have reached the White House. If you know your party's extens—" Emily hung up and tried the next number. No one answered at the Pentagon either. She tried the numbers for the FBI, the CIA, the Smithsonian, and every police precinct and hospital within a fifty-mile radius. When she exhausted New York State's political party HQs, she moved on to numbers in California.

The only voices she heard belonged to ghosts.

Right around two in the afternoon the three cups of coffee took their toll and she had to stop what she was doing and use the bathroom. She was beginning to get hungry too, so she decided to take a break and grab something to eat. She warmed up a can of clam chowder on the stove and added a few saltine crackers to it. She ate her lunch quickly and quietly, and then returned to her phone calls, choosing key numbers in Kansas this time.

By three-thirty, both Emily and her cell phone were precariously close to empty. She hung up from her last call, snapped the phone shut, and almost threw it at the wall in utter frustration. Instead, she walked into the kitchen and attached it to the charger she kept permanently plugged into a wall socket. It would take a few hours for it to fully charge, so now was a good time to go grab those supplies she needed. When she got back, she could start working on checking the social-networking sites for any signs of life.

Got to keep your chin up, girl, the ghost of her father said inside her head as she grabbed her keys from the kitchen counter and headed out the front door.

CHAPTER EIGHT

Emily stepped onto the concrete terrace outside the apartment block and stared up at the clear sky.

Even though the shadow of the building protected her from the full glare of the sun, she still found herself squinting at the dramatic change in brightness. After a day of being cooped up in the apartment with just artificial light, this sudden exposure to actual sunlight was a shock to her retinas, and she quickly found herself raising a hand to her brow in a semi-salute to protect her strained eyes.

For the first few minutes, as she allowed herself time to acclimate to being outside, Emily could almost believe that nothing had really changed—that maybe, just maybe, yesterday really had been just a dream. But, as the seconds ticked by and her eyes became accustomed to the daylight, she began to sense just how truly profound a change had swept over her beloved city.

Besides the gentle rustle of a flag on a nearby pole, there was no sound at all: no cars, no people, no music, no birds twittering, no dogs barking, no couples arguing, nor babies crying. None of the background noise of a city full of people chatting on phones and to each other, nothing but the rhythmic thumping of her heart and a stillness that seemed to triple the weight of the air around her.

When she was a kid, Emily had gone on a school trip to a bird sanctuary over in Black Hawk County. The school bus was packed with kids, and all the way there and all the way back the bus was filled with the constant innocent chattering of the children; the bus had buzzed with conversation and life. When the trip was over, the school bus driver dropped the kids off directly outside their homes. Emily lived the farthest away and hers was the last stop. By the time the driver pulled up outside her parents' home, the bus was empty save for herself and the driver, who wasn't particularly chatty on the best of days and even less so after spending four hours with a busload of overexcited kids. The noise of forty chattering kids that had filled the bus quickly evaporated, and young Emily had felt the first disquieting sense of absence, of how life can suddenly change.

Now, as she stood in the sunshine of what should have been a beautiful New York day, Emily had the same sense of absence she felt when she was the last kid on the bus, magnified a million times. All sound had left the city, and in the vacuum it left behind there was nothing but peaceful, pure, perfectly terrifying silence.

The city smelled different too. It smelled clean. Yes, that was exactly it, she thought. That quintessential aroma of New York—a mixture of carbon monoxide, burgers, hot dogs, dry cleaners, and bakers, mixed with the sweat of eight million people—had also vanished.

Sometimes, after a heavy rain, the city almost smelled this way, like crisp fresh linen. It would linger for a few minutes, but even then, there was always an underlying flavor to the air that never really disappeared—until now. This morning the city smelled pristine and the air tasted sweet, free of all pollutants, dirt, and everything else that made it so special to her, that gave it its unique character. It was all gone.

Emily's sense of scale of the previous day's events suddenly exploded.

Her apartment had acted as a buffer against the desolation that now covered her hushed city like a shroud, insulating her from the power of the true gravity of the emptiness that surrounded her. Nobody and nothing but Emily Baxter remained alive for miles around.

She could feel the void of its passing deep within her core. She was a single cell flowing through a city that was now nothing more than a dead heart lying within an already decaying body. A profound sense of solemnity snatched her up into its grasp. Emily knew that she was, quite possibly, the sole witness to something few other humans had ever experienced: the passing of an entire civilization, maybe the entire human race.

"Fuck!" she said aloud, surprising herself with how loud her voice sounded on the empty concrete terrace.

That single expletive was not exactly what she would describe as the most profound statement on the world's passing, but it summed up her feelings quite succinctly, she thought.

"Fuck!" she said again, glancing around at the empty street. "Oh, fuck!"

Except for a few scattered and presumably abandoned vehicles, the roads were empty. Had everyone managed to get out of the city before the plague, or whatever it was, hit?

She supposed it made sense. There had been enough warning in the hours after the red rain had fallen for even the most technologically unconnected of New York's residents to learn what was happening in the rest of the world and decide whether to stay or go home. Who could blame them? After all, wasn't that what she had decided to do? And she didn't have any family here to speak of.

In the hours after the rain, the news would have quickly percolated down to every level of the city. People would have been faced with the same decision: stay or go? It looked like most of them had decided to go home to their families. Somewhere they felt safe, protected.

Of course, there could be other survivors holed up around the city or maybe even some that had hunkered down in their offices. There could be hundreds or even thousands of others just like her who'd survived and had decided to wait it out for a couple of days, to see how things panned out, in the hope of rescue. It was such a seductive, comforting thought, but surely, if there were survivors, they would have tried to make others aware they were alive, right?

It didn't feel right to her. As weird as it sounded even to Emily, she had no sense of anyone else being alive in this city; there was a distinct lack of...what? Spirit? Life? The very air—so crisp and clean now—felt bereft of energy. It was as though the very life force of the city had suddenly gone AWOL. She didn't know why she felt the way she did, but with each passing minute, she was growing certain she was the last living person for many miles. Life as she knew it had come to a very abrupt stop on good old planet Earth.

Directly across from the apartment block was a row of offices and stores, and as Emily scanned the buildings for any sign of life, her eye caught an indistinct shape curled up in the recessed entranceway to the florist. It was hard to make out exactly what it was from where she was standing so she took a few extra steps closer. Stopping at the curb, Emily instinctively looked both ways before stepping into the road.

She stopped in the center of the road, and stared at the shape in the doorway. It was a body. She was pretty sure she could see a pair of scuffed black boots sticking out from beneath a blanket.

"Hello?" she called out, her voice surprisingly squeaky to her ears. "Can you hear me? Are you okay?"

There was no reply and no movement from the blanket-covered shape. Emily took a few more steps toward the doorway, stopping when she was about ten feet away. It was definitely a person; she could make out the shape beneath the ragged, dirt-stained blanket covering everything from the head down, except for the aged boots. It looked as though whoever was under it had simply curled up in the doorway and pulled the blanket up over his body, like a child trying to hide under the sheets.

"Are you okay?" Emily repeated as gently as she could. Again, there was no answer from the bundled form. With a deep breath, Emily walked the few remaining steps until she was standing next to the huddled shape. She reached down and slowly lifted one frayed edge of the blanket.

The man beneath the blanket was dead, of course. He looked to be in his late forties; a thick beard streaked with gray covered his lower jaw, echoed by a smattering of stubble across his cheeks. His skin was tanned leather brown from too many years exposed to the elements and a skein of tiny blue veins extended like a road map over his nose and cheeks. The vagrant's black, blood-clotted eyes regarded the equally dead and wilting flowers of the florist's window display. The dead man clutched a half-empty bottle of cheap vodka to his chest with both hands, like a child holding onto his favorite toy.

There was something not quite right with the scene, though.

It took Emily a minute to realize it was an absence that had caught her attention; there was no blood anywhere on the dead man. Instead, a nimbus of fine red dust outlined the man's head where she thought the blood should be.

The same red dust coated the blanket covering the man and, as she pulled it back farther down the corpse, the tiny particles floated gently up into the air, then slowed and began to fall back toward the dead man, settling on his exposed skin. As Emily watched, she saw more dust float down and settle on the pale skin of the dead vagrant, as though the corpse was attracting it with some weird magnetism. In fact, it wasn't just the red dust she'd disturbed on the blanket that Emily could see moving toward the body. More of the red dust was floating in from outside the store's entryway. If it hadn't been for the afternoon sunlight streaming in at just the right angle she wouldn't have even noticed it moving toward this man's impromptu burial plot. Her memory recalled the way the red rain had dissipated yesterday, how it had seemed to break apart and float away rather than evaporating.

An impulse overcame her, and before she knew why she was doing it Emily exhaled a long strong breath aimed at the particles floating around the cubby of the florist's entrance. Her breath pushed the tiny red specks back out into the street, but, instead of being blown away from her, the particles slowly began to float back toward the dead man. They weren't *just* floating, Emily corrected; they were actually moving horizontally, as though powered by some inner force, drawn toward the dead skin. But not to her, she noticed, only toward the corpse beneath the blanket.

"No way," said Emily in disbelief. "No—freaking—way!"

Fascinated, Emily continued to watch as, in a matter of minutes, the entire exposed portion of the man's face became covered by a layer of the red dust to the point she could no longer make out any of his features. It looked like he was wearing a red mask.

Once the dust touched the man's skin, the particles seemed to jostle and jiggle with each other for position, rearranging themselves so they filled in any exposed areas of skin.

Just like iron filings on a piece of paper when you move a magnet underneath them, she thought.

Emily resisted the urge to touch the red layer of dust. She was beginning to come to terms with the probability that by some strange twist of fate or good fortune of her DNA, she was a survivor of whatever this event was, but she didn't feel the need to push her luck. It was bad enough that she was probably inhaling this stuff with every breath she took.

Of course, there could be any number of reasons for what she had just seen happen. *Maybe* the dust was attracted to the man's skin by static electricity. The blanket was made of polyester, so when she pulled it back it could have generated enough static to cause the red dust to be attracted to the man's skin. Surely though, if that was the reason, wouldn't the dust just have headed to the blanket instead of the dead man?

Still not 100 percent convinced that what she had just witnessed was real, Emily carefully pulled back the rest of the blanket from the body, listening for the telltale crackle of static electricity while exposing the man's hands to the open air. Instantly, she saw the red motes of dust still circulating in the entranceway begin to head toward the exposed leathery skin of the body. There was no mistaking it this time; the dust was making a beeline straight toward his hands. Emily watched a dust particle that had, until moments earlier, been heading out toward the street perform a meandering U-turn before descending slowly down toward the corpse and settle into place on the man's left hand. It had been about four feet away from her, too far to be affected by any kind of static, she was sure. It had unmistakably changed its course and headed methodically down before joining the other particles that moved gently back and forth on the dead skin like the gentle swell of lake water, as they rearranged themselves into a uniform layer.

More particles fell toward the man's hand, and Emily decided to test her experiment a little more. She pulled the blanket back up to the vagrant's chin, careful so as not to create even the slightest disturbance to the air, while keeping her eyes on the descending particles of dust.

As soon as the blanket covered his hands, the dust that had been heading toward them slowed and turned leisurely in the still air to begin moving back out in the direction of the street.

What did I just see? The thought lodged in the center of Emily's brain like a splinter and throbbed almost as painfully. First the red rain, now this weird dust. She had the feeling something far larger and far more complex than a simple virus was responsible for this strange new world she found herself in.

While she might be the last living human for God-knew-how-far, Emily had an uneasy sense that she was no longer alone.

■ ■ ■

As hard as she tried, she could not shake the idea something intangible was becoming aware of her. Maybe it was paranoia, but Emily felt as though a million hidden eyes had focused suddenly on her, watching her, examining her every move. Although she knew it was impossible, the feeling of disquiet it created proved just as impossible to shake. There was no explanation Emily could think of that could adequately explain the events taking place around her.

She felt bad for leaving the dead vagrant in the doorway, but what could she do? She supposed she could drag him somewhere and bury him. He looked like he weighed less than she did, probably even less now that he was a regular at the great barroom in the sky. But bury him where? There wasn't anywhere she could put him for miles. That would be a job for the rescue services if they ever came...*when* they came, she corrected herself.

So she had left him to the red dust that swarmed and whirled around him like flies. Where *were* the flies? She hadn't seen one since the red rain. The thought flitted across her mind for a second but she dismissed it. All she could do now was carry on with her plan. She had already lost enough time trying to figure out just what she had observed with that freaky flying show the red dust had performed. She had bigger problems to worry about and it was time for her to pull herself together and to get back on track.

Two buildings down from the florist was the corner convenience store where she had witnessed the near-riot the day before. The street was clear now. There was no sign anything untoward had happened except for a few crushed cans of what had probably been green beans on the road outside the store. The door to the shop was unlocked; she pushed it open and stepped inside.

Bing-Bong!!!

Emily let out a screech of surprise as the electronic door chime activated. For a second she thought she was going to pee herself with fear. Her heart was pounding hard enough to shatter her ribcage as a sudden surge of adrenaline pumped through her veins.

She wasn't sure how many more scares like this she could take before she simply went into cardiac arrest and keeled over. To be honest, the thought wasn't so bad, she admitted. The idea she might be the last living human was petrifying and made a sudden death seem almost attractive.

"Don't be stupid, girl," she said aloud and then began to giggle. The giggle turned into laughter as the full weight of what had transpired over the past two days and the growing realization of her predicament finally hit her.

It was an absolutely absurd situation to be in. Emily had spent the majority of her life feeling as though she was prepared for anything, confident in her own capabilities and focused on moving forward, just like everyone else she knew. But now, here she was: completely alone and unprepared, at a complete and utter loss as to what she should do next. And, wasn't it truly ironic that the sole surviving human—that's what she felt like, after all—would be a journalist? The biggest news story ever and there was no one left alive to tell it to. It really was just too much.

Emily's legs felt like they were ready to give way as the laughter suddenly turned to snuffling tears and a hot well of fear and desperation bubbled up from inside her. She tried to force the emotion back but she didn't stand a chance. Emily covered her face with her hands and began to weep at the thought of everything she had lost.

Everything dear to her was gone, swept away from her in an instant. Her parents, Nathan, music, TV, the theater, her friends and workmates, her job—everything that made life worth living had been stolen from her in just one day, leaving her alone and wrecked. She may as well have been on Mars for all the good being alive without all of those things meant.

Her sobbing turned into a wail of despair as she realized that none of those things would ever be coming back either. It wasn't like the human race had stepped outside for a quick cigarette break and normal service would resume when it got back;

humanity was gone, finished, snuffed out in a single day. She knew it with a certainty as strong as she had ever felt anything.

"Dear God, what am I supposed to do now?" Emily mumbled through lips trembling with the unburdening of the pent-up emotion. Her shoulders heaved and shuddered as she collapsed to the cold floor of the store, knocking over a stand of magazines and sending them slithering over the tiles. She picked a magazine up and tossed it at the door, screeching in pure frustration. She felt her body sink to the cold floor again, curling herself into a fetal position as the pain just kept coming.

A few minutes later, emotionally washed out, her body exhausted, Emily fell into a deep sleep, hoping she would never wake up.

■ ■ ■

Emily's eyes flickered open.

The cramp in her shoulders from lying on the chilly tiled floor of the store meant she must still be alive.

She felt better. At least, as better as she was going to feel under the circumstances. Ridding herself of her emotional burden had released her from its weight and allowed her mind, and her heart, to expel the pain. That was a good thing.

Emily pushed herself to her feet, stretched her stiff legs, and flexed her aching arms as she looked around the small store's interior. How long had she been asleep? It must have been a couple of hours because the inside of the market was much darker than when she first entered. In fact, as she stared out through the storefront window, she guessed it must be close to sunset because the streetlights were beginning to flicker on one by one, their sodium-vapor bulbs casting a warm glow across the street.

Emily's breath caught in her throat. Outside the store, illuminated by the glow of the nearest light, she could see a mass of red dust. The orange flush turned the dust an ominous black, but what truly disturbed her was how much of it she could see as it floated past the light. Uncountable dots of the dust moved along the street, silently flowing in a bizarre rhythmic undulation, driven by what exactly? No wind disturbed the leaves and branches of nearby trees. It was almost as though the dust had combined into a single giant creature, and that creature was now roaming the empty streets, searching for something only it knew.

The cloud of dust moved like the giant dragon puppets she had seen in Chinatown when they celebrated the New Year; up and down, a sinusoidal wave of dust undulating past the window. It was a mesmerizing sight, but at the same time, the implication of what she was witnessing chilled the blood in Emily's veins.

She walked to the window and stared out at the whirling dust on the empty street. Just yesterday she had stood in the café and watched as the red rain had fallen; the world had changed so much since then. As clichéd as it sounded to her writer's brain, it truly seemed to have been a lifetime ago. And, Emily supposed, it may just as well have been a different life, because when the rain fell, her old world, the one where Emily was just another woman trying to make it through the day as unscathed as she could, had died too.

Okay, pull yourself together. You've got to get a grip on this situation, she chided.

She was resisting the urge to speak her thoughts aloud. The temptation to talk to herself was almost overwhelming. It was less than a day since she had heard another human voice, but she never would have imagined the effect it would have on her.

Whatever was happening outside the shop's window, there must be some kind of explanation for it. She was looking at the greatest story of her life; hell, for all she knew, while she might not be the last human left, she might well be the world's last reporter. So if she didn't document this, and if she didn't at least *try* to figure out what was going on, then who would?

So, no! No talking to myself just yet. Not until I've figured out exactly what's going on here.

"Damn right," she said aloud, allowing a flicker of a smile to cross her face as she turned her attention away from the strange red storm raging on the other side of the window, and back to tracking down supplies.

The store had been stripped clean of almost everything. Two rows of metal shelves had once held an assortment of canned food and bottled water. One of the shelves had toppled over and now leaned against a wall. Both shelves were empty save for a torn packet of instant mashed potatoes that had spilled most of its contents over the floor.

Emily carefully picked her way through a minefield of shattered liquor bottles and crushed cans, their contents spilled and worthless after a day's exposure to the air. Scattered pages from a broadsheet newspaper spread over the tiled floor, moving gently in the breeze of a fan whirling quietly on the counter.

Behind the cash register was a recessed pigeonhole where the owner had displayed his stock of cigarettes. It was empty now but Emily glanced behind the counter anyway. On the ground were a couple of crushed soft packs of Marlboro Lights and an occasional orphaned cigarette. Emily wasn't a smoker, so the cigarettes held no interest for her, but what did catch her eye was a can of condensed soup—it was tomato; she *hated* tomato soup—that she picked up and placed on the countertop. Emily moved back behind the counter into the clerk's area and opened a couple of small storage cupboards the looters had apparently missed. There were a couple of cartons of cigarettes that looked like they were well past their sell-by date and…score! Pushed almost to the back of one cupboard Emily found a package of two gas-fueled lighters.

She added the lighters to the soup on the counter.

A small room at the back of the store acted as the stockroom. The wooden door was wide open, hanging from a single hinge, the imprint of a large boot near the broken lock.

Emily poked her head into the storeroom; it was dark inside so she felt around on the wall until she found the light switch. A single shadeless bulb hung from the ceiling, but it was sufficiently bright to push the darkness back far enough for Emily to see there was little left to scavenge. The room had been picked over and it was as much of a shambles as the front of the store; the floor was covered in torn cardboard packaging and broken bottles of Budweiser and Miller Lite.

A plastic pint bottle of water caught Emily's eye. It had rolled against the far wall of the stockroom. She retrieved it and slipped it into her pants pocket. She pushed a few of the larger pieces of cardboard aside and found another can of soup—this time it was vegetable, not her favorite but a step up from tomato, at least—and a four-pack plastic pod of mixed fruit. Two of the pods had been crushed, so she pulled those off and tossed them away.

A couple of minutes of more searching turned up a blister pack of six C-type batteries, a tin of Spam, another plastic four-pack of mixed fruit and, tucked away beneath a shelf, a pound bag of jerky strips. She also found a box of chocolate-chip cookie mix but she discarded that, knowing the chances of her finding fresh butter or eggs was going to rapidly head toward zero.

Confident she hadn't missed anything else, Emily left the stockroom and headed back out to the front of the store. She placed everything she had just found next to her stash waiting on the counter and then loaded it all into a bright blue plastic shopping basket from a stack located next to the door.

It wasn't much of a haul, she thought, but it was better than nothing. It would buy her another day and give her time to formulate a better plan or for the authorities to show up. She knew she would have to head to one of the larger food stores soon and see if she could find a bigger supply, assuming the other stores hadn't been wiped clean too. The power was still up and running, but who knew how long that would last? As soon as the electricity went down her water supply would disappear right after, as would her heat and any way of cooking her food, so it was imperative she find a stock of water and anything she could eat out of a can that didn't need to be cooked to be consumed.

Emily picked up her basket of trophies and headed to the exit. A small refrigerator near the door hummed quietly to itself. She hadn't bothered to check it when she came in, sure it would be empty, but as she passed it she stopped and pulled back the sliding glass top, peeking inside. Emily fished out a pint tub of Häagen-Dazs strawberry ice cream. "You're coming home with me, big boy," she said with a smile, and added it to the basket.

Outside the store, full darkness had descended on New York but Emily could still see the storm of red dust swirling in the glare of the streetlights. In fact, the storm seemed to have only increased in intensity. She could barely make out the vague shape of her apartment block across the road. The building's external security lights created a beacon that she could orient herself by, but only just. There was still just enough light to see and she knew there really wasn't anything in the road she could stumble over, but if this red storm was going to keep getting worse it was best if she left now.

Carefully, Emily cracked open the door to the street, holding onto the door handle to keep it from being ripped from her hands.

She had readied herself to be pummeled by a burst of wind, but there was nothing, not even a hint of a breeze.

Motes of red dust rushed through the gap in the doorway and into the empty store, whirling around her. Within seconds, the cramped space of the convenience store filled with a whirling storm of tiny red particles.

Emily stood still, her eyes blinking mechanically as ribbons of dust flew toward her but inevitably swerved around her, continuing into the store as if she did not exist. As she watched, the dust seemed to maneuver its way through the space of the building. The dust's movement reminded her of a dog when it first entered a new home, methodically moving around the room as though it was searching for something and, not finding it, flowing back out through the doorway again, only to be replaced by more dust.

Emily raised a hand to push an errant lock of hair from her face. Amazingly, as she moved her arm toward her forehead, the flow of red dust maneuvered around it like smoke in a wind tunnel blowing over a car, completely avoiding contact with her. She tried the same thing with her other arm and then stepped to the side. The flow shifted with her but never touched her, leaving an inch or so of space between her body and the mass of whirling particles.

My God, it's as if it's intentionally avoiding me.

The thought of the dust she had seen earlier attaching itself to the skin of the dead vagrant leaped to the forefront of her mind.

Was it searching for the dead?

The idea made her flinch. That just could not be. It *had* to be a coincidence. There *had* to be some other explanation. Yet as she stood in the doorway watching the continuous stream of dust enter on her left, whirl around the room for a few seconds, and then exit on her right, with not even a hint of a breeze to propel it, Emily had the unsettling feeling that that was *exactly* what was happening.

If—and it was a very big if—she was correct, then she truly was observing something far more profound than a simple chemical spill or natural disaster. If—there was that word again—the phenomenon she was witnessing was actually real then it could only mean there was some kind of intelligence behind the event, driving the dust to seek out the dead. That meant it was synthetic. That thought was even more terrifying and yet, on some level, predictable to Emily. That humanity had screwed itself over once again, this time apparently permanently, did not surprise her. It had been in the cards for years, she supposed. And after the ineptitude she witnessed on an almost daily basis, well, it came as no great surprise that someone, somewhere, might have screwed the pooch big time.

With a sigh of resignation, Emily dipped her head against the flow of red dust. She picked up the plastic shopping basket from the floor, stepped out onto the pavement, and began heading back in the direction of the apartment block.

■ ■ ■

The trip back was not nearly as strange as she had expected. It was, however, more difficult than she anticipated. The twisting eddies of dust made it almost impossible to see more than a few feet in front of her. It was like walking through one of those snow globes she'd had when she was a kid, eerie but also strangely beautiful. The dust still kept its seemingly self-imposed distance from her, whipping past in twirling ribbons of red as it scoured the streets in search of only it knew what. It was almost as if there was some kind of shield surrounding her that the dust was just unable to penetrate. The dust made a low shushing sound as it passed her, like sand dropping onto paper.

Very fucking weird.

While the contents of the basket were not heavy, the basket itself was another matter. The thin metal handles dug into the palm of her hand and the plastic cage of the basket kept banging against her thigh as she tried to maneuver her way through the thick swirls of dust. Half-blinded by the storm of red surrounding her, Emily did not see the raised curb of the pavement, clipping it just hard enough with her shoe to send her sprawling onto the sidewalk, spilling the basket and sending half her supplies spinning off into the darkness.

A few frantic minutes of searching recovered everything but the can of tomato soup. *No loss there.* Completely disoriented during the search, she wasted another ten minutes heading in the wrong direction, ending up a block away from where she thought she was.

Almost thirty minutes after leaving the store, a frustrated Emily finally pushed the door to the apartment open and stepped into the building's lobby, a streamer of the red dust following her inside before the door closed, severing it. The stream of dust whirled around for a second within the lobby, then dissipated.

She dropped the basket to the ground and stared at the white welts left by the handles on the palm of her hand. She could barely feel her fingers. She flexed them a few times to try to get blood flowing back into them before she made the long climb up the stairs to the apartment.

The elevator still held the body of the woman she'd found on her floor and Emily wasn't interested in spending any more time in the presence of dead people, thank you very much.

Giving her fingers a few extra flexes for good measure, Emily picked up the basket and began to climb the stairs to the seventeenth floor.

■ ■ ■

Emily stood at her window looking down over the streets below. She had already put her precious supplies away, taking stock of exactly how much food she had collected with what she already had in the pantry. It wasn't much. She estimated there was maybe three days' worth of food and enough drinking water to last her a minimum of a week, longer if she rationed it.

She had decided to fill the bathtub with as much water as she could before she went to bed—just in case—along with a couple of empty plastic gallon containers she could use before she broke out the bottled water. She would use the water in the bathtub for cleaning herself and her clothes; she could transfer it to the washbasin from the tub as needed. Emily didn't know whether the purification process the city used to sanitize the water they supplied would function for long without human interaction, so it was probably best to err on the side of caution and not drink water from the faucet after tonight. Who knew what was happening out there or what contaminants could have entered into the supply with several million dead people just lying around. It wasn't worth the risk of drinking tainted water when there was so much bottled water available from local stores and other apartments in her block. But she was going to allow herself one final indulgence before she resigned herself to austerity and caution.

Emily moved from the living room into her bathroom and turned on the bath's hot and cold faucets, filling the tub until the water lapped precariously close to the brim. She threw in some bath salts, grabbed the tub of Häagen-Dazs ice cream she'd liberated from the store, stripped off her dirty clothes, and climbed into the steaming bath.

She soaked her tired muscles for forty-five minutes. By the time she climbed out, the water was tepid and she was as wrinkly as a shar-pei dog. The tub of ice cream was empty, but Emily felt almost human again. The bath had been a luxurious treat that she knew she would not be able to look forward to again for a very long time.

She emptied the bathwater and then refilled the tub with cold water while she toweled herself down. She pulled on her favorite pink flannel dressing gown and walked back into the living room.

Now she stood staring down from her lofty perch into the darkness. The street below was virtually invisible. Even the streetlights were barely perceptible beneath the thick river of red dust that seemed to be growing larger by the minute. It had been too dark to confirm it by the time she arrived back at the apartment, sweaty and exhausted, but Emily would bet her last dollar that what she had witnessed from the confines of the little corner store was happening throughout the city, maybe even across the whole country.

A sense of relief settled over her as she sat entranced by the whirling spirals of dust moving through the street. This was something so massive, so completely out of her control that it was actually quite liberating to know there was not a damn thing she could do about it. All she had to do was sit back and watch the show, see what happened, and hope she would be able to get out the other side when the dust—*pardon the pun*, she thought—finally settled.

The shucking of responsibility felt good, she admitted, to be just an observer, unbridled by the politics or angles she usually had to fight through for almost every story she had ever covered. This was simple, even pure in some respects.

Emily watched the ebb and flow of the river of red dust as it surged through the streets for almost an hour before she felt her eyelids beginning to droop. She let out a long yawn, pulled the drapes closed, and walked to her bedroom, closing the door on both the world and the day.

DAY THREE

CHAPTER NINE

Emily woke with a start.

She popped her head out from under the covers and glanced at her bedside alarm clock; it showed 8:23 a.m. in bright red numerals. The bedroom felt overly warm; the air-conditioning should have kicked in by now. Obviously, the power was still on because her alarm clock was still working. Maybe there was something wrong with the thermostat.

She climbed out of her bed, pulled on her dressing gown from the hook on the back of the bedroom door, walked out into the living room, and emptied enough water into the coffeemaker to brew six cups. She had the distinct feeling this was going to be a six-cup kind of a day.

She had slept well and this was the first morning since the world ended that she actually felt normal, clearheaded enough that she could turn her mind back to figuring out how she was going to reach whoever was still alive out there. It was obvious from her efforts yesterday that simply calling locations she thought might be the logical centers for an organized rescue just wasn't going to work. She couldn't be the only person left in the world; she was certain of that. The law of averages made it next to impossible for her to be the sole survivor. So today was going to be the day she figured out how the she was going to contact them.

Grabbing a fresh mug from the cupboard above the sink, she filled it with coffee and wandered over to the living room window. The question burning in her mind was how she was supposed to locate other survivors when there were no clues as to who they were, their location, or whether there was even anyone alive to contact.

How? How? How?

Emily reached out and drew back the drapes from the window.

Outside her window—she corrected herself; outside her *seventeenth-story* window—was nothing but a whirling mass of the red dust. Emily could not move, could not look away; the swirling flow of the red storm was mesmerizing.

It filled the entire skyline, silently blocking the view of everything for miles. Below, she could vaguely make out the very dim glow of the streetlights, their light-detecting circuits deceived by the dense swarm of red dust into thinking darkness had arrived early. It crawled over the exterior of the window like flies on a rotten carcass. In fact, now that she stopped to think about it, that was exactly the analogy she had been looking for. The behavior of the dust was just like a swarm of insects methodically searching for its collective next meal.

Could she have been mistaken? Was this stuff she thought of as dust actually some kind of animal? She leaned closer to the window, trying to follow one of the motes as it hit the pane of glass, but it moved across the glass too quickly for her to follow and whisked away before she could get a good look at it, only to be replaced by another, slightly larger piece. In the few moments she was able to briefly track the larger particle of dust she could see it certainly didn't resemble any kind of bug she had ever seen. It looked, well, like dust. Actually, it was more like plant pollen. It had an irregular bulbous shape with sharp points sticking out at odd angles, but rather than appearing solid, the particle she was staring at was diaphanous and almost as delicate as the dandelion seeds she'd seen floating on the wind back home in Iowa.

It was impossible to tell with the limited perspective the window offered just how much of the city was enshrouded by the dust storm. If she wanted to do that, she was going to have to leave the apartment. Hopefully it was just some kind of localized effect that had caused the dust to collect on her side of the building. The idea that this might be happening all over the city was unnerving.

Emily unlatched the security lock on the apartment door and opened it, but stopped dead before she even set a foot outside the entrance.

Running along the ceiling just outside her front door was a tendril of the red dust. Emily poked her head outside the apartment doorway and glanced quickly down the corridor toward the elevator. The dust spiraled and twisted about an inch below the ceiling; it seemed to be coming from the direction of the exit to the main stairwell. A few feet into the corridor, it split into two branches, with one tendril heading toward the apartments to the right of the stairwell and the other inching its way in her direction. But that wasn't all it was doing. The dust was also splitting off at each doorway. Branches of the dust spiraled down over the doors of each of the corridor's apartments like smoke pulled along by some unfelt breeze. *Or, like the tentacles of some giant monster*, Emily thought, with a creeping sense of horror. As she watched, she saw a strand of the dust break off from the main root and descend down to the door of Mrs. Janowitz's apartment just three apartments down from her own. The strand descended over the doorway, the tip making small movements left and right as though it was feeling its way. When it found the keyhole, the dust disappeared into the tiny opening as a second strand continued down to the base of the door. When it reached the floor, the tendril began to probe at the narrow space between the base of the door and the floor, as it looked for another entrance into the apartment.

That was it, Emily decided. This was just too fucking much. She slammed her own door shut and sprinted to the linen closet. She flung the closet open and snatched up a handful of the thickest towels she could find, then ran to the kitchen, almost slipping as she rounded the corner but recovering enough she didn't fall headfirst into the corner of a cupboard. She threw the towels into the sink and turned on both faucets full force. Sure that the towels were absolutely soaked, Emily raced to the front door and threw the sopping wet towels down onto the floor to block the crack, pushing them tightly into place as though she were trying to stop smoke from a fire. The edge of the door where it met the doorframe looked secure; the apartment owner had installed a plastic dust excluder that sat between the door and the frame, so she wasn't worried that anything could get through that. The keyhole was another matter though; it was too small to block with a towel and she didn't want to plug it with wet paper because that would be a bastard to get out and there was no way she was going to risk not being able to lock her door—or worse, trapping herself inside.

Emily ran back into the kitchen and began pulling out each of the drawers. She knew she had a roll of duct tape around here somewhere. She found it after she pulled out the contents of her third drawer, tucked at the back behind a bunch of plastic grocery bags she had always meant to return to the local market.

Racing back to the front door, she tore off two eight-inch strips of the gray industrial-strength tape with her teeth. She pressed the pieces over the keyhole just as the first few particles of the red dust began to float through the hole. She watched the dust float away from the door toward the kitchen. Emily tore off a third piece of tape and stuck it diagonally across the other two she had already applied, *just to be on the safe side,* she thought.

She stepped back from the door and gave it the once-over, taking care to look for any telltale signs the dust might have found some other way through she hadn't seen. But there was no indication she'd missed any gaps and, after a tense minute of double-checking, she exhaled a heavy breath.

"Shit!" she said aloud as another thought struck her. The air-conditioning had failed to kick in this morning. The apartment block used a central forced-air system that fed all of the apartments in the building from two external industrial-sized air-conditioning units on the south side of the apartments. The two massive units fed the apartment block through a series of ducts that interconnected throughout the walls of the building, supplying the ceiling vents in each room. Of course, it could just be a simple technical problem with the machinery. A couple of days of no human intervention may have created some mechanical problem causing them to overload and stop working. But, after witnessing the methodical way the dust had seemed to search out every possible entry point into the rooms on her floor, Emily doubted it was anything as simple as mechanical failure. The unit's sudden demise was more likely because the red dust had found some way into the machinery, overloading the air-conditioning unit somehow. Even now it could be making its way through the miles of ducting, looking for a way into every goddamned apartment.

Grabbing the roll of duct tape, she raced back down the corridor to the living room. The vents were too high for her to reach so she had to double back into the breakfast nook and grab a chair. A vent sat directly over the glass table in the breakfast nook, so she climbed up onto the chair and pushed the thumb-slider to the closed position, sealing it. Even with the vent closed, she could still see a small gap between each of the vent's oblong fans that she was sure was more than large enough for the tiny particles of red dust to make it through. Also, the cover of the vent was held in place by two flathead screws and she could clearly see a black line of shadow between the edges of the vent cover and the white paint of the ceiling. That meant the vent casing wasn't sitting flush with the ceiling.

She began tearing off strips of duct tape and sticking them over the exposed seams between the vent cover and the ceiling, carefully pushing them into place with her fingertips to make sure it made a tight seal. Emily tore off more strips and attached them across the panels, completely obscuring the vent. She hoped she had enough tape to cover all the apartment's vents. If she didn't, well she'd be up the goddamn creek without the proverbial paddle.

Twenty minutes later, Emily placed the final strip of tape against the vent in her bedroom. She'd managed to cover all of them and, glancing at the roll, it looked like she still had enough left for a couple of strips to patch up anything she might have missed, but she was confident she had effectively made her apartment airtight.

That was going to be her next problem, she realized. With no air-conditioning the apartment was going to get warm quickly. In fact, she thought she could already feel the temperature in the bedroom beginning to rise. It could just be her imagination; after all, she'd just spent the last thirty minutes or so rushing around like a mad woman and she was sweating profusely. Imaginary or not, she was going to use up all the air in the room and things would get very uncomfortable. At some point, she would have to open up the apartment to the outside and allow some fresh air in. When she did would depend on how long the dust decided to hang around, of course.

She had managed to cover all the possible ways into the apartment she could think of, and Emily felt her panic finally begin to subside. She began to run back the mind-bending events she had just encountered, analyzing everything she saw, or thought she had seen, through the filter of her reporter's brain.

To her mind, the obvious intelligence the red dust had exhibited to coordinate entry into the apartments was incontrovertible proof that what she had observed over the past forty-eight hours or so was not some coincidental cluster of unrelated events but actually part of a far bigger phenomenon. That phenomenon was itself a part of a larger process or plan—she was not sure which yet—but she could sense that the answer was just out of reach of her senses. Whatever the answer was, Emily understood something massive had been set in motion with the fall of the red rain, and it was moving methodically and systematically toward its final goal.

■ ■ ■

Emily quickly tired of checking the window to see if the maelstrom of dust had receded. Each time she pulled the curtains aside and peeked out it seemed the storm had only become worse. It was so thick now that glancing down toward the street she could not tell if streetlights had simply stopped working or if the cloud of dust covering Manhattan was so thick the light just couldn't make it through.

As the hours passed, Emily paced the apartment, turned on the TV, and scanned every channel in the hopes that some station somewhere would be broadcasting something, anything to give her a clue or an indication there was somebody else alive. All she found was static from channels that had gone off the air or emergency service broadcasts that did nothing but loop, warning people they should stay in their homes until the crisis was over. Oddly enough, many of the satellite channels were still broadcasting. She guessed that was because the systems had been preprogrammed weeks in advance, so the computers controlling the broadcasts would probably just trundle along until the power went out or the satellites fell out of orbit.

She decided to try her luck with the Internet. Pulling her laptop from its bag, she connected it to the docking station she kept on a small desk in one corner of her bedroom. She expected the Internet would be down, but to her surprise, when she plugged the ethernet cable into the connector on the side of her computer, she saw the connection indicator in the bottom right-hand corner of her monitor turn from red to green. She was online!

Emily tried all of the major news sites first. CNN was still up but displayed the same headline it had the day of the red rain. The same was true for MSNBC and Fox. Up, but no new news. When she tried to load up the website of one of the local TV channels all she got was a 404-error message: "The page you are looking for cannot be found." Undeterred, she began working her way through the list of social-networking sites she had compiled the day before, looking for any hint someone had posted a message they were still alive. It was like looking for that proverbial needle in a haystack, only this haystack spanned the entire globe.

She logged in to her Twitter account and read the messages she'd missed. She hadn't accessed it since the red rain had first fallen, so the bulk of the messages expressed concern or fear over the event. Some messages explained that their authors were hunkering down and hoping to ride out the storm; there were even one or two that dismissed the threat as nothing more than mass hysteria.

How'd that work out for you? Emily wondered.

There was no sign of any new messages posted to Twitter since the red plague had hit though.

On each social media website or platform she visited, she left the date, her telephone number, and a simple message: "I am alive. Please, contact me!!!" She did not think it would be a good idea to leave her exact address, so she just wrote "New York City." That was close enough.

Emily spent the next four hours checking in to every website and web hangout she could find, looking for any sign of recent activity that might indicate someone, somewhere, was watching. She found nothing. She left her message on every one of them and, where possible, activated the option that would notify her if there were any new updates to her post.

By the time she exhausted her list of websites, Emily's eyes had begun to ache from the strain of staring at the screen for so long. She could feel beads of warm sweat dripping down her back and across her chest from the steadily growing humidity in her sealed-off apartment.

She headed into the bathroom. The bathtub still held her emergency supply of water, which meant she would have to drain it if she wanted to take a shower. Instead, she filled the basin with water, stripped out of her clothes and rinsed herself off with a facecloth. The cold water felt wonderful against her clammy skin. Refreshed, she threw on a fresh T-shirt and panties.

She was beginning to feel her hunger pangs howl so she pulled a can of soup from her cache and heated it on the stove, raising the temperature in the apartment even further, but *Hey! I have to eat.* Sitting cross-legged on the sofa, she devoured the soup with the last few slices of bread she had left. While she ate, she turned on the TV and found a movie channel that was still broadcasting.

Restless and unable to focus, Emily switched the movie off before it ended and went to check the window one final time. The red dust still beat against the glass and she'd be damned if she could tell whether it had gotten worse or stayed the same. If she was perfectly honest with herself, at that particular moment, she didn't care whether it had or not. She'd felt the depression begin to set back in after she'd logged off from the last website. It was hard to fight off the nagging feeling that, despite her best efforts to remain upbeat and reassured, she really was the only person left alive on this lump of rock the human race had called home.

The steadily growing temperature in the apartment and her own agitated nerves slowly sapped away at Emily's energy, darkening her mood even further. There was little more she could do today, other than sit and brood the rest of the evening away. That wouldn't help. She wanted to rest, but the clammy heat made her sticky and uncomfortable, and besides, she was tired but not sleepy. She grabbed a bottle of over-the-counter sleep aids she kept in the medicine cabinet in the bathroom, popped two of them into her mouth, and swallowed them with a swig of water before climbing onto her bed and burying herself in the welcoming coolness of the comforter.

Outside the apartment window, the red dust continued to scratch against the glass, blindly looking for a way in. Emily didn't care. Within minutes, the stress of the day and the sedating effects of the sleeping pills pulled her down into sleep.

DAY FOUR

CHAPTER TEN

Emily awoke to the faint but unmistakable sound of a baby crying.

At first, as the sound penetrated her diphenhydramine-induced sleep, Emily thought she was simply dreaming.

She felt damp and she could sense tiny pinpricks of perspiration all over her skin. With no air-conditioning to cool her, the temperature had continued its gradual rise overnight. She'd kicked off the comforter at some point and now lay spread-eagled diagonally across the bed. The medication she'd taken had left her feeling woozy while it continued to try to drag her back down into sleep.

Of course it's not a baby. Just a dream. Go back to sleep. No need to wake up yet, her addled mind whispered to her.

Then the sound came again: a drawn-out wail that was unmistakable. Adrenaline instantly pumped into her body, negating the pills' effects. She bolted upright, listening intently to make sure she was not just hearing some sound created by the building.

Wagghhhhh!

The sound floated to her again. It was undeniable now. That was the sound of something alive, distant, but definitely in the building and somewhere above her. Maybe on the next floor up?

Waggggggghhhhhh!!!!!

The cry sounded stronger this time, and her ears were sharp enough to distinguish that it did indeed sound as though it was coming from the floor above hers, or possibly the one above that. It didn't really matter; she hadn't a second to lose. All this time looking for survivors and it hadn't even crossed her mind there might be kids out there. A child wouldn't understand the implications of a fire alarm and a baby couldn't let her know it was there other than by doing the one thing it instinctively knew would attract attention: bawling its eyes out!

Stupid! Stupid! Stupid! All this time and I was so sure I was alone in this place. How fucking dumb am I.

The poor kid must have been on its own from day one of this disaster. It sounded young, probably no older than a year. God knew what it had gone through for the past few days, stuck in the room on its own, its parents surely dead.

She would have to move fast if she was going to help, but first, she needed to check on the red dust.

While she was still 99 percent convinced the dust wasn't interested in her and that probably extended to the baby too, she didn't want to risk overexposure to it, just in case. She was dealing with unknowns and the situation was all so freaking weird, who knew what the long-term effects of contact with that shit would do to her. That was the least of her concerns. Right now, what mattered was finding that baby and finding her quickly.

While she stumbled her way to the living room window, Emily threw on a pair of jeans and tucked in the T-shirt she'd worn to bed. Throwing back the drapes she was greeted by a beautiful blue sky and a view of the city that stretched for miles, and not a sign of one piece of dust—nothing. Just sunny skies.

She stood, mouth agape, staring at the view outside the window. Not a trace of the dust could be seen, at least not from up here. What was going on? It was as though the storm she'd witnessed over the last two days had never happened. If she was—

Wagghhhhh!!!

The baby's cry broke Emily from her thoughts and she immediately dragged her attention away from the dust-free sky to finding the child.

Of course, just because the outside of the building was clear didn't mean the dust wasn't still lurking inside the apartment complex somewhere. She jogged back to the bedroom, grabbed her sneakers from beneath the bed, quickly laced them together, and started to make her way to the door, but before she got there she had another thought. She needed a blanket. Who knew what the poor kid had been exposed to; she needed to make sure she had something she could wrap the child in when she brought it back to her apartment. Emily rummaged through the linen closet and quickly found what she was looking for: the baby blanket her mother had swaddled her in when she was a child. There was something very poignant in grabbing this particular blanket. Emily had never expected to have kids of her own and, at her age, the prospect had looked pretty bleak. It was something her mother and father had hinted at whenever she visited them. She laughed for a second at the thought of her mother's not-so-subtle probes about her love life and whether there was anyone special.

Who knew, Mom? All it took was the end of the world for you to finally get a grandchild.

Looking through the apartment's peephole out into the main corridor, Emily could see no evidence of the probing red dust that had caused her to turtle up the previous evening. Of course, the peephole only allowed for a limited view of the hallway and for all she knew the dust could be sitting just out of sight, like some coiled snake waiting to strike. That, of course, was just her nerves playing havoc with her mind. She'd been in contact with both the red rain and the red dust with no ill effects—*yet*, she cautioned herself mentally—but that didn't mean she should start getting careless.

Even though the adrenaline pumping through her body was urging her otherwise, Emily decided to take her next step cautiously. Instead of pulling away the towels (now long dried out, she noted) from the base of the door and tearing the tape from the keyhole, she decided to remove just the towels first. She did this, making sure she kept them within easy reach in case she needed to throw them back in place. With the towels out of the way Emily slid the security chain off its fastener, thumbed the button on the door latch, and gently twisted the door handle.

The door swung open just a crack and Emily felt a refreshing wave of cool air sweep over her. Thank God, the air-conditioning was back on again. *That's a good omen*, she thought hopefully.

Emily allowed herself a few short seconds for the air to cool her while she peeked through the crack. Her eyes quickly scanned up and down, first checking the ceiling then the floor of the corridor. No sign of anything. She opened the door an inch more, her eyes fixed on the corridor for any movement, ready to slam the door shut at the slightest hint of trouble—still nothing. Emboldened, she pulled the door wide enough to slip her head outside so she had a full view of the corridor in both directions.

There was no movement, no sign whatsoever of the strange red tendrils that had seemed so intent on insinuating themselves into every nook and crevice of the apartment and the city. Except that wasn't entirely true. Here and there, scattered over the floor of the corridor, was a fine red residue that stood out against the light blue carpeting. While it retained some similarity to the red dust, it was now more of a pink color, and seemed to have lost the diaphanous structure that had allowed it to move so easily. Whatever this residue was, it seemed brittle, granular even, and nothing like the delicate structures she had seen propelling themselves through the air. It reminded Emily of the pink Crystal Light powdered drink she would sometimes mix up over the summer.

Emily stepped out of her apartment, quietly closing the door behind her, listening all the time for any indication of the baby. It was only a few seconds later and she heard the telltale wail of the infant. In the corridor the baby's cry was much louder and was definitely coming from somewhere above her. She began jogging toward the stairwell.

Crunch!

The sound surprised her and, as she looked down at her feet, Emily saw she had stepped on a pile of the seemingly inert dust, shattering it with a sound like crisp autumn leaves. Lifting her foot she saw the residue of the dust had turned to powder under her foot, leaving bits stuck to the soles of her sneakers. She had no idea what this signified, but she got the impression that whatever had happened while she was asleep, this powdered residue was all that was now left of the dust.

Doing her best to ignore the constant crackling of the desiccated dust under her feet, Emily continued on her way to the stairs. She would head up to the eighteenth floor first and listen for the child there. If she could not pinpoint where the plaintive cry was coming from she was going to have to start going door to door and listening.

A sudden thought struck her as she climbed the stairs up to the next level: what if the kid wasn't the sole survivor? What if there was someone else alive? That would explain how the kid had survived all this time without access to food or water. The thought excited her more than she would ever have expected.

For most of her life, Emily had been a loner. That she had gone into a profession bringing her into contact with people on such a regular basis had surprised both her parents and her few close friends. She had explained it easily enough: as a reporter, contact was always on *her* terms. She dictated the start and finish of her interaction with every person she interviewed. It was simple really: she maintained complete control of the amount of exposure she had with people, and when she tired of them, she just ended the interview. Easy, really.

So why was she so excited at the possibility of seeing another human being? She couldn't answer that. She was a reporter, not a psychiatrist, but the idea of being no longer totally alone, of having someone, anyone, to talk to was the most astonishingly important thing to her right now.

Emily smiled widely at the thought. It had created a brightness in her that she had not known had left her, and as she opened the door onto the eighteenth-floor landing she began calling out.

"Hello?" she yelled as loud as she could. "Is there anyone else alive here?"

As if in answer to her yell she heard the cry, this time louder and definitely somewhere on the same floor with her.

Wagghhhhh!!!

She paused for a second to try to identify which direction the cry was coming from.

Wagghhhhh!!!

From her left, definitely. And not too many doors down either, by the sound of it.

"Hello," she continued yelling. "I'm here to help. Can you hear me?"

Waggghhhg! Waggghhh! The reply came, doubled to match her own urgency, and luckily too, because she had passed the door to the apartment where the cry was coming from. She doubled back and stood outside the door. Placing her hand flat against the wood of the door she gave it an experimental push: locked! Of course it was; what had she expected?

Emily slapped her hand twice against the door.

"I'm outside your door," she yelled. "You don't have to worry, I didn't get sick. I can help you. Please, just let me know that you're okay. Please." The sentence came out almost as a single word, she was speaking so fast, babbling with excitement, she realized.

As if in answer, the cry sounded again, this time it was a single, long-drawn-out syllable.

Aaaaaaaaaaaaaaaaaaaaaaa!

It was then that Emily realized with an abrupt certainty that the kid was in there on her own. *How do I know she's not a he?* she thought, but it sounded better than calling her "it." Somehow, she had survived for all this time on her own and now it was up to Emily to help. She had to rescue the child. But how the fuck was she supposed to get into the room?

She could try kicking down the door but she didn't think she'd have much luck with that if it was anything like the entrance to her own apartment. Years of cycling had given her strong legs, but she knew she was not strong enough to break down a secured door. No, this was going to take a more focused application of force to open.

"Of course!" she said. She ran back to the stairwell. On either side of the doorway was a large red fire extinguisher, housed in its own box behind a pane of glass. Next to the fire extinguisher, on the opposite side of the doorway, was a similar red box and behind its glass was a large and equally bright-red fire ax. A small metal hammer, about the size of an ice pick, hung from a metal chain on the right side of the box. She grabbed the hammer, turned her eyes away, and hit the glass with as much force as possible. It shattered with her first strike. Gripping the ax with both hands, she pulled it from its retaining clasps and sprinted back to the apartment.

The apartment complex owner hadn't skimped on anything when he built the complex, and that attention to detail also extended to the doors of each apartment. They were made of a high-density wood mix that could withstand a fire for up to an hour. Hacking her way through the door would probably take her a month of Sundays so there was no time to spare.

Rather than try to chop a hole large enough to fit through, Emily decided to concentrate on disabling the actual locking mechanism of the door instead. If she could get to the lock, she should be able to gain access to the apartment.

Emily planted her feet shoulder-width apart with enough room between herself and the door that she could put some real momentum behind her swing. The ax weighed about thirty pounds but she managed to heft it up to head height and take aim at the lock tumbler. She drew in a deep breath and brought the ax down with as much force as she could muster against the face of the door. The impact transmitted waves of pain through her arms and up to her shoulders but she was rewarded with the satisfying sound of wood splintering as she saw the ax blade bite deep into the wood. She had to wiggle the haft of the ax up and down a few times to free it from the door, but once it was out she could see a six-inch-long, inch-deep gash just to the right of the lock.

As if in encouragement to her attempt at breaking and entering, the child inside the apartment let out another mournful wail. As the cry reached her, Emily raised the ax again and sent it down into the door. This time the shockwave of pain was worse as she felt the blade of the ax hit the metal shaft of the lock's cylinder. Sweat had already begun to trickle down her forehead and she felt an uncomfortable wetness under her armpits, but it was worth it because she could see the lock was canted at a slightly different angle than when she first arrived outside the door.

This explains why I became a reporter and not a firefighter, she thought as she felt the dull ache of the pain in her muscles.

Emily summoned her energy again and drew the ax back up above her head. Holding it there for a second, she sucked in as big a gulp of air as she could before exhaling it in a scream that was half frustration and half anger. The ax plummeted down, scoring a direct hit on the lock, dislodging it from the receiver and sending it whistling toward her, missing her head by mere inches.

"Jesus Christ!" Emily exclaimed as she turned to follow the trajectory of the six-inch piece of metal as it clattered to the floor behind her after rebounding off the opposite wall. When she turned back, the remainder of the lock lay on the floor too.

The door to the apartment was now ajar.

The line of work Emily was in had long ago taught her to trust her gut instinct. For some unknown, subconscious reason, she hesitated at the threshold of the apartment, the flat of her left hand resting against the door, her right hand clenched so tightly around the ax handle that she could feel her nails digging into the flesh of her palm. Something did not feel right, she realized. She couldn't put a finger on it, but she had a definite sense of *offness* about what she was hearing. From the dark apartment beyond the door the wail of the child sounded again, louder now that she was so close, breaking through her indecision.

Wagghhhhh!!!

A scene from the movie *The Shining*—the one where an insane Jack Nicholson chops down the door to his kid's room with an ax—leaped unbidden into her mind, sending a shudder of unease down her spine, but she dismissed it as just nerves.

"Here's Emily," she croaked as she pushed open the door and stepped into the apartment.

CHAPTER ELEVEN

The stench of ammonia hit Emily the second she eased the apartment door open wide enough for her to slip inside. It filled her nostrils and seared the back of her throat, instantly triggering her gag reflex. She spent a full minute trying not to throw up before she could move any farther into the apartment.

The smell was not what she had expected. It wasn't the bittersweet stench of putrefaction. This was more like a hundred cats had spent a week peeing freely in the apartment and then sealed the place up for another week.

Waves of heat rolled out through the open door. Emily felt beads of moisture condense against her skin. What had the kid's parents been keeping in here? Were they running a meth lab or something?

How had the kid survived so long breathing this air?

If she had a towel or a rag on hand, Emily would have soaked it in water and used it to filter the cloying, ammonia-laden air. She was tempted to use the blanket but decided against it. Instead, she untucked her T-shirt from her jeans and pulled it up until it covered her nose and mouth, keeping it in place with one hand. It wasn't perfect, she knew, but it should help keep some of that vomit-inducing stench at bay. Gritting her teeth against the smell, Emily stepped into the apartment's entranceway.

It was dark inside but she quickly found the light switch and snapped it on. The overhead lights revealed an empty corridor with just a single painting on the right wall for decoration. The humidity in the apartment was almost as overwhelming as the smell of ammonia. Within seconds of her entering, she was soaked through with sweat and moisture from the air.

"Hello?" she called out. She lowered her hand from her mouth and instantly regretted it. She sucked in a huge gulp of fetid air and felt a chemical burn as it scorched the roof of her mouth and back of her throat. Emily tried to resist but the stink and stinging irritation were just too much this time. She vomited onto the white shag carpet. She wiped her mouth with the back of her hand and quickly brought the T-shirt back up to her mouth. The ammonia was biting at her eyes now, raising tears that blurred her vision so badly she had to wipe them away every couple of seconds with the baby blanket. She wouldn't be able to handle this for very long without passing out, going totally blind, or choking on her own vomit. She needed to find the kid as quickly as possible and get them both out of there. She had to move fast.

The apartment was the next model up from Emily's. It had the same basic layout but came with an additional bedroom. She knew the kid's parents would have put the child in the smaller second bedroom, so she made her way to it, pushing the door open while fumbling for the light switch. She flicked the switch and revealed what was definitely a nursery. A cute crib sat against the right wall, and suspended from the ceiling above it was a child's mobile. Large pink plastic animals hung from the main frame of the toy; *lions and tigers and bears. Oh my!* White wallpaper, decorated with colorful flowers and butterflies, covered the room's walls. Across from the door, she could see a changing station and a high-back chair where the parents could sit and spend some quality time with their kid. Emily walked over to the crib and pulled back the expensive-looking wool blanket. There was no child hidden beneath it.

As if sensing her presence, Emily heard the child's wail echo into the room. Instead of immediately rushing toward the source of the cry, Emily stopped midstep. Her gut was trying to tell her something that her brain did not want to hear; *something is not right here*, it screamed at her, and this time she listened to its advice.

Waggghhhhrrrrrgh!

The cry came again, more insistent. Emily realized, now that she was so much closer to the source, that she could hear an odd trill to it that made it seem far more complicated than the simple cry of a child. It almost reminded her of the tones she'd hear when she was forced to use an old-fashioned dial-up modem to connect to the Internet. The sound was, what was the word? Mechanical? Yes, that was close enough. Now that she could hear it clearly, without the layers of flooring and walls to filter it, the cry sounded less like a child.

Of course, it could just be her imagination. The strange edge to the cry she heard could just be the result of the kid being stuck in this toxic room for so long, but Emily had the sudden overwhelming urge to quietly leave the apartment and never come back.

But as strongly as her instincts might be telling her to leave, she couldn't do that. She had to find out what was making that noise.

There was more caution in her step as she exited the child's bedroom and began creeping toward the master bedroom directly across the corridor. She nudged the door open with the tip of her shoe and cautiously reached inside for the light switch. She poked her head in and quickly scanned the room: a king-size bed, neatly made and waiting for sleepers who would never lay their heads down on the pillows again; a bookcase filled with paperbacks; a dresser; and a tallboy, but no sign of the apartment's tenants.

Emily turned her back on the room and made her way down the corridor, heading in the direction of the kitchen and living room areas. The curtains were drawn closed, filling the living room with gloom. With every step Emily took she felt the temperature increase and the cloying smell of ammonia become stronger, until it was almost unbearable. Even though the area was dark, Emily had a sense of *something* moving in the living room and she froze, the hairs on the back of her neck bristling like spines on a porcupine.

A sense of panic had crept almost unnoticed up her spine and, as she moved unsteadily through the apartment, it had begun knocking on the back of her skull like a hammer, yelling at her to get the fuck out of there, pronto. But her journalistic inquisitiveness and her overwhelming need to rescue the child overrode her sense of self-preservation—*again*, she thought—so Emily began blindly running her hand along the wall looking for the switch that would turn on the living room's overhead lights. The wall's surface was sticky with something that Emily didn't even want to think about at that moment; it felt like someone had sneezed big-time. She wasn't sure which was worse: the stink and the heat or the idea that she'd just put her hand in a huge pile of snot. Neither was terribly appealing, she thought, just as her fingers found the wall switch and filled the room with light.

It took just a second or two for her eyes to adjust to the brightness, but when she finally stopped squinting Emily started screaming.

It seemed as though she had turned on a light that shone directly into the center of a nightmare. In the middle of the room, covering what had probably been the family couch was something that looked as though it had crawled right out of the deepest, darkest corners of hell.

What she was looking at was the source of both the cat-piss smell and the apartment's incredible humidity. That much Emily's brain was able to process, but it stalled when it tried to make sense of what her eyes were relaying to it.

There *was* a child, or at least she supposed that it must have been a child at some point, and the parents were with it. The three had merged into a single mass of fat and tissue that hung from the ceiling in the far corner of the living room. The bottom half of the child's body had disappeared, subsumed into the pulsating bulk of the mass, but its torso and one hand were still free. The hand moved feebly back and forth, almost as though it was waving a friendly "hello" to its new playmate. But that was impossible too, because Emily knew the child couldn't see her; it had no eyes, after all. They were gone, replaced by empty black sockets. It was from the kid's mouth that the eerie ululation was emanating. As she stood transfixed, its mouth opened wide and the bone-chilling sound of its cry spilled out, filling her ears.

Wagggghhhhhhhh!!

The parents were barely recognizable within the pulsating bulk. If it hadn't been for a disconnected foot with a man's shoe still attached to it that lay a few feet (*pardon the pun*, she thought) from whatever *this* thing was, and an obviously female arm that dangled limply from one flank, Emily would not have known what the damn thing was made of. *And that would be fine by me.*

Thick gobs of red *stuff* moved over the skin of the mass, pulling pieces of the main body with them and then moving them to other parts, almost as if it were putting together some kind of puzzle. As she watched the bizarre rearrangement, her mind just a single step from insanity at the utter horror before her, a large globule of the red substance left the body and reached out for the severed man's foot. It deftly surrounded it, shoe and all, and began moving it back to the main body, just like she'd seen ants transport leaves and other dead bugs back to their nest.

This was utter madness, she realized. What she was seeing simply could not exist; it was impossible, so she must be dreaming. But as she continued to watch in horrified amazement as the foot was dragged back to the main mass, and the child's head began a gradual clockwise rotation until it had moved through 180 degrees. The eyeless sockets now stared at her from where the kid's chin should have been, the mouth opened wide and let out a long piercing wail that resonated off the apartment walls and cut through her skull with the precision of a surgeon's scalpel.

Wagghghhghggggggggg!

Emily's courage finally gave in. She exhaled a piercing scream and ran for the door.

■ ■ ■

Emily exploded from the apartment.

Her normal cognitive processes had been superseded by a blind animal survival instinct of the most primitive kind, instincts most humans had not felt since their caveman ancestors first began exploring their new world.

Her feet slid out from under her as she hit the corridor and she went down hard, knocking the air from her lungs, but she was up in a heartbeat, arms flailing as she sprinted toward the stairwell. She took the stairs down to her floor three steps at a time, her feet working on autopilot. Somehow, miraculously, she did not stumble or trip.

Emily kicked open the door leading from the stairwell onto her corridor so hard it slammed back against its hinges, the aluminum handle taking a chunk out of the interior wall. Still sprinting toward her apartment, Emily found the door keys in her jeans and pulled them free. She tried three times to put the key into the lock but her right hand was shaking so violently and the key seemed so massive compared to the tiny slot that she had to steady it with her left hand. Finally, the key found its mark and the door opened. She leaped inside, slamming the door shut behind her with a boom that echoed throughout the entire apartment complex. She fumbled the security chain into place, quickly followed by the thumb lock, and sprinted down the hallway.

Emily's mind did not register these events because all it was concerned with was the dreadful baby-thing that lived in apartment twenty-six on floor eighteen. Caught in a processing loop as it tried to assimilate exactly what this latest assault on her sanity was, her mind refused to do anything but force her feet to move.

When Emily's brain finally returned control of her body, she found herself standing in her bedroom, leaning rigidly against the door. Her first thought was *How the fuck did I get here?* Her next was that she needed to change her underwear and jeans because for some reason she just couldn't fathom, she had wet herself.

With control of her mind and body now returned to her, the full, terrible truth came flooding back to Emily. She understood why she was bracing her bedroom door closed. She knew why she had peed herself. It was because the thing upstairs should not, *could* not, exist.

And yet it did.

Her eyes drifted to the bedroom's ceiling. That *thing* was up there, just feet above her head.

Another terrifying thought struck Emily like the proverbial thunderclap from on high and, given the absolute insanity of the last few days, this latest thought most certainly did not seem to be outside the realm of possibility: What if what she had just seen in the apartment upstairs was able to get out of the room? And what if there were more of them out there? What was she supposed to do about that? What if she, Emily Baxter, really was the last human being left on earth, the sole surviving woman in a world full of monsters?

What if she *was* completely and absolutely alone?

It was at that very moment, with so many questions exploding in her brain like dark fireworks, that Emily heard her cell phone ringing on the table in the kitchen.

CHAPTER TWELVE

I'll call them back later, Emily thought, her mind still trying to wrap itself around the events of the last thirty minutes. *They can leave a message.*

Only after the third trill from her cell phone did the fog filling her brain clear enough for her to grasp what she was hearing. Emily was out the bedroom door and halfway to the kitchen before she even realized she was moving. Grabbing the phone from the table, Emily flipped it open, pressing it to her ear.

There was silence on the other end of the line.

"Hello?" she whispered, her voice barely a croak. "Please, be there. Please." She was no longer surprised at how desperate her voice sounded.

The silence continued for a second, but then Emily heard someone take in a deep breath and a man's voice broke through the silence: "Is this Emily Baxter?"

Emily had been sick once when she was a kid. Really sick. The doctor had informed her parents it was probably just food poisoning, but to Emily it had seemed as though she was dying. The pain had been excruciating; two days of vomiting and diarrhea had left her exhausted and dehydrated. She had eaten nothing and drank little but cool water fed to her by her mother with a spoon. On the third day, as she began to recover, Emily's father brought her a can of her favorite orange soda with a cute pink straw in it. It was one of those straws with a concertina section two-thirds of the way up, so you could bend it toward your mouth. She had drunk that same soda a hundred times before she had become sick, but this time, this time the soda tasted like pure liquid heaven to her parched throat and deprived taste buds. The flavors were so intense, the bubbles so exciting on her tongue, and the cold rush of the soda as it exited the straw and hit the back of her mouth so exquisite, it was as though she was experiencing it in a completely new body.

The smooth resonance of the stranger's voice in her ear had the same effect on her now. She felt as though she had received a call directly from God himself.

"Yes, this is Emily," she managed to blurt out before she broke into a flood of tears.

■ ■ ■

"It's okay! It's all right!" the man's voice on the end of the telephone line said softly. "You're not alone."

At that moment, if the stranger had asked how she was feeling, Emily would have been unable to articulate the rush of different emotions she felt sweeping through her. Gratitude, fear, happiness, sorrow, all simultaneously took hold of her body; but greater than all of those emotions combined was an overwhelming sense of hope. The flood of emotions coalesced into an immobilizing mixture that, for the first ten minutes of the conversation, such as it was, refused to allow Emily to respond to the man's questions other than with a faint, bleated yes or no. Attempting to say anything more than that was futile; the second she tried she dissolved into a huffing bout of tears.

Until this moment, Emily had no inkling she was so totally and overwhelmingly terrified. Even the memory of the horror she had witnessed minutes earlier seemed to have diminished as she allowed the relief of knowing she was not the only person left alive to wash her fear away. Finally, as the rush of endorphins subsided and her self-control began to exert itself again, Emily found her tongue and began answering more fully the patient questions her caller was asking.

His name was Jacob Endersby, he told her. There were eleven other people with him, eight men and four women in total. They were a team of scientists, techs, and support staff working at a remote climate-monitoring station on a tiny, frozen island off the northern coast of Alaska, part of a small cluster known as the Stockton Islands. Their group was, at least until the red rain came, a research team from the University of Alaska Fairbanks Alaska Climate Research Center, and they'd been stationed on the Stocktons for just over three months, gathering climatological data as part of a semiannual study.

Jacob explained that no red rain had fallen anywhere near their base in the Stocktons, but that Jacob's wife, Sandra, who was stationed several hundred miles south of his team's location, back at the university in Fairbanks, had reported the phenomenon falling as far north as the Noatck Preserve, which was about 180 miles southwest of Jacob's location.

Jacob became silent for a minute at the mention of his wife. Emily listened patiently, a light static hiss buzzing in her ear, not sure whether he was still on the line or not.

Eventually, she spoke quietly into the receiver: "Jacob? Are you still there?"

"Yes," he replied, just as quietly. Emily could hear his barely concealed pain vibrate in his voice. This man was carrying a burden of loss as great as any she was feeling over the passing of her family and friends.

"We had a TV satellite feed, so we were following what was happening throughout Europe after the rain had fallen," he continued. "Sandra said the rain had fallen all around the university; not much, just a smattering, but that I shouldn't worry because she hadn't been in contact with it. The university was going into lockdown and they were quarantining everyone who had any contact with the rain, as best as they could.

"Sandra said she'd managed to contact a few other weather and climate-monitoring stations scattered south of her and across the border in Canada. They all reported significantly decreased amounts of the red rain the farther north they were. Eight hours after I last spoke with my wife, I tried calling her again on the shortwave but she didn't answer. *Nobody* answered." Jacob whispered the last sentence between a barely restrained sob and a ragged intake of breath.

The climatologist paused again as he collected himself before continuing. "We have a couple of satellite phones, so we all took turns calling family, friends, and colleagues at other research sites around the world. We called everyone that we could think of, but no one picked up. Since then, our tech guys have been scouring all the major websites and listening on the shortwave, trying to find someone, anyone, who is still alive. That was how we found you, Emily. And we are so very glad to hear your voice."

No one on his team had a solid theory for what exactly had happened, Jacob told her, just some wild conjectures. They were, for the most part, baffled. But one thing did seem quite obvious to the team of scientists: from the data they had managed to collect before losing contact, the red rain phenomena covered a significant portion of the globe, and in Jacob's opinion, it seemed to be an almost directed action against the most populated areas of the planet. As far as they could tell, not one country was left unaffected; there was not a major city, town, precinct, or village anywhere south of latitude 68° north that had not been decimated.

Emily was the first person his team had made contact with. They'd picked up a few fleeting messages on the camp's shortwave receiver but the signals had been too weak and too garbled to make any sense of—but it was a good indication, Jacob said, that others had survived the catastrophe, somewhere.

"Of course, logic dictates there *must* still be pockets of survivors out there, probably small groups like us who live in the colder areas. Maybe there are some military installations left. I guess submarine crews are the most likely to have been unaffected by all of this, but who knows what will happen to them when they surface," Jacob explained.

"What about you and your team?" Emily asked. "How do you think you survived?"

"There's no way for us to understand whether this phenomenon is virus based, a nerve agent, or something else completely. We're guessing that, for some reason, whatever kind of agent the red rain is, its ability to multiply and spread is affected by the cold, which is why my wife reported so little of it in Fairbanks and the other stations north of her. Of course, it appears that even minimum exposure to the rain proves fatal. Unless we can contact other survivors in colder areas across the globe we won't be able to confirm that hypothesis. For all we know, the moment we set foot inside the contamination zone, we'll drop dead. Same could happen to any other survivors outside the areas where the rain fell. You can probably guess that no one here wants to put that theory to the test."

Emily listened intently to everything Jacob had to say, but in the back of her mind she found herself wondering whether she should mention what she had experienced with the red dust storm or the thing she had seen in the apartment on floor eighteen. Would he think she was crazy? If she were in his shoes, she sure as hell would. Telling him she had seen some kind of a monster made up of the young family that once lived in the apartment wasn't exactly going to lend any kind of credence to her story.

"I saw...something, Jacob," she finally blurted out before she even knew she had made up her mind. "Something strange. Not normal."

Jacob stopped midsentence. "What do you mean 'not normal,' Emily?"

Oh, shit! Now I've done it, she thought, doubt filling her mind again. But she *knew* she had seen what she had seen, that it wasn't a figment of her stressed-out brain. She just had to tell him.

"There's other stuff that happened after everyone died. The rain turned into some kind of autonomous dust and..." she paused, drew in a deep breath and then blurted out, "something is happening to the family in an apartment on the floor above me. They're dead but...they're...changing into something else."

"Ooo-kaaay," said Jacob, his voice taking on a confused tone.

"Look," she continued, "I know this will sound crazy. I know you're going to think I'm out of my mind. I mean, I'm questioning my own sanity right now, but I swear I'm not making up what I'm about to tell you."

Emily told Jacob about the strange storm of red dust she had seen, how it had seemed to be attracted to the dead vagrant and then later attempted to invade her apartment. She thought to gloss over how she had heard what she thought was a baby crying, tracked it down to the level above, broken down the door, and found the monster inside, but the truth was, everything she had already told him sounded crazier than a soup sandwich anyway. So why not?

When she was done recounting her story, Emily waited to hear the click of the phone as Jacob hung up. She could imagine him wondering how on earth he had managed to connect with the last crazy person alive in New York.

"Interesting," he said finally.

Well, that certainly wasn't the response she'd expected.

"You believe me?" she asked, still not sure what to make of his response. "I'm not crazy?"

"I can't speak to what you've experienced since the red rain, Emily. And, to be totally honest, I think we both know that if you'd told me the same story before everything that's happened over the last couple of days, my response would probably have been different. But, after what you…what *we* have all experienced? I can't discount any evidence, no matter how subjective it may be."

There was silence for a few seconds as both strangers considered what to say next. Finally, Jacob spoke.

"I told you we really only have conjecture to work with, but we've had little else to do around here than run ideas past each other since everything"—he searched for the right word—"ended. We've parsed every possibility we could think of as a group, no matter how far-out-there it might seem, and eliminated the majority of them as either impossible or highly improbable. What we're left with is, well, to quote you, Emily, is 'crazy' sounding."

Emily heard Jacob take a swig of something, swallow, and then carry on the fast-paced delivery of his idea.

"What we're sure of," Jacob continued, "is *something* far outside the realm of probability has happened across the globe. That *something* is so unlikely it might just as well be defined as a random event because it's so far off the scale of probability. When we throw in the new data you've supplied us, it pretty much removes the possibility of the red rain being a manmade event; there's no way human technology could have the kind of rapid effect on a human body you described, which means we're back to trying to define that elusive *something* again. So, if we rule out manmade technology then we're left with only two probable causes for the red rain and what you witnessed. The first is that our *something* is a part of the natural cycle of the earth, an extinction-level event, similar to the 'great dying' in the Permian-Triassic period. That one event wiped out about 70 percent of land animals and 96 percent of marine life. And there's plenty of data to suggest mass extinctions happen—on a planetary timescale, at least—pretty regularly, *and* we're long overdue for the next one. So, maybe the red rain is part of a cycle that kicks in every few hundred million years or so and wipes the planet clean. It's just the delivery of this event that's *so* strange, *so* unexpected. It just doesn't seem likely that we would have missed some kind of evidence of it in the fossil record."

"And what's the second possibility?" asked Emily, not sure she really wanted to hear the answer.

"Well, again," said Jacob, "you can call me crazy but the only other possibility we can come up with is that this is some kind of extraterrestrial event."

Emily was stunned. "What? You mean like ET? We've been invaded by little green men or something? You're kidding me, right?"

"Yes, well, kind of. It depends on your definition of 'invaded.' What we could be experiencing here is a kind of extraterrestrial biological entity. Our planet is really just a massive superorganism. The red rain could be the equivalent of a virus, but one that exists *out there* in the vastness of space and affects planets instead of individuals." Emily could imagine Jacob energetically waving his hands toward the roof of his office all those thousands of miles away from her. "It just floats around until it randomly lucks on a suitable host planet and then *boom*…mass extinction's the result. The theory is really kind of fascinating when you look at it dispassionately." Jacob seemed to realize that getting excited over the reason for the almost total extermination of humanity might not seem quite so attractive to anyone else outside of his small band of colleagues.

"I'm sorry," he apologized. "I didn't mean to sound so enthusiastic about it all. That's what happens when you spend too much time cooped up with scientists twenty-four hours a day for months on end."

"It's okay," Emily told him. "I understood what you meant." And, if she was honest with herself, Jacob was right; it *was* a fascinating concept. Terrifying, but also incredibly interesting.

"So that's just two of the prime possibilities we came up with," the scientist continued. "Hell, for all I know we could have been on the receiving end of the equivalent of a galactic bug-bomb. We just don't know and I don't believe we'll ever find out the real cause. But what we are sure of is that something unprecedented in the entirety of human history has occurred, and all the old rules, well, they've been thrown right out the window. And, if we factor in your encounter, then the logical conclusion would seem to be that something far greater than a simple random catastrophe is at play here. Which means that that *something* is probably much more complex than we can even begin to estimate at the moment."

There was a long pause and then Jacob's voice filled her ear again, crackling with static. "So, what are your plans, Emily? How are you going to get out of New York?"

Jacob's question caught Emily completely off guard. "What? I'm not planning on leaving my apartment, let alone New York. Why would I need to get out of New York?"

The earlier excitement Emily had heard in Jacob's voice vanished, replaced by a patient, quieter tone that she thought he probably reserved for first-year students at the university and kids—and now he could add crazy reporters to that list.

"There are a couple of good reasons for you to get out of the city. First and foremost, you're surrounded by several million dead bodies that are already well on their way to decomposing. At some point, that's going to bring you into contact with God knows how many potentially fatal pathogens: cholera, typhus, you name it, it's all going to be floating around out there. It is not going to be a very healthy place for you to be."

Jacob hesitated before continuing, but when he did Emily could sense his words were couched by a level of misgiving bordering on reticence, but she couldn't tell whether it was directed at her or was Jacob's doubt at voicing his own thoughts.

"If you're right about what you saw then who's to say it's not happening everywhere? It's not my intention to scare you, Emily, but maybe we need to consider that this event will have even further-reaching effects than we've imagined so far. I hear myself say the words and I know how screwy I sound, but have you considered that the transmutation you saw with the family might be happening elsewhere? Because if it is, then we're talking about an unprecedented shift in the biological hierarchy of this planet, and to be quite frank, that scares the living shit out of me."

"But that's just—" Emily started to answer but Jacob cut her off as if she had not even spoken, his voice insistent.

"Either way, you need to get out of there, Emily. And If I were you, I'd be heading north as fast as I could."

"So what am I supposed to do? I can't drive and I'm pretty sure you guys aren't going to volunteer to come pick me up. How do I get out of here and where am I supposed to go?" Emily could hear the whine of desperation—or panic—begin to creep back into her voice again.

"How do you get out of New York? That I can't really help you with, but where you need to go, that's simple; you need to head as far north as you can. Come to us; we're not going anywhere. The colder it gets the better your chances probably are of surviving this. But you have to prepare and you have to go soon, Emily."

From upstairs, Emily heard the wailing of the thing in the apartment. The idea that there could be who-knew-how-many more of them all around her turned her blood to ice. It was all she could do not to throw the phone to the floor, rush to the closet, and hide until she woke up from this nightmare.

"Okay," she said before she even realized that she had consciously made the decision to leave. "Tell me what I need to know."

■ ■ ■

"First things first," said Jacob. "The power's not going to stay up forever and we need to make sure that you have some way to stay in communication with us. Do you know where you can lay your hands on a satellite phone?"

As it happened, Emily did. The paper had a pair of them they handed out to correspondents covering foreign events or who had to head out to remote areas where regular cell phone coverage was either poor or nonexistent. The paper had put all their reporters through a two-hour-long training course when they'd bought them; Emily had even had a chance to make a couple of calls, so she knew how to operate one. These units were state of the art and even came with a small 12-watt portable solar panel that could be set up in a couple of minutes and used to charge the battery when there was no access to a regular power source.

"That's excellent," Jacob said when she told him. He gave her the number for their sat-phone. "Just in case things start shutting down faster than we anticipated."

"I'll head over to the paper once we're done. Keep your fingers crossed nobody was using them when the shit hit the fan."

The difficult part wasn't going to be getting out of New York, Jacob explained. There was close to 4,500 miles between Emily and Fairbanks; that meant months of hard traveling just to reach the university. Then, once she arrived in Fairbanks, there was another four or five hundred miles of travel over some of the coldest and roughest terrain in North America, with no major roads, to reach the Stocktons. She'd either have to complete that last leg on foot, or hope that the snowmobiles Jacob told her she would find at the university were still where they should be and in working order.

"Don't worry about that right now," Jacob told her. "Worst-case scenario, we can come and get you once you make it to the university. What's important is that we get you out of New York while this event is still in its early stages. We can narrow down a better plan once we know you're safe."

They talked for another hour, exploring plans and ideas for the best course of action to get her on her way. Eventually the conversation turned to personal protection and the need to defend herself. "Who knows what's out there, Emily. You need a weapon of some sort. Do you know where you can lay your hands on a gun?"

Emily's mind instantly flashed back to Nathan. His service revolver had still been in its holster when she dragged his body into the apartment down the hall. She mentally kicked herself for not grabbing the pistol when she had a chance to, but, she reminded herself, she had other things on her mind at the time. And how was she supposed to have known she would even need it? She had been so sure help was going to be on its way. No one in their right mind would have guessed she would need to defend herself against some freak of nature made up of a dead baby and its parents. And what if what she'd witnessed upstairs was also happening to her dead boyfriend too? Did she really think she could handle that? So no, no way was she going to try to get into that room and put what was left of her sanity at risk. She'd worry about a weapon when she had to.

"I'm going to have to get off this phone if I want to get to the paper and back again before it gets dark," Emily told Jacob finally.

"Okay, well, you have the e-mail and the sat-phone if you need us. Just remember you're not alone, Emily. You can call us anytime; someone will always be up, okay?"

"Okay," she replied. The idea of hanging up, of severing the only connection she had had with anyone for the last few days was excruciatingly hard to do. Jacob must have sensed that.

"Emily, don't worry; everything is going to be just fine, I promise you. We'll speak again soon, okay? Good luck and be careful." Jacob hung up, leaving nothing but dead air between them.

Everything was going to be just fine, he had promised her.

Emily doubted that very much.

CHAPTER THIRTEEN

Emily closed her phone and glanced over at the clock on the stove. It was three thirty in the afternoon. That gave her about four hours of sunlight, which should be more than enough time for her to make the ride to the *Tribune*'s offices and get back before sunset.

Emily went to the closet in her bedroom, raised herself on tiptoes, and started feeling around on the top shelf. Eventually her fingers found what she was looking for and she pulled out a large military-style backpack. It was basically an oversized knapsack with several extra-large storage pockets, a relic from the one time she and Nathan had taken a weekend camping trip up at Bowman Lake State Park. They'd bought the backpack from a military surplus store in Chinatown.

It had rained the entire time at the lake, but that hadn't mattered. It had been great, and she smiled at the memory. It all seemed so very distant now.

Emily shook her head to dispel the melancholia she sensed creeping up on her. The backpack would be useful; if she was going to make the trip out to the paper, she may as well make a stop at one of the big stores nearby and grab some supplies while she was out.

She took the backpack and left it near the front door while she grabbed her jacket. She was reaching for the door handle when a thought stayed her hand. Emily walked back to the kitchen and pulled a twelve-inch long butcher's knife from the block she kept on the counter next to the stove. She wasn't sure how much use the knife would be against the thing upstairs—or any of its relatives, for that matter—but as she hefted the blade in her hand it at least gave her some reassurance.

She slid the knife into the inside pocket of her jacket. It wasn't a perfect fit but she didn't think it could fall out, and the jacket was loose enough that she wouldn't end up accidentally stabbing herself. *Better to be prepared*, she thought, as she grabbed the backpack, swung it over her shoulder, opened the door, and stepped out into the hallway.

The hallway was empty, but as she made her way to the stairs she paused as the sound of something shuffling on the floor above her echoed down the corridor. It was a low rumbling sound, like something was being dragged across the floor. Emily paused for a second, her heart beating loudly in her ears. She waited to see if the sound came again, but there was nothing. Taking a deep breath, Emily commanded her legs to walk. They objected for a second but then she was on the move again.

There was no denying it: she was spooked.

Emily knew she was no longer alone, but the closest human being she was aware of was several thousand miles away. If the thing upstairs was moving around, how long would it be before it decided to leave that stinking apartment and explore the rest of the building? What if it was already wandering the hallways? She gave a little shudder as she reached the door to the stairwell, pausing only to peek through the glass security window and make sure the passageway beyond it was empty. Seeing nothing, she pulled the door open and headed down to the ground floor.

■ ■ ■

Emily's bike was exactly where she had left it, chained to the security stand out front of the building. She unlocked it and swung herself into the saddle, glad to be free of the confines of the apartment block. Once she was comfortable she used her feet to get some momentum going and freewheeled down the steps in front of the building bump by bump.

There was no sign of the red dust storm from the day before other than a few drifts of the same glass-like residue piled up against walls and collected in the entranceways to the shops and offices she passed as she pedaled north toward the *Tribune* offices.

She passed a few abandoned vehicles, all of them empty. In fact, during the entire trip she did not see a single corpse. Even the dead birds that had littered the roads and sidewalks seemed to have mysteriously disappeared. Maybe they'd be blown away in the red dust storm, she thought. As much as she would like the explanation to be true, it didn't make much sense because, from what she had experienced during her trip back through the storm, there had been no wind propelling the dust.

So that left what? They'd somehow magically walked away? Or was there a more sinister explanation to the lack of dead on the streets? She sure as hell didn't want to think about it right now so she shifted her focus back to her riding. As she rode through the deserted streets, she started running back over some of the plans she and Jacob had talked about during their phone call. She'd need supplies: fresh water and nonperishable food would be the most important items. And of course, the farther north she traveled the colder it was going to get, so she'd also need to pull together a suitable wardrobe: warm clothes, boots, maybe even skis or snowshoes.

She did not think she would have much of a problem finding shelter on her trek north; there would be so many empty—*hopefully* empty, she amended—buildings between here and her destination in Alaska that she could use to hole up for the night. Her biggest problem, the one she had no real idea how to overcome, was how she was going to transport all of this stuff on her bike. She was so caught up in the minutia of planning her trip as she rode that she soon found herself just a block away from the paper, having traveled the majority of the distance on autopilot.

She pulled up to the building and set her bike down in her usual spot. She instinctively went to lock it but decided against it; she didn't think it risked getting stolen anytime soon. It was also doubtful she was going to need the backpack just yet either, so she swung it off her shoulders and hung it by its straps from the seat of the bike.

The door to the *Tribune's* offices was unlocked. *Thank God for that*, she thought as she pushed through the set of revolving doors and stepped into the deserted foyer.

The place smelled musty, as though it had been deserted for years, like an old, empty library. She supposed that was what the place was now. Emily very much doubted there would be news coming out of this building ever again. That realization struck a poignant note of discord within her; the paper had been her entire world for so long she hadn't really given any thought to its passing. It was almost as painful for her as the loss of her family and friends—more so really, as the paper represented so much more than any individual could. It was an integral part of civilization as a whole. Without it, who would write this world's epitaph?

Jesus, when had she decided to start waxing so lyrical?

"Hello," Emily called, hoping that she might hear Sven or Frank reply. Her voice echoed through the once bustling reception area. There was no answer to her greeting so she began to make her way to the stairs leading up to the second floor and the secure storage area where the paper kept all the expensive gizmos it loaned out to its reporters.

The staircase was one of those spiral affairs, winding up to the second floor like a corkscrew. Made from ornate wrought iron, it was easily wide enough to accommodate four people standing abreast of each other and must have cost a small fortune to have built and installed. Emily had always thought it was quite beautiful, but as the metallic echoes of her feet rang around the empty building she began to feel a sense of unease nibble at her mind and a cold rivulet of sweat roll down the small of her back.

Paranoia came as part of the territory for every reporter Emily had known; she'd received enough threats over the years from the targets of her stories to know a little suspicion was actually a healthy thing. How did that old saw go? *Just because you are paranoid doesn't mean they're not out to get you, right?* And after everything she'd witnessed and experienced over the last few days, well, a hefty dose of suspicion might just be what was needed to keep her alive.

The top of the stairs opened out on to the second-floor landing and a small waiting area. A row of comfortable-looking seats, where visitors could look out through the windows to the street, lined one wall. At least that was the idea, but since Emily had worked for the paper, the windows had always been too grimy to see much of anything. An office-lined corridor led away from the landing; this was where the editors had their suite of offices and also where the main meeting room and the publisher's office could be found.

The security locker was in the editor in chief's office, the last office on the right, almost at the end of the hallway. For the entire time Emily worked at the paper she had only been "upstairs"—as anyone who wasn't a member of senior staff called the second floor—three times: once for her initial interview and the other times for staff meetings. It wasn't a place a staff reporter ever felt comfortable visiting. If you found yourself on that floor, it usually meant you'd been summoned by the editors, which in turn meant you had probably screwed up.

Emily padded her way down the corridor. She found the door she was looking for at the end. A brass plaque fixed to the door had text embossed on it that read JUSTINE GOLDBLOOM and below that, EDITOR IN CHIEF.

Justine was—had been—a great editor and boss. She kept out of the way of her reporters for the most part, giving them just enough freedom to feel like they weren't chained to their desks, but she was always willing to get down in the trenches with the rest of the staff if the need ever arose. Justine had started out as a stringer with the *Tribune* thirty-odd years before Emily had arrived, clawing her way up to the top. Emily regarded her very highly. She had managed to keep her femininity intact while still commanding the respect of both her male and female staff. That hadn't made Justine a pushover by anyone's measure. She was still more than capable of busting your balls if the transgression called for it.

Tough but fair; that was Justine. Emily would miss her.

Emily pushed down on the door handle and stepped into Justine's office. A large mahogany desk occupied the center of the room, and three matching mahogany bookcases, filled with old copies of the *Tribune* and reference books, sat off to one side. On the wall behind the desk, Justine had framed and hung some of the awards she had won over the years. A cubby room sat adjacent to the main office area, set back slightly off to the right. This was where Justine kept the security cupboard and where Emily hoped she would find the sat-phones.

The cupboard was far less imposing than she had imagined it was going to be. In fact, it was just a large metal storage cabinet with a tough looking padlock looped through the handles to make sure no one walked off with the cabinet's contents. Emily gave the padlock an experimental wiggle just to make sure it was locked; it was.

"Great," she sighed.

She felt around the top of the cabinet to see if the key was there but found nothing but dust bunnies. It wasn't pinned to the wall or anywhere else in the cubby that she could see so Emily moved back into the main office and began systematically searching Justine's desktop, and when that turned up nothing, she began rifling through the drawers.

No luck there either, which meant she was going to have to resort to other, more primitive methods.

She wished she had thought to bring the fire ax she had used on the door to the apartment with the baby-monster. It would have made short work of the lock, but it was still sitting where she had dropped it outside the apartment that housed the monstrosity. The knife in her jacket pocket would surely snap in an instant if she used it to try to pry the doors apart, of that she was certain, and the cabinet's hinges were securely located behind the doors, safely out of reach of any pry bar or screwdriver. Her only other option was to find something heavy and try to bash the lock off.

There was a janitor's closet on the ground floor where the cleaning crew kept their brushes, mops, and other equipment. If Emily was going to find anything capable of opening the cupboard it would likely be from there.

She left the office and retraced her steps back along the corridor and the stairs, heading down into the main news-desk area. As she opened the door into the newsroom, Emily was struck by a pungent, yet strangely familiar smell: ammonia! She stopped with one hand still holding the door ajar.

"Oh shit," she hissed.

There was one of those things in there. The urge to turn and run was overwhelming, but the smell, while unmistakable in its cat-piss aroma, was nowhere near as strong as she had encountered in the enclosed space of the apartment—but it was definitely in the air, tickling at her nostrils like week-old laundry.

Emily looked around the expanse of the newsroom. Everything was just as she remembered it. In fact, it looked like everyone had just left for the day, which, she supposed, they had; *never ever to return*, her mind sang to her. The rows of L-shaped desks, neatly lined up like soldiers on parade, still held paperwork and notes. There were even a couple of laptops exactly where their owners had left them, their monetary importance trumped by the need of whoever had owned them to get to the safety of their homes or to be with someone they loved. The TV screens on which she had watched the breaking newscast from Europe now showed nothing but gray and black dots of static.

A wild sensation overtook Emily. She was tired of being alone, tired of being afraid, and even more tired of not knowing what the fuck was going on. It was time to take charge, to take back some control of her life. She pulled the kitchen knife from her coat pocket and stared at it for a second. If it came down to it, could she really stab whatever was in here with her?

"Fuck yes," she said aloud, and kicked the door closed behind her.

■ ■ ■

Emily moved over to the right side of the newsroom. Her sneakers squeaked against the vinyl-covered floor with each tentative step she took. She was tempted to slip them off, but the idea of having to make a rapid shoeless exit did not really hold much appeal for her.

The wall on her side of the room was pretty much clear of obstructions, except for a large photocopier and a table used for collating next to it. If she kept her back to the wall, she would have a clear view of each row of cubicles and still give herself some protection.

Emily inched her way along the wall, one hand flat against its cool surface, the other, the one with the knife, extended out in front of her to ward off any swift attacker. With each crab-like sidestep she forced her eyes to scan the dim recesses and shadows of the cubicles, watching for any movement or sudden explosion of motion. She'd seen enough horror movies in her life to know the threat always came when the character least expected it; no way was she going to fall for *that* trick.

She had just passed the midpoint of the room when the dim outline of a shape across the far side of the room caught her attention. It was impossible to tell what it was exactly, but Emily was familiar enough with the layout of the room to know that whatever it was hadn't been in the room when she left the day of the red rain. It had been invisible to her while she was in the doorway, attached just out of sight to one of the large silver air-conditioning ducts that ran along the room's ceiling and down the opposite wall. Emily stood motionless, her eyes locked on the indistinct shape, waiting to see if it would move. It was difficult to get a clear view of what it was because of the deep shadows surrounding it. Just enough of it was visible to have caught her eye. If she had been focusing solely on the cubicles she would probably have walked right past it.

Emily took a tentative step forward. There was no sign of movement from the thing on the wall but she kept her arm extended out in front of her anyway, pointing the steel tip of the blade directly at the shape. If it leaped off the wall at her she was going to make damn sure it hit the knife first.

With each step closer to whatever this thing was, Emily was able to make out a little more detail: it was about six feet long and two feet wide. The head—if you could call it that—was rounded, almost bullet shaped, while the body tapered off to a flat base at the opposite end. Its skin glistened a pinkish-red, shot through with brighter red veins that crisscrossed over the entire length of it. As Emily took another step closer, she could see the veins periodically pulsing as some kind of liquid pumped along their length. The skin was translucent and she could make out the shadow of a darker shape inside periodically flexing and rotating. It kind of reminded her of an insect pupa or a chrysalis.

Emily's feet caught on something lying on the floor. Her attention was so focused on the thing on the wall that she hadn't paid attention to where she was stepping and she went sprawling, her hand instinctively letting go of the knife and grabbing for the nearest desk to steady herself. She missed and instead struck the edge of the desk with her right forearm, sending a lightning bolt of pain shuddering up her arm and into her shoulder. Her mind registered the sharp edge of a desk flashing toward her and she willed her body to roll as she continued down. Her head barely missed the corner of the desk and instead hit something firm yet yielding. She let out a muted "oomph" as the rest of her body hit the floor, forcing the air from her lungs and sending another bolt of pain down her arm.

Confused, Emily's mind tried to reorient itself to her sudden relocation from upright to horizontal. She pulled in a deep breath of air, sure that she had cracked a rib when she fell—and, knowing her luck, punctured a lung. She was going to drown in her own damn blood, she just knew it.

Goddamn it!

How could she have been so stupid not to look where she was walking?

She lay motionless on the floor for a few moments trying to regulate her breathing and slow her throbbing heart while she listened to the signals from her body. There was none of the telltale pain that she knew would come with a broken rib, no wet rattle of a deflated lung, just a sharp sting in her wrist and an even more painful, but thankfully dull, throb in her shoulder. Emily flexed her fingers a couple of times while she extended her damaged arm in a slow reaching movement; nothing broken either. She had been lucky this time. She raised the arm to eye level and examined the skin. It wasn't cut but already a dull-looking patch of blue and brown was spreading from her wrist toward her elbow. It was going to develop into one hell of a bruise, she was sure.

Emily craned her neck back over her shoulder trying to get a visual of the thing on the wall. It was still, thankfully, exactly where it had been before her little trip.

Emily used her good left arm to push herself to an upright position, careful to feel for any other signs she had broken something or otherwise hurt herself, but there was only the pain in her shoulder and wrist. Once she was in a sitting position and sure nothing else was damaged, she rolled over onto her knees; that way she would be able to use her left arm and the desk she had almost collided with to help pull herself back to her feet.

Emily stared at what had caused her to trip.

It was another one of those things, a pupa. This close to it she could feel warmth spilling off it—nothing like the dense waves of heat the thing in the upstairs apartment had exuded, but more like the warmth of a naked human body. She could clearly see the thick viscous fluid as it pumped through the arteries just below the surface of the skin. In fact, this close to it, she could see an even finer network of veins, like spiderwebs or varicose veins, spread across its entire surface. And beneath that surface, another shape moved slowly, churning in a light pink fluid filling the interior cavity behind the pupa's thick outer layer.

Before she realized what she was doing, Emily reached out her unhurt arm and placed her hand against the pupa's shell. She had expected it to feel slick or slimy, but instead it was surprisingly dry and smooth, hot beneath her fingers. The dark shadow inside the husk gave a sudden twitch and Emily pulled her hand back, abruptly aware that she was touching something that had once been human and was now in the process of becoming something else entirely. She doubted anyone had simply wandered in from the street to take refuge here, so this…this changeling… had been someone from the paper, someone she had known. Her mind sped back to the day the rain arrived. To a conversation held in this very room.

"Oh no," she said aloud. "No."

These two obscenities were all that remained of Konkoly and Frank Embry?

"No," she said again as she looked at what she knew could only be the remains of one of her friends. This had once been someone she had worked with, talked to, interacted with on a daily basis. Now he was this…this…alien *thing*.

The red rain had arrived from nowhere. Killed everyone she knew and loved, tearing her world right out from underneath her. But that hadn't been enough, no; now it was changing them into something else, something alien, with no resemblance to the person they had once been. The idea revolted her.

Emily looked around for her knife. It had spun out of her hand when she'd fallen, but she thought she had heard it clatter off into one of the nearby cubicles. She used her good arm to push herself upright, her eyes unable to break away from the monstrosity at her feet, fascinated by the rhythm of the fluid pulsing through the thing's veins and the oddly slick-looking yet surprisingly dry skin. Finally, she managed to tear her eyes away, turned, and stepped into the cubicle where she thought she had heard the knife land.

She found it lying near a next-to-dead potted palm tree the owner had placed in her cubicle. Grabbing the knife's hilt, she checked the blade. It looked more or less fine except that the tip was broken, snapped off during its unexpected escape attempt. Still, she was sure it would be more than up to the task she had planned for it.

Exiting the cubicle, Emily stepped over the pupa on the floor and placed a foot on either side of its strange bulk. She stared down at it for a few seconds—it really was quite fascinating, almost hypnotic, to watch—then raised her good arm to shoulder height and plunged the knife down into the thing.

There was a wet "pop" as the blunt tip of the blade punctured the shell of the pupa. Emily was hit by a nausea-inducing stench of ammonia as a spray of thick red mucous exploded from the body, splattering across her face, chest, and arm. Some of it managed to land in her mouth and she quickly batted at it with the back of her gore-soaked hand, but that only served to push more of it into her mouth. *Tastes like month-old rotten fish*, she thought just as she felt her gag reflex kick in for the second time that day. She continued to spit the crap out of her mouth, the taste of vomit preferable to whatever it was she had just swallowed.

Emily forced herself to grab the hilt of the knife and push the blade even deeper into the casing of the chrysalis. When it was plunged all the way to the hilt she began drawing the blade down the length of the pupa. The thing inside the shell began to convulse violently, bucking and writhing beneath her as she methodically drew the knife—this time using both her good and injured arm—down the length of the shell like she was gutting a deer. Pink, stinking fluid oozed out from between the lips of the gash and the stench of ammonia became even stronger as the creature trapped inside writhed and twisted in pain.

Something glistening and dripping red goo rose from within the bifurcated shell with a wet slurp. Emily watched in horrified fascination as a red-tinted tentacle extended from within the shell. The tentacle whipped back and forth through the air spraying more of the red crap over the floor and Emily. It was about two feet long with three thick cords of flesh coiled around each other to form a single helix-shaped appendage. The tentacle was tipped with what looked like a black beak but as she watched, Emily saw the beak break open into three triangular pieces, articulated by a fleshy joint at the base that attached each piece to the tentacle. The tentacle ceased its thrashing and suddenly turned to face Emily. The weird beak-that-wasn't-a-beak opened even wider until she could see, nestled snugly in the center of the three triangular pieces, a lidless eye that regarded her with a cold malevolence.

A fucking eye!

It looked nothing like a regular human eye, or that of any other earth-born creature she had ever seen, but she was equally sure that it was still most definitely an eye. And it was staring directly at her.

Emily tugged the knife from the shell of the monster, the pain in her arm and shoulder forgotten temporarily, replaced with an anger-fueled bloodlust. With a flick of her wrist she severed the tentacle in two. The end with the eye fell, bounced once off her knee, and hit the floor with a wet splat. The bottom half, presumably still attached to whatever was growing inside the pupa, snapped from side to side, spraying more of the disgusting red goop before disappearing back within the protection of the shell. Emily raised the knife, and then plunged it deep into the pupae, aiming for the black shadow hidden inside it. The knife found its mark and the rolling of the creature became more violent as its sanctuary suddenly became its execution chamber.

Again and again she stabbed at the thing hidden in the pupa, ignoring not only her own pain but also the stench and taste of the fluid that sprayed from it. When at last there was no longer any movement from whatever was hidden at the center of the shell, Emily dragged herself to her feet and let the knife fall to the floor. She stood over the now dead thing like some ancient blood-splattered gladiator over his defeated opponent.

"One down, several billion to go," she mumbled and spat the last of the bloody crap from her mouth.

Emily glanced at the other alien pupa; if she had the time (and a ladder) she would take care of that one too, but right now she needed to complete what she had come here to do. The pain in her shoulder was already beginning to filter through the adrenaline high and Emily knew if she didn't break into the security cabinet soon and get on her way, she'd have problems making it home before dark.

An open box of tissues sat on the desk of whoever had owned the nearly deceased palm tree. She pulled a handful of the tissues from the box and batted at the gore she could feel splattered on her face. When she was done, she balled up the pink-stained tissues and tossed them at the remains of the cocoon on the floor before heading toward the back of the office to find the janitor's closet.

■ ■ ■

It took just three strikes from the ball-peen hammer Emily found in the janitorial closet to snap the padlock, but that was more than enough to set her injured shoulder on fire. Emily was beginning to suspect that the fall might have done a bit more damage than she had first thought.

With the lock dealt with, she dropped the hammer and pulled the metal cabinet doors apart. Inside she found what she was looking for on the top shelf: a canvas carryall about the size of a handbag with the word "Iridium" stenciled on the sides in large white letters.

She pulled the bag from the cabinet and lowered it to the floor, unzipped it, and began pulling out the contents, laying them next to the bag: a sat-phone, charger, operating instructions, a spare battery, and a solar charger in its own impact-resistant case.

Perfect.

Emily quickly repacked the components back into the bag and gave the cabinet another once-over for anything else that might be of use. There was nothing left but a cashbox that probably contained a couple thousand dollars. No use to anyone now.

As Emily closed the door to the cupboard, she spotted the hammer she had used to break the lock lying on the floor where she had dropped it. She grabbed it by the shaft, dropped it into the bag with the phone equipment, and zipped it closed again.

Picking up the bag with her uninjured hand, Emily retraced her steps back along the corridor and down the metal staircase. She winced in pain as, unthinking, she used her injured right arm to shoulder through the main door out onto the street. If she had thought about it she should have looked for a first-aid kit, or some painkillers at least, but it was too late now. The adrenaline rush from her little chainsaw-massacre moment had worn off and the throbbing in her shoulder had evolved into a sharp teeth-clenching pain that Emily suspected might be a torn muscle or—and she hoped to God this wasn't the case—a dislocated shoulder. She was still able to move her arm before the pain really kicked in, so she suspected she could disregard the dislocated shoulder theory, but her first-aid training was minimal and the last class she had taken was back in her high school days.

There was no way she was going to have the time or the ability to do any of the extracurricular shopping she had planned, not today. What was most important now was to get home without doing any more damage to herself and treat her injured shoulder and arm; the supply run would have to wait until she was feeling better.

She lifted the backpack from its resting place around her bike's saddle and pulled open one of the pouches; slotting the sat-phone bag into it she secured the pouch and hefted the backpack onto her left shoulder. This next part was going to hurt, she knew, but there was no way she was going to leave the backpack behind on the street.

Her right shoulder screamed at her, the pain bringing tears to her eyes as she gingerly manipulated it through the backpack's shoulder straps. She had to keep her elbow akimbo and slide it through, while pulling the strap across her chest with her good left hand. Without the injury it would have taken her mere seconds, but instead it used up precious minutes of daylight and left her sweating like a horse that had just run a steeplechase.

The buildings threw long shadows across the street as the sun dropped behind them. A row of streetlights had already begun to brighten as she swung her leg over the top bar of the bike, settled herself into the saddle, and used her feet to kick some initial momentum into the bike. She had to keep her right arm bent and resting against her chest as though it were in a sling, as she could no longer extend it far enough in front of her to reach the handlebar. That made the bike less stable, so she also had to fight her instinct to pedal at her normal rate. Instead, Emily reduced her speed to a safer, but far slower level to ensure she wouldn't fall off the damn bike and do even more damage than she already had.

It took her almost three times as long to get home as it had taken her to get to the *Tribune*'s offices. As twilight slowly edged toward dusk, Emily slowed her speed even more as the pain in her shoulder became a second-by-second distraction to her. She had to avoid any kind of bump or rut in the road, because hitting one caused her shoulder to explode in agony, sending spots of blackness across her vision that would in turn send her careening off course. Twice her vision had cleared just in time for her to narrowly avoid slamming into one of the few parked cars still left on the empty streets. The second time she'd almost gone over the handlebars when she pulled the brake lever too hard, forgetting she only had her front brake. The bike had reared up on its front wheel in a reverse wheelie and she had tottered there for a second before the back end had bumped jarringly back to the road.

As Emily rounded the final corner before the apartment complex, she let out a sigh of relief and began to relax, in spite of the pain. When she got home, she was going to risk draining the water she'd collected out of the tub and running another hot bath. She was going to soak in it for as long as she needed.

Purposely overshooting her destination by a half block, Emily rode the extra distance to a pedestrian crossing where she knew she would find a disabled-ramp she could use to get her bike off the road and onto the pavement, avoiding the guaranteed pain of jumping the bike up the curb. She circled back toward her building and pulled up in front of it, exhausted, bloodied, but alive and still in one piece.

Dismounting as carefully as she could, Emily left the bike lying on the pavement in front of the entrance and headed toward the welcoming warmth of the brightly illuminated apartment block. She pushed through the building's front door, careful to avoid her damaged shoulder this time, pulled the door to the stairs open, and readied herself for the seventeen-floor climb ahead of her.

And that was when all the lights went out.

CHAPTER FOURTEEN

Emily had never been afraid of the dark.

When she was a child she had laughed at the other kids who insisted they sleep with a night-light on. She had never believed there was a monster hiding in the dark recesses of her closet and she definitely had no problem taking a wander out into one of her parents' fields after sunset, just to sit in the long grass and stare at the moon and the stars.

But this was a very different kind of darkness. It was so deep and absolute, she might as well have been blind as she cautiously maneuvered her way up each level of stairs toward her apartment, carefully feeling for the landing at each new level so she could make the 180-degree turn needed to continue up the next flight of stairs.

The stairwell was a completely enclosed space with no windows. There was supposed to be an emergency generator down in the basement that should have kicked in and turned on the backup lights when the power went down, but that, apparently, was not going to happen.

No light meant no floor numbers either, so Emily had to count each level as she climbed and hope she didn't make an error in her calculation and end up a floor above or below her apartment's level. *Especially* not a floor above.

It was incredible to her how the removal of a single sense, albeit the one she relied on completely, could have such a profound impact on her interpretation of the world. Alone in the mine-black darkness, with only her four remaining senses to guide her, she became acutely aware of how ironic it was that she was now in exactly the position she had once relished as a child: alone in the dark, surrounded by the unknown. Back then it had been exhilarating and inviting; right now, with the events of the past few days and the stench of the creature she had killed earlier still filling her nose, she was absolutely and profoundly terrified.

It wasn't often Emily wished she could go back to being a kid again, but she could use an ounce or two of that childhood bravado. Of course, being surrounded by some unknown menace didn't exactly help either.

To distract herself, Emily began counting each flight of steps out loud. It wasn't long before the sound of her voice echoing up the empty shaft of the stairwell began to make her more uneasy than the silence, and she reverted to counting the steps off in her head instead.

By the time she reached what she was 99 percent positive was her floor, Emily was barely able to put one leg in front of the other. The strap of the backpack was digging into her right shoulder and felt more like a knife than a foam-padded support strap. Her head ached from the overdose of adrenaline and her back and knees objected to every step she asked them to take.

She felt around for where she thought the door should be. It wasn't there, so she moved her hands to the right and found the crack where the door met the frame. A few inches in, her hands found the coolness of the pane of security glass in the door's center panel and she inched her hand down from there until she located the aluminum bar-handle.

She was about to pull the door open when a faint noise dragged her attention back to the stairwell. It was distant, but definitely coming from within the building somewhere, she was sure of it. The sound was a warbling ululation unlike anything she had ever heard before. It echoed eerily through the stairwell, bouncing off the walls. Emily had the unnerving thought that she might be the first human to have ever heard this strange, unearthly cry.

The sound came again, a lone voice probing into the darkness. As she listened, more warbling voices joined the first, answering the call and, as Emily stood mesmerized by the strange chorus filling the blackness of the stairwell, a final voice joined the choir and this one was much closer.

This one was in the stairwell with her.

■ ■ ■

Emily flung the door open and stumbled blindly out into the lightless corridor, rushing headlong into the opposite wall, her face impacting painfully with the drywall. Luckily, she had been in the process of fishing her keys from her pants pocket so her head was turned just enough to the left that she didn't hit nose first. A busted nose would just have been the icing on a perfect day. Instead, her cheek and, of course, her injured shoulder took the brunt of the collision. The pain was so intense she literally saw stars, tiny white motes of light that danced around her sightless eyes. She felt like a cartoon character and wondered whether those same stars bouncing around her vision were circling around her head.

No time to think about that, her panic driven brain reported to her. *Got to move. Got to get to safety*.

The braying cry of the unseen creature again echoed up from the stairwell, puncturing the darkness and paralyzing Emily for a second before her brain regained control over her feet and forced them to move. She was totally disoriented; the corridor was almost as dark as the stairwell, and she had no idea whether she was facing toward or away from her apartment.

She had to stop for a second and reorient. Convincing her brain that this was a good idea was next to impossible; the primal flight or fight instinct had kicked in and her brain had made its decision quickly and decisively: *run like fuck!* But if she followed that impulse she could end up in completely the wrong half of the corridor, so she forced her feet to remain rooted to the spot.

Emily's heart crashed in her chest, reverberating in her ears; unfortunately, it wasn't loud enough to drown out the cacophony of calls that now seemed to fill the night. Emily could hear other noises too, shuffling and clunking sounds that filled the empty air, seeming to come from every floor of the apartment block. Emily's mind instantly imagined the unimaginable: from all around her came the sounds of creatures emerging from their cocoons and beginning to explore their surroundings for the first time. The strange cries and warbles belonged to things that weren't of this world and whose bodies were designed for other, far distant planets. They had woken from their slumber and were even now moving and shuffling as they called out to their brethren.

She was surrounded. Emily Baxter, until just a couple of days earlier a reporter for a mildly respected newspaper, was now the last living woman in a city that might as well be on another planet.

"Screw that," she breathed, barely able to hear herself above the growing cacophony of calls.

She reached into her jeans and pulled her apartment keys from her pocket. These were her lifeline. Even though she couldn't see them, the reassuring jangle of metal against metal was a welcome sound of normality and, if she could just find her door, a promise of safety. The reassuring feel of the keys in her hand was enough to force her body back under her control.

Emily drew in another deep breath and reached out with both hands, ignoring the pain in her shoulders and the twinging throb in her cheek. Her hands connected with the plasterboard of the wall and she took a step to the left, feeling her way along the surface of the wall, looking for something that she could use to orient herself within the corridor. She took another step and repeated the process but didn't find what she was looking for, so she turned around until she was relatively sure she was facing the opposite wall and took two tentative steps forward until her palms again touched a wall. She reversed the process she had begun on the other wall, taking baby step after baby step until, finally, her hands found what she had been searching for: the solid bulk of the stairwell door she had exited through. Now that she was oriented, Emily knew which direction to head, but she was going to have to rely exclusively on her sense of touch to locate her apartment.

From the other side of the stairwell door, Emily sensed rather than heard something large move. It was just the tiniest of sensations, a disturbance in the air brushing against the small hairs of her face, a vibration transmitted through the door and to the tips of her fingers. In the pitch-black hallway, her remaining senses had switched to a heightened state and Emily knew that the owner of the cry she had heard in the stairwell earlier was now *much* closer.

As if to confirm her thought, an ear-piercing scream exploded from the thing in the stairwell, battering her remaining senses. The sound was so strong and so close the vibrations of its ferocity ran through the door and flowed up Emily's arms, resonating and buzzing in her brain like a swarm of angry wasps. This time the sound had the opposite effect: instead of freezing, it galvanized Emily into movement. She turned her body in the direction of her apartment, clutched her keys firmly in her hand and pushed her thumb through the loop of the key ring, just in case she stumbled or fell.

She began walking as quickly as she dared toward her apartment, her left hand trailing behind her as it traced the contour of the wall. She let out a sigh of relief as her fingers felt the sudden lift and then dip of the frame surrounding the door of the first apartment.

"One," she counted off and then began moving forward again through the darkness.

Her fingers touched the frame of the next door and she whispered, "Two"—her voice almost drowned out by the cries of the thing in the stairwell. It seemed to be closer still. *Just two more doors,* she told herself as terror began to creep back into her heart, *just two more.*

More steps, this time rushed, as she gauged her chance of falling versus remaining in that haunted corridor a second longer than she had to.

"Three," she said as her fingers found her neighbor's door. Emily ran the last few steps, the skin on her fingers tingling with the friction generated as she felt along the wall. Her hand contacted with her door just as she heard another click and the unmistakable squeak of the stairwell door opening.

Emily stopped, listening.

The squeak of the door's hinges opening farther reached her ears and then...another noise. Emily's breath froze in her throat as the sound of something large squeezing itself through the doorway echoed down the corridor. It was followed by another noise, like stiletto heels on tile, the sharp "tap, tap, tap" of multiple feet drumming against the floor as whatever had just entered the corridor began moving in her direction.

She was no longer alone, Emily realized with a growing sense of horror.

Tap...tap...tap... The rapid staccato sound edged closer to her, then stopped for a second before continuing.

Emily's mind frantically worked to make a familiar association with the sound of the fast-approaching creature but she came up blank. While her imagination could not piece together what was in the corridor with her, her instincts had no such qualms and screamed at her something she already knew: whatever was drawing closer in the darkness was searching for *her*.

She began quickly feeling around the door for the lock. Finally, she felt the cold metal of the knob beneath her trembling fingertips. Her fingers, clammy with sweat, tugged at the keys looped over her thumb. They were stuck on the knuckle of her thumb and would not budge. She gave an extra hard tug and felt the key ring pull free of her thumb. Emily let out a small cry of dismay as they slipped from her damp fingers and clattered to the floor, invisible in the darkness. She dropped to her knees and began to feel around for the lost keys. How could it be so damn hard to find them? They had to be right in front of her.

Tap...tap...

The sound was closer this time. Her breath began to come out in short ragged bursts as her heart played a drumbeat behind her ribcage while she frantically felt around in the darkness for the lost keys.

As if the creature at the other end of the corridor could sense her panic, Emily heard a sudden acceleration to its movement.

Tap…tap, tap, tap…

The thing skittered even closer to her through the darkness.

Then—*thank you, God*—she felt the shape of the key ring beneath her fingertips. She snatched it up, feeling for the telltale rubber cover she had placed over her front-door key. The fingers of her right hand searched for the keyhole again, and, as she felt the outline of the brass lock cylinder beneath her fingers, she brought the key up and guided it into the lock. Turning the key, Emily was rewarded with the familiar click of the lock's tumblers falling into place. The weight of her body pushed open the door and she stumbled into her apartment. She pulled the key from the lock, slammed the door shut with all her remaining energy, and searched for the thumb lock. With the thumb lock securely in place, Emily patted around above it until her hand swatted the security chain, which she fumbled with before finally fastening it.

In the total blackness of her apartment, Emily Baxter crawled along the corridor on her hands and knees until she found her bedroom. She crept inside, still on her hands and knees, over to the walk-in closet on the far side of the room. Opening the door to her closet, she pulled herself inside and closed the door securely behind her.

That night, cowering in the corner of the closet, Emily listened to the calls of an awakening world.

DAY FIVE

CHAPTER FIFTEEN

Emily did not know what time the creatures stopped their wailing. As the night wore on, her mind gave her the only protection it could, providing her with a buffer against the overwhelming sense of dread that gripped her as she listened to the cries of the creatures calling to each other.

Her mind retreated into itself, filtering out the strains of the alien dissonance that pummeled her senses. Emily found herself regarding the situation from a place where, if she had cared to try to explain it, she could only describe as the center of her mind. It was so quiet there. Not the scary quiet she had experienced after everyone else had died, but a peaceful, warm quiet. Her pain, both physical and mental, became a distant distortion, more fascinating to her than distracting.

At some point during the night, her body, shocked and in pain, had demanded to shut down and, despite Emily's best efforts to remain awake in that beautiful island of peace her mind had taken her to, she had slept.

When she awoke, the memories of the previous night came flooding back to her, and they brought with them a new fear: that while she slept the creature she had heard in the corridor might somehow have made it into her apartment.

She had no idea how long she had hidden in the closet or even what time it was. Her closet-sanctuary was almost as dark as the corridor she had fought her way through the night before, but a bright line of light filtering through the crack at the bottom of the door could only mean day had arrived, and that at least helped to alleviate some of the fear gnawing at her courage.

As her head began to clear, her injuries also began to make their presence known. Emily winced as she eased her body away from the wall she had been leaning against, and her legs complained as she unfolded them from beneath her.

She gave her injured right arm a cautious experimental flex. A dull throb, starting in her deltoid muscle and continuing down into her triceps, pulsed with each movement she made. It hurt but it wasn't debilitating. Next, she tried lifting her elbow to shoulder height but only managed a few inches before a sharp burst of pain in her neck made her grimace and decide it probably wasn't such a good idea to try that again for a while. Looking on the bright side though, the pain level wasn't as bad as last night. It was just an eleven on a scale of one to ten, instead of a fifteen. Hopefully, that was a good indicator her injury wasn't as severe as she had first thought. Still, it hurt like a son of a bitch and was going to slow her down for sure.

"Okay, on the count of three," she whispered. "…Three." She used her left arm to help push herself to a standing position, coddling her right arm, keeping it tight to her body, but the pain was still enough to force a hiss of air from her as she raised herself to her feet.

She allowed herself a moment for her strained muscles to relax. As she stood in the darkness, she turned her thoughts to her next problem: whether she had picked up a new roommate overnight. It could have been her imagination, of course, but the thing in the corridor had seemed very interested in her last night. Emily was sure the sound of her door being broken down by some multiple-legged freak that used to be one of her neighbors would have gotten her attention, even given the almost catatonic state in which she had spent the night. Still, given the magnitude-ten on the weirdness scale of the past few days, it was better to err on the side of caution from now on. She was hardly in a fit state for another fight, after all.

Emily reached for the closet's doorknob and, ever so cautiously, twisted it, cringing as the latch squeaked back. Keeping her hand firmly on the handle, Emily pushed the door open until a crack large enough for her to view her bedroom and the door leading into it was visible. She was ready to snatch the closet door closed again if she spotted anything out of place, but everything looked normal to her. There wasn't any sign of a disturbance, so she pushed the door open a few more inches until the gap was large enough for her to stick her head through. She scanned the rest of the room and the back of the door, just in case anything was lurking out of sight back there—nothing.

With the coast apparently clear, Emily cautiously slipped out of the closet and into the bedroom. Only when a loose tie-down caught on the door handle did she realize that she was still wearing the backpack she had slept with the damn thing on her back all night. With a little luck, she hadn't damaged the sat-phone while she was asleep. She'd check later but right now she needed to recon the rest of the apartment.

Emily crossed over to the bedroom door and looked out into her hallway, but again, there was nothing. The front door was in one piece with the thumb lock and security chain both still in place. She began to breathe a little easier, but she'd need to do a full survey of the apartment before she could relax fully.

Pushing the bedroom door closed with a click of the lock, Emily moved to her bed and undid the quick-snap belt from around her waist, dropping the backpack onto the comforter. She winced as a jab of pain shot across her shoulder like an electric shock.

She had left the knife next to the remains of the pupa back at the paper, but the hammer she had used to break the lock of the security cabinet was still in the sat-phone bag, so she quickly undid the flap covering the main compartment of the backpack, pulled out the sat-phone bag, and located the hammer. The weight of it in her hand felt good, even if she would have to carry it in her left hand. It wasn't as comforting as the knife but it sure would put a dent in the day of anything that might be lurking elsewhere in the apartment.

With hammer in hand, Emily opened the door of the bedroom and began searching the remainder of her apartment. Quickly moving from room to room it was soon clear to her that whatever had been lurking in the corridor had apparently lost interest in her and had failed to breach her apartment's defenses. The place looked exactly as she had left it; nothing waited for her in any of the closets or behind the breakfast nook or even under the bed.

Her place was clear.

Returning to the bedroom, Emily unpacked the sat-phone and accessories, inspecting them all for any damage. Everything looked to be in good shape, but when she pressed the power button for the phone the display remained black; the battery was dead. She popped the plastic back panel off the phone, pried out the old battery, and inserted the spare, hoping there might be some charge left in it, but it too was spent. She would need to charge them both as quickly as possible.

Emily glanced over at her bedside alarm clock. The alarm's display was blank. She walked over to the light switch on the wall, flicked it on and off a couple of times but the light above her head remained dark.

With the power still down—and with little chance it was ever coming back—she was going to have to use the solar charging unit she had picked up with the sat-phone to charge the batteries.

It was imperative that she reestablish a line of communication with the scientists in Alaska as quickly as possible. They had to know what was happening.

Emily unboxed the solar charger and scanned over the instructions on how to operate it. The device came with a separate battery unit that plugged into the collapsible solar panel. This separate unit would hold a charge up to six times longer than a regular battery and would allow her to then charge the phone's batteries from the unit. This meant she would always have an extra charge available. Simple. The only problem was it was going to take about nine hours to fully charge the solar unit and then the phone. Emily took the battery unit and solar panel into the living room where it would get the most sun. On the way in she checked the clock on the cooker, realizing she had no idea what time it was. With the power off, though, that clock was also dead, so she had to backtrack into her bedroom to read the battery-powered analog clock on the wall: 11:07 a.m. the hands showed. That was good; it gave her at least seven hours of sunlight, which should be enough to get a full charge.

Using the instruction book to guide her, Emily made quick work of assembling the unit, snapping each piece into place and then moving the completed unit to the sideboard close to the window where the solar charging panel could gather the energy it needed. Almost immediately, a small red LED indicator on the top of the unit began flashing to show it was indeed charging.

Emily's stomach grumbled loudly. She had ignored her hunger pangs while she worked to get the unit up and charging. With that chore out of the way, she figured she had time to grab something quick to eat.

She opened the refrigerator; the air was still cool inside but that wouldn't last long now that the power was down. She had half a pack of honey-roast ham left and decided it was best to use that up before it spoiled. She pulled a couple of slices from the packet, rolling them into a tube before biting a chunk off the end. The remaining meat she put between two slices of bread, smothered them in some mayo, and chowed down, savoring the flavors while wondering whether this would be the last time she ever tasted any of them. She chased the sandwich with the last of the milk along with a couple of extra-strength Tylenol from the medicine cabinet in the bathroom.

With her belly full, Emily turned her mind to the next item looming on her agenda: how was she going to get out of New York?

For anyone else, she supposed the option would be clear: grab any of the tens of thousands of vehicles left abandoned on the side of the road or parked in apartment garages, and head out of town, but Emily had zero driving experience. She had never had a need for it. She supposed that she could try and learn to drive but there was always the chance that she'd crash the damn car and end up dead—or worse still, trapped in a wreck with no hope of rescue and only a slow painful death to look forward to. Besides, while the roads were pretty much clear around her patch of Manhattan, who knew what they were like on the routes out of the city. She could spend the time hunting down a suitable vehicle and trying to learn to drive while not killing herself, only to find the roads blocked somewhere along the way. She'd be in a worse position than she was now and without the security of her apartment, the mobility of her bike, and the chance to plan far enough ahead. Besides all of those reasons, Emily had a creeping suspicion that last night's chorus line was only the beginning of a totally new act in this bizarre show. She could not afford the time she would need to spend screwing around with learning to drive when she could be using it to gather supplies and start on her way. No, when she left, it was going to have to be with the help of her trusty bike and her own two feet.

Her first objective, then, was to gather more supplies. She was confident that when she left the city, *if* she chose the right route, she could avoid the major population centers. If she stuck to the rural areas, she could still scavenge for food and find somewhere safe to rest each night while lowering her chances of running into anything nasty. If she could do that then she wouldn't have to worry about carrying more than a few days' worth of food and water with her, which meant she could move faster. Of course, she would have to take the time to track down provisions and shelter on a daily basis, but she was confident that would not be too much of a problem. When you were conceivably the sole remaining human being left on the East Coast, the world was pretty much your oyster.

Most homes, she thought, would have a supply of canned goods in their pantry. She was sure those nonperishables would last for months, if not years, before spoiling. She would collect food as she traveled. The extra space she gained from carrying minimal provisions would be taken up with other essentials like a medical kit, spare parts for her bike, the sat-phone equipment, and extra water—and, of course, some kind of weapon. At some point she was going to have to address that, the sooner the better she supposed, but the idea of entering the apartment where she had left Nathan with the dead family frightened her. She wasn't afraid to admit it. The possibility he had become one of whatever she had encountered in the darkness last night—well, that was not something she was sure she could face.

The one thing that could prove to be a problem was finding spare parts for her bike; a punctured tire, snapped brake line, or a broken chain could be hard to fix and slow her down by days if the bike was damaged in the middle of nowhere. And, she suspected, the fewer reasons she had to travel into major population areas the safer she would be.

If she was honest with herself, her current bike was not exactly in its prime anymore. It might be worth paying a visit to her local bike store one last time. First, Emily needed to change her clothes and wash up because she stank worse than a pissed-off skunk on a summer's afternoon. Her clothes were torn and covered in whatever the thing she had killed in the newsroom called blood.

Just because it was the end of the world didn't give her an excuse to start acting like a bum.

■ ■ ■

The image that greeted Emily in the bathroom mirror was unnerving, to say the least. She raised a tentative hand to her cheek and touched the purple bruised skin beneath her right eye. The throbbing pain in her shoulder had distracted her from the fact that her face looked like she had gone a couple of rounds with Manny Pacquiao. While she lightly probed around the puffy broken skin with her fingers, Emily's mind drifted back to the events that had caused her to run headlong into the wall. Looking back at it now, in the clear light of day, she began to wonder whether the creature she thought was chasing her had been nothing more than a phantom created by her stressed-out, overexcited mind. She hadn't *actually* seen *anything*, right? But it had been too damn dark to see anything in that corridor, and what about the caterwauling that had caused her panic in the first place? Emily *knew* she hadn't imagined that.

She smarted as her fingers pressed against the inflamed skin of her cheek a little too hard. An inch-long cut just below her right eye stung every time she blinked. It wasn't too deep and had already scabbed over. Emily was confident she would live.

It was okay to joke but Emily knew she was going to have to be extra cautious when treating any open wounds she suffered from now on. A minor cut could easily become infected and, with no access to a doctor, she would be on her own. She made a mental note to look for a supply of antibiotics before she left.

And what was with her hair? It was a matted mess and looked like a family of sparrows had built a nest back there. The final addition to her end-of-the-world makeover was the flaky streaks of dirt slashing diagonally across her face like camo paint from some war movie.

"Well, don't you just look lovely," she told her reflection, before bending to the cupboard beneath the bathroom sink and pulling out the small first-aid kit she kept there. She unclipped the lid and rifled though the contents until she found an antiseptic pad, which she set on the glass shelf underneath the mirror. She'd need to clean herself up before she used the pad, but the idea of washing in cold water held no appeal for Emily. Instead, she chose the next best option: wet-wipes. She pulled the plastic packet from the medicine cabinet on the opposite wall and began wiping as gently as she could at the dirt and dried blood on her face. It took most of the pack before she felt she looked presentable again and had cleared the dirt and muck away to reveal the full extent of the abrasion on her cheek.

"Son of a goddamn bitch!" she yelled as she wiped the antiseptic swatch across her grazed skin, the pain in her shoulder forgotten for a moment, as the sudden burning of her cheek demanded all her attention. She hoped the extra abuse she was putting herself through was worth the effort. She'd cut her cheek over eight hours ago and wasn't sure her late attempt at first-aid would actually do her any good. But in the spirit of her earlier commitment to an overabundance of caution when it came to medical issues, she wiped the antiseptic pad across the gash on her face a couple of more times.

With her bout of self-torture finally over, Emily slipped out of her disgustingly dirty shirt and jeans, pulled off her panties and socks, balled them all together, and tossed them into the far corner of the bathroom. With no electricity for laundering, she wasn't going to be wearing them again, but Emily was confident she wasn't going to be here long enough to worry about cleaning up after herself.

The air was cool against her exposed skin as Emily moved from the bathroom into her bedroom. She pulled a clean T-shirt and jeans from the same closet where she had spent the night. As she pulled on her fresh set of clothes, she caught a whiff of her own body odor, but there wasn't much she could do about that. She would need to figure out a way of heating water at some point. She didn't think she could handle her own stench for too many days.

A few minutes later, wearing her fresh clothes and another pair of sneakers—*whoever came up with the idea of replacing laces with Velcro strips was a genius*—Emily felt she was finally ready to start moving forward with the next part of her plan.

■ ■ ■

This time, she would be ready for any trouble. She gathered together a collection of essential items: her trusty hammer, a large bottle of water, several snack bars she found hidden behind a bag of flour in the pantry, and, determined to never be caught in the dark again, a six-cell Maglite flashlight she kept in her bedroom tallboy in case of a brownout. The flashlight would also double as a baton if it came down to it. She packed everything except the hammer into the backpack and shouldered it, slotting the hammer into the waist belt.

The pain pills she had taken with her late breakfast had kicked in and the pain in her strained muscles was already beginning to fade to a sufficiently ignorable level. Feeling as ready as she was ever going to be, Emily checked the corridor outside her front door, looking through the security peephole for any sign of the creature she thought she had heard in the darkness. It looked clear, but she decided to err on the side of caution and pulled the hammer from her belt before slowly opening her front door.

Nothing lay in wait for Emily outside her apartment. The corridor was as empty as she remembered it being when she left the day before. There was *something* different though. On the opposite wall from her apartment, a number of ragged holes punctuated the wall. They were spaced almost evenly apart, and as she looked closer, Emily could see they left a trail that extended along the wall back toward the door to the stairwell before curving up onto the ceiling and ending at the stairwell entrance. She leaned in to get a closer look at the holes; they were large enough for her to place her pinky finger in and looked to have been cut by something sharp enough that it left a clean hole with no rough edges.

They were track marks, she realized.

Something *had* come up through the stairwell last night. While she had struggled in the darkness, it climbed along the corridor wall after her and stopped outside her apartment. The hair on the nape of Emily's neck stood erect. Emily wasn't sure she felt any better knowing she hadn't imagined the incident, because now she was truly unnerved. Instinctively she looked up and down the corridor again, double-checking to make sure whatever had made these tracks was not hiding somewhere nearby.

The divots in the drywall were spaced in two parallel arcs, six on each side. Emily placed her left arm in the space between the two sets of tracks, her fingertips touching the top set of holes; her elbow didn't even reach the center of the gap between the two tracks. Whatever had come through that door was big, at least four feet across, if her rough measurements were anything to gauge it by. Her grip on the shaft of the hammer grew tighter as her imagination spiked into overdrive, conjuring up images of what could create the kind of marks she was looking at on the wall. Emily quickly dismissed the thoughts. She knew that no matter what imaginary creatures she created, the reality was going to be far more alien than her tired mind could produce.

She had always considered herself willing to confront anything—a reporter who wasn't able to face down opposition wouldn't last very long—but this whole situation was just too far out, too strange. The drive to hide and pretend it was all okay was overwhelming, but if she gave into it, Emily knew she would surely die. Her only hope of survival was to move forward with her plan. That meant leaving this city and heading north as quickly as she could.

■ ■ ■

Emily's trip down the stairwell was far simpler this time than her previous night's adventure. She followed the tracks she found outside her door as they continued along the wall of the seventeenth floor and eventually into the darkness of the stairwell. Her flashlight illuminated her way down each flight of stairs as she tracked the holes down another two floors until they disappeared when the spider-thing, as she had come to think of it, presumably decided to stop using the wall and instead jumped to the stairs like any other self-respecting New Yorker would.

The foyer of the apartment block was clear. Nothing looked disturbed or out of place, but she did notice three more sets of tracks leading from the ground floor and out through the building's main doors. That could only mean there were more of the spider-things on the loose, but at least the tracks appeared to be heading out of the building and away from her.

Stepping into the open air and the beautiful day that greeted her, Emily felt her spirits surge. The apartment, now that she was fully committed to leaving, had gradually become more and more claustrophobic and stuffy to her, but out here in the sunshine, it was simply glorious.

The sun shone brilliantly, framed by a clear, cloud-free sky, much the same as the day the red rain had fallen. Emily didn't care about the similarity; the warmth of the sun against her skin felt fabulous and she paused for a moment, closed her eyes, and allowed herself to simply bathe in the radiated warmth of her planet's star. For that moment, as she stood rejoicing in the simple act of sun worship, the orange warmth permeating through her tightly closed eyelids, she could imagine that this was just another day. That the sights and sounds that were this great city's heartbeat had simply paused for a moment to allow her these few seconds of bliss and that when she opened her eyes, the world would be as it once was, as it had always been, as it should be.

Of course, when Emily finally allowed her eyes to flutter open again, the world was as empty as when she had closed them. It was okay, she supposed, because she was still alive, she knew that she was not the only survivor, and today would most likely be the final day she would have to spend in this vast city of ghosts and scuttling unseen monsters.

Emily let out a sigh of resignation. Her aching body was already complaining about the prospect of this latest jaunt. The painkillers she had taken earlier were still doing their job but they weren't powerful enough to blunt the pain completely.

Her bike was where she had dropped it the night before. For some reason she thought it would be gone, spirited away by whatever she had heard awakening in her apartment complex last night. In fact, there was no sign of any of the owners of the fricative alien voices that had serenaded the city, and Emily pondered whether they had some kind of aversion to daylight.

Maybe they are just late sleepers, she joked to herself. She didn't laugh.

Bending over to lift the bike caused a warning spasm of pain to quiver through her shoulder. Even though the discomfort was numbed by the painkillers, she had to keep in mind that her body was beat up, and her injuries could easily be exacerbated if she overexerted herself. Any other time and she would put herself on light duty, but time had run out for both Emily and the human race. She could no longer simply take to her bed for a couple of days while she healed.

She had to be extra careful from here on out, she reminded herself again.

Emily scooted her bike around until it was facing east, mounted it and began pedaling at a leisurely pace, resisting the urge to pick her pace up to her normal cruising speed. There was no need to rush today; it was more important to ensure she didn't put her recovering body under any more stress. Besides, at her current speed she could also keep her eyes open for any of the owners of the strange cries she had heard last night.

There were several bike shops within a few miles for her to choose from but she decided to head to her favorite, the oddly named Steals on Wheels over on Lexington and Seventy-Fifth. It wasn't one of those megastore we-sell-everything emporiums where you could buy just about anything but where no one knew you from Adam. No, this was just a small-time boutique bike shop, owned and operated by a lifelong cycling enthusiast named Mike Stanley who stocked what he liked to call "the best bargains on two wheels." Despite the store's name and Mike's motto, the bikes he sold were anything but cheap, but they were most definitely some of the most robust, reliable, and well-made bikes you could pick up anywhere in the city. Plus, it was only a block or so away from a Whole Foods Market that had opened up just a few months earlier. With a little luck she could find a new bike plus all the spare parts she could carry at Mike's store, and then head over to the market and stock up on the supplies she would need for the first leg of her trip.

She pedaled southwest on Amsterdam Avenue, past the eerily empty stores and businesses and the equally deserted sidewalks. When she made the left onto West Eighty-Sixth Street, Emily had to swerve and brake suddenly to avoid a huge delivery truck jutting out from the semi-collapsed building it had collided with. The road was littered with kegs of beer. They lay scattered across the road like mines, their silver casks glinting in the sun and mixing with the debris from the decimated building.

The cab of the truck had buried itself deep inside the shattered building. Splintered floorboards, pieces of ceiling, and plasterboard hung from the mouth of the building, reminding Emily, oddly, of the Christmas decorations that had always seemed so appealing to her when she visited Santa's Grotto as a child. *Strange how the mind works*, she thought as she slowed to a stop.

Emily dismounted and propped her bike up against the curb using the flat of the left pedal. The truck's cab was barely visible through the tangle of fallen debris. She had to pick her way toward it, carefully avoiding the sharp splinters of wood jutting like stalagmites and stalactites, seemingly from every angle. She reached the front of the vehicle unscathed; the doors to the truck were both closed, but the driver's-side window had an almost perfectly circular hole in it measuring a couple of feet across. Emily used the truck's footplate to step up and examine the hole; it looked as though someone had taken a circular saw and cut through the glass. She ran her fingers over the edge of the opening. The edge felt sharp, serrated almost, as though whatever had made it had gnawed through the glass.

Peering through the hole into the cab, Emily could see that nothing remained of whoever had been in the delivery truck. They were gone and in their place was the remains of one of the giant pupae she had seen—and splattered, she reminded herself—at the paper yesterday.

Both doors of the truck were still locked from the inside of the cab, which meant that whatever had emerged from the pupa could only have escaped through the circular hole in the glass. The hole was just too neat to have been caused by the crash, so the logical assumption, Emily concluded, would be it could only have been cut by the thing trapped in the cab. The transformed driver was, she hoped, long gone, because Emily did not even want to imagine the kind of being that had climbed out from the cocoon and then been able to bore through the truck's window with such precision to escape.

Emily turned her attention back to the remains lying on the floor of the truck's cab. The pupa had split open along its middle like a giant clamshell. The inside was a dull brown now but Emily could make out several slimy looking tubes that she guessed had acted like umbilical cords to feed the creature the nutrients it had needed. The faint reek of ammonia still filled the truck's cabin.

She climbed down from the truck and cautiously made her way back out into the sunshine, but even as the warmth of the sun welcomed her back, an icy tentacle of fear wrapped itself around the base of her spine and began to tighten its grip.

■ ■ ■

Emily sped across the junction of Central Park West and Eighty-First, her head instinctively flipping right and left despite the dead traffic lights and mostly empty road.

A single police car, its front driver's side and passenger seat windows wound all the way down, blocked the right lane of the entrance onto the Seventy-Ninth Street Transverse, positioned to stop any traffic continuing past it, she guessed. Emily could imagine the cop sitting in his car, arm resting on the sill of the open window, but she had no idea why he would have chosen to stop there.

Emily had already cycled several hundred yards past the abandoned police car when she had an idea. She slowed the bike and circled back to the cop car. Not bothering to dismount from the bike, she pulled up alongside the driver's side, opened the door and leaned in, her eyes quickly searching the interior of the black-and-white. She found what she was looking for secured between the passenger and driver's seat.

Emily mentally crossed her fingers before giving the shotgun a sharp tug.

"Yesss!" she yelled in victory as the Mossberg 500 pump-action shotgun pulled free of its security rack. A bandolier of spare shells rested in a recess beneath the weapon, alongside a full box of extra shells. The shells would be useful but the bandolier would be uncomfortable to wear with the backpack so she pulled the cartridges from their individual holders and added them to the box, tossing the empty bandolier back into the cab of the patrol car.

The previous summer, Nathan had insisted on teaching Emily how to shoot and had taken her out to the gun range. While she had enjoyed learning the ins and outs of firing a handgun, she had *really* enjoyed shooting the shotgun. She liked the heft of it but most of all she enjoyed knowing that whatever she pointed it at was probably going to be hit. It could effectively hit a target out as far as seventy yards or so, but at close range, it was absolutely deadly. The Glock 15 Nathan had handed her was cute and had left neat little holes in the paper target she was firing at, but the shotgun, well, that had cut the paper target in two.

Dismounting from the bike, Emily quickly removed her backpack and pushed the spare shotgun shells into a side pouch. Once she had fastened herself back into the backpack she looped the strap of the Mossberg over her head and across her chest. It wasn't particularly comfortable but it would do for now.

While she wasn't sure just how effective the shotgun might be against the creatures roaming her apartment's corridors, she certainly felt more secure knowing she now had something to defend herself with.

■ ■ ■

The shoulder-high sandstone retaining walls on either side of the two-lane road were almost entirely obscured by a green waterfall of plants that clung to every inch of the gray stone. The lush foliage spilled over the cold stones and drooped toward the pavement. The road Emily was riding cut directly across Central Park and avoided what would normally have been paths crowded with pedestrians and tourists. Emily slowed her speed slightly, marveling at what a couple of days of no traffic could do for the air. Despite her many trips down this same road over the years, this was the first time she could actually smell the park and its plant life. The air was thick with the fecund aroma of vegetation; it tickled her nostrils and filled her mind with images of sweeping fields of grass. It was intoxicating.

Under any other circumstances, this would probably rank right up there on her list of perfect days: the sun, warm and welcoming on her skin; the road empty before her; the heady aroma of eight hundred acres of grass, trees, and flowerbeds. If it had not been for the rest of the city's occupants lying dead around her and in the process of being consumed by some strange menace, then, yes, this would certainly have ranked right up there.

Despite the obvious drawbacks, Emily allowed herself to bask in the simple illusion as she pedaled onward. The road dipped beneath a footbridge and she swept past a row of dilapidated storefronts on her right. She could be anywhere in the world right now, she thought. The old stone architecture reminded her of pictures she'd seen of Europe and she allowed herself to imagine she was riding through the back roads of Provence, or maybe Tuscany; she had always wanted to take a trip to Italy.

Her daydream ended when she rounded the final bend approaching the exit onto Fifth Avenue and Seventy-Ninth. Three cars, or what was left of them at least, had collided at the junction. Two were full-on yellow, with NYC Taxi stenciled on their doors. The third was a white Nissan Pathfinder SUV. One of the taxis had T-boned the Pathfinder, and the second taxi had apparently careened into the back of the first taxi, effectively blocking the junction. Three police cruisers, one at each junction, had positioned themselves to stop traffic from getting past.

The accident must have happened just as the majority of Manhattan's workers learned of the approaching disaster, because in the lanes blocked by each patrol car were row upon row of empty vehicles. Most bore the same yellow livery as the crumpled taxis involved in the accident, but Emily could see the occasional delivery truck, a couple of tour buses, and even a motorcycle or two here and there lying on their sides in the road.

Caught up in this traffic snarl, every driver had undoubtedly been sitting impatiently behind the wheel of his or her vehicle, unaware that it would be their final resting place.

The exit lanes leading away from the lights were more or less empty, apart from the occasional car caught in the process of making a U-turn, hoping to head in the opposite direction of the accident before it was too late. Emily saw one car that had run through a bus stop, scattering bits of the decimated shelter across the sidewalk and road. There wasn't any sign of an ambulance, so the accident must have happened just minutes before death stepped into the city.

Emily slowed her bike to a walking pace and made a wide curve around the debris field of the accident. The vehicles' engines must have all been running at the time the red plague struck because, in every vehicle she looked into, the keys were still in the ignition. Most had their doors closed and locked, she noted. Some of the unlucky drivers had apparently managed to get their doors open before succumbing to the effects of the red rain (or maybe they had simply opened them to yell and scream at the drivers in front of them in true New York fashion). But every locked vehicle Emily passed as she freewheeled slowly down the center divider between the two lanes had one thing in common: they had an almost perfectly round hole in one of their windows as she had seen minutes earlier in the beer delivery truck.

The crush of cars disappeared as she crossed over Madison Avenue. The road was virtually clear of vehicles as she continued heading east along Seventy-Ninth Street, except for a few stragglers who must have managed a U-turn before they got caught up in the traffic snarl ahead. When she hit the Lexington junction she hung a wide right and continued down the next four or five blocks until the road met with Seventy-Second Street.

Steals on Wheels was another block farther on, nestled between a Wells Fargo bank and a Starbucks. Emily pulled to a halt with a squeal of brakes in front of the bike store. She pulled her bike up onto the pavement and leaned it against a parking meter just outside.

The door to the bike store, unsurprisingly, was locked. She could see a bunch of bikes in the window, all neatly arranged in order of price, but Emily knew the bike she was looking for would be inside, safely away from the window just in case somebody decided to do exactly what she planned to do next.

Emily was getting a little tired of having to commit a B and E every time she needed something, but she guessed she would have to get used to that from now on. The majority of storeowners, Emily thought, would probably have shut up shop and headed home as quickly as they could, locking their stores behind them. Emily wondered how many of them had really believed they would ever return.

Pulling the hammer from the pack, she flipped it over so the ball-peen would act as the business end. She was going to have to use her damaged right arm for this little exercise in vandalism. She still couldn't raise that arm much above seventy degrees and she needed to cover her eyes from any flying glass, just in case. Only her left arm was flexible enough for that.

She slid out of her jacket and rolled it around her right hand until only the shaft of the hammer and the head were visible, then, turning sideways to the plate-glass window, positioned her feet in a wide stance. She turned her face away from the window, burying it deep into the crook of her elbow.

Emily struck the window with the hammer with as much force as she could muster.

The glass shattered with the sound of a thousand icicles smashing to the ground, amplified to a nerve-jarring level by the empty streets. As Emily took a step back to escape the rain of shattered glass, she felt something tug at the leg of her jeans. Looking down she saw a four-foot-long triangular shard from the shattered window protruding from the cloth of her jeans. Just an inch or so to the left and the spike would have speared her leg instead of the hem of her jeans. She reached down with her gloved hand and took careful hold of the lance of glass while she held the pleat of her jeans with her other hand. She tugged at the glass. It came away after a few pulls with a ripping sound, leaving an eight-inch hole through both sides of her jeans leg. Emily tossed the deadly piece of glass away and cringed as it smashed to pieces on the sidewalk, shattering the silence of the dead street once again.

Mental note: need more jeans.

Turning to look at the front of the store, Emily examined her handiwork. Almost half of the window now resided in a million pieces on the pavement. A few stubborn fragments of glass protruded here and there from the metal surround that had held the window in place, but they disappeared under the might of Emily's hammer.

The broken glass crunched beneath her sneakers as she stepped up and into the front display area of the store. If the power had still been on, the alarm system would have been screaming bloody murder at her and the cops would be there in, let's say, thirty minutes, give or take an hour.

Instead, only the sound of broken glass crunching beneath her sneakers accompanied Emily as she edged past the display of bikes and stepped down onto the main floor of the store. She was glad she had brought the flashlight with her, as the interior of the store gradually became darker the farther back she walked.

She fished the flashlight out of her backpack switched it on, and twisted the beam adjuster until it gave off a wide angle of light that pushed back the remaining darkness. There was almost enough light to see by without the flashlight, but the weight of the Maglite in her hand added an extra sense of security she welcomed and meant she didn't have to unstrap the shotgun from around her chest.

Spare wheels, frames, and bicycle forks lined the walls on either side of the store. Everything a cycling enthusiast would need to build her own bike from scratch or replace a broken part was available somewhere in the store. On the main shop floor, two rows of bicycles formed an honor guard on either side of a wide strip of industrial-strength carpet that stretched down into the darkest end of the store. From her previous visits, Emily knew Mike liked to keep the cheaper bikes at the front of the store; the deeper into the store one walked the more expensive the bikes became.

The bike Emily wanted was about three-quarters of the way down and on the right. She'd been eyeing it for months, slowly stashing away a little bit here and there from each paycheck. By the time the red rain came, she was still a couple of months shy of having the twelve hundred bucks she needed to buy it. Of course, money was no longer an issue for her now; she could choose whatever bike she wanted, but there was something about this particular model that just spoke to her. She followed the carpet pathway toward the back of the store, sweeping the flashlight left and right as she walked.

Emily didn't think there would be any kind of threat in the store; Mike was too smart to have stayed. He would have gone home and died with his family just like millions of other Americans probably had. But she was learning to be cautious, so she made sure to check out the entire store, poking her head warily into all the corners and cubbies where one of the creatures could have gestated. She needn't have worried because, just as she had expected, there was no sign of any kind of a threat. Satisfied she was alone in the shop, Emily headed back toward the center of the store and quickly located her new bike.

It was the perfect bike for the grueling trip that lay ahead of her: a Novara Randonee touring bike in dark green with FSA Wing Compact handlebars and a Shimano Deore LX derailleur. It had a saddle that was the closest thing to a La-Z-Boy recliner, and puncture-resistant inner tubes. Most importantly for her, it weighed less than thirty pounds.

Emily pulled the bike from its stand, giving it a quick once-over to check that the tires were inflated. She lifted the back wheel off the ground and used the pedal to get it spinning while simultaneously running up and down all the gears, checking for any slippage. Satisfied everything worked just as it should, she pushed her new set of wheels to the front of the store and leaned it against the cash desk.

Next she walked back along each of the walls and grabbed everything she thought she might need for her journey: puncture kits and spare inner tubes, brake-blocks, a hand pump, a can of WD-40, a rain smock, a set of pedals, brake cables, a couple of plastic drinking bottles she could fit to the crossbar of the bike, a multitool, and finally, a GPS unit. The GPS had a specially designed clip to mount it on the handlebars of her bike. By the time she collected everything she could think of, a large pile of items had collected on the glass counter of the counter. Emily had to draw the line at a spare pair of wheel rims though. There really was nowhere for her to carry them. She would just have to hope she wouldn't need them. However, she could deal with the pile of spare parts she had accumulated.

Emily walked to the farthest end of the store, shining her light into the darkness until she found what she was looking for, a display rack of panniers. She picked out the two largest sets she could find: one to fit over the back wheel and a second, smaller pair that would fit nicely over the front wheels. The addition of the two pairs of modern-day saddlebags would greatly increase her ability to carry extra supplies.

Emily fitted both pairs of panniers to the new bike using the multitool she had found earlier. Then she placed all of the spare parts she had collected into one of the rear carrier's pouches. She gave a final mental run through her list just to make sure she hadn't forgotten anything; once she was on her way, she didn't want to find herself without the means to fix her only form of transportation. She was sure she hadn't forgotten anything—apart from those spare wheel rims; leaving them really irked her—so she hefted the bike onto her left shoulder, marveling at how light it was, even with the panniers and extra parts she had picked up, and carefully made her way out of the shop. When she was clear of the debris field of broken glass, she set the bike down, leaning it against its kickstand.

Emily looked at her old bike, battered and bruised after so many years of use, and a tinge of betrayal touched her heart. She felt like she was about to shoot a faithful but old horse while picking up a younger replacement.

"Don't be so damned ridiculous," she said to herself and started to wheel her new bike away. But after just a few steps, Emily dropped the bike's kickstand again and, with a resigned sigh, walked back to where she had set her old bike to rest, picked it up—good God it was heavy by comparison to the new one—and carried it into the store, setting it down in the space left by her new Novara.

"You're a freaking idiot," she told herself. Then she turned and climbed back through the broken window, leaving the last vestige of her old life behind.

■ ■ ■

The new bike handled like a dream, and Emily found herself quickly shifting up through the gears as she sped east along Seventy-Ninth Street in the direction of the Whole Foods Market.

The tires made a satisfying purr of rubber against macadam, and the efficient metallic whirr of the drive chain complemented it perfectly, creating a simple tune of efficiency that was perfection to Emily's ear.

She pulled over in front of Whole Foods.

Outside the store's entrance, a confusion of plastic shopping carts lay scattered on the pavement. Spilled bags full of food had emptied their contents onto the sidewalk and road, dropped by their owners as they fled the market or maybe in a crush of looters, like she had seen at the little store next to her apartment.

The store's automatic doors were closed, and for a moment, Emily thought she was going to have to smash yet another window. They weren't locked, though, and Emily was able to slip her fingers between the rubber seals and push one apart until there was enough room for her to squeeze through into the entrance area.

The stench of rotting meat and vegetables greeted her as she walked through the entrance and headed toward the produce section. Where there had once been rows of apples, organic tomatoes, and other assorted veggies, there was nothing but a rotting mass of almost unrecognizable decay. There were no flies buzzing around the decaying food, Emily noted. The place should have been black with them and Emily began to wonder just how far along the food chain the red rain's impact had been felt.

There was obviously nothing worth scavenging in this section, and even if there had been, Emily wasn't going to spend any more time breathing in that stink than she had too. She pulled a shopping cart from a row stacked in front of a checkout and pushed it toward the opposite end of the huge store. The front left wheel seemed to have a life of its own; it squeaked insistently and refused to go in the same direction as the other three. The world as she knew it had apparently ended, humanity was on its knees, and an inscrutable menace threatened her very survival, but *still* she managed to choose the one wonky cart in the store. Typical!

As Emily squeaked her way up the aisles, she spotted a pallet of gallon bottles of drinking water on an end rack. She pulled four of them from the pallet and set them down in the aisle. She would pick them up on her way out of the store. If she limited herself to a liter or so of water a day she would have enough drinking water to last her almost two weeks, as long as she didn't exert herself too much. She made a mental note to grab some of that instant energy powder too. She could add it to her water for when she was riding.

Next stop, canned goods. The aisle was mainly full of soups, so Emily grabbed as wide a selection as she could. She wasn't a soup fan but it would be easy to prepare, hot, filling, and most importantly, it had a long shelf life. Worst-case scenario, she would simply drink it right from the can. She made sure to grab only the cans that had the pull-tab tops so she wouldn't have to worry about a can opener. She spotted a selection of canned meats and added four cans of organic corned beef.

She pushed the cart up and down the rows of aisles, grabbing cans of vegetables, canned fruit—no peaches though, definitely no peaches—and chili.

Then it was on to the health supplements aisle. She pulled out enough bottles of multivitamins to last her a year. It couldn't hurt to start adding them to her daily regimen; she wasn't exactly going to be eating a balanced diet from this point onward. On the same aisle, she also found the powdered energy supplements. She added a handful of boxes to the basket.

Emily snatched up two large boxes of oatmeal, placing them in the rapidly growing pile of food in the cart. The cartons were bulky and the oatmeal would need to be heated before she could eat it, but Emily thought it would be worth the extra space the packaging took up. Hearty and filling, it would be a good way to start her day and a great source of energy; she was going to need as much of that as she could get over the next few months.

Her final stop was at the feminine hygiene section. She added enough boxes of tampons and panty liners so she wouldn't have to worry about that particular problem, at least not for a couple of months.

Emily maneuvered the cart in the direction of the front of the store and picked up the four containers of water she left there earlier. As she moved toward the exit, she spotted something she had forgotten near one of the checkout lanes—candy. She pushed the squeaking cart to the checkout and grabbed a handful of chocolate bars, chewing gum, and mints, and tossed them into the cart with everything else. She took a final moment to think about what she might have missed. Satisfied she had everything she was going to need for at least the next week or more, Emily squeezed the cart between the exit doors and back out into the sunshine.

■ ■ ■

Emily had never ridden a bike carrying as much weight as she was about to. She guessed the secret to assuring she stayed on the road, instead of ending up in a ditch, was to spread the load as evenly as possible and make sure the bike stayed balanced. The last thing she wanted to do was change the dynamics of her new ride and find out about it when she least expected it. She unpacked the provisions she had collected from the shopping cart and loaded the majority of them into the backpack. The remainder went into the panniers. Emily made sure to distribute the weight evenly over both sides of the bike. When she was finished, she buckled down the tops of each pannier and then pushed the kickstand up with her foot, testing the bike's balance with the extra weight. The addition of the supplies certainly made a difference to the feel of the bike. She wouldn't be taking corners anywhere near as sharply as she was used to and it was going to be harder to get it rolling from a dead stop. Overall, though, she was happy with the feel of it.

She swung her leg over the saddle and started in the direction of her next stop. The bike felt a little unsteady at first. Now that she was on the move, the dynamics were harder to gauge than she had expected, but after a few minutes she became accustomed to the changes and barely noticed the difference.

There was one final place she needed to stop before heading home. The power was down, most likely gone forever, but that didn't mean she had to suffer through cold meals for the rest of her life. A couple of blocks farther on from the Whole Foods Market was an outdoor sports and camping store. She was hoping she could pick up some camping gear to help make her trip just a little more comfortable, and that was where she pointed the bike.

A few minutes later, she pulled up outside and leaned her bike against the storefront window. Emily didn't plan on wasting any time inside. She knew exactly what she wanted, but she took the shotgun with her anyway.

The door to the camping shop was, surprisingly, unlocked so she stepped inside. A large sign hung from the ceiling by fishing wire directed Emily to the back of the dark store for camping gear. She followed the sign's instructions and was soon rooting around a selection of portable propane-fueled stoves. She was tempted to take the largest one but it was just too bulky and would add far too much weight to her pack. She settled for a double-burner model that was one-third the size and half as heavy. A couple of shelves up from where she found the stove was a row of the small green propane tanks that powered it. She grabbed four of them, then added a lightweight pot and pan and a utensil set. She was tempted to take some dehydrated food supplies with her but decided against it. She had enough food to last her and she was still confident she could scavenge whatever she needed as she traveled. On her way back toward the exit, she spotted a box of long-stem candles and picked up a box of twelve.

Emily left the camping store and packed the stove and fuel in the bike's rear set of panniers. When she finished tying the panniers' flaps down, Emily mounted the bike and pushed off in the direction of home.

■ ■ ■

She found herself making much better headway than she had expected as she again approached the traffic jam of empty vehicles on Seventy-Ninth Street. Rather than take the same route she had arrived by, Emily decided to cut through Central Park instead and test her new bike's performance on the weaving paths that interlaced it.

She zigged off the road to her left and then up onto the pavement using the curb ramp, aiming her bike at the park entrance between two five-foot-high pillars of sandstone. She passed by an abandoned hot dog stall, the stink of rotten meat fleetingly filling her nostrils; then she was into the park and the welcoming smell of grass and trees quickly replaced the stench.

The concrete path forked after a couple hundred feet and she followed the branch curving off to the left. Emily allowed the bike to tilt gently into the curve, applying the brakes just a touch. She continued down the path, past empty benches and the occasional abandoned picnic lunch. She deftly maneuvered around an empty baby stroller resting on its side in the middle of the path.

The pathways through the park were convoluted affairs, designed more for the walker to enjoy than to quickly get you from point A to point B. Apparently, whoever had designed their layout did not believe in straight lines. Emily eased her bike to the right and cut across the grass. To slow her speed sufficiently she had to drop down to second gear and pedal just a little harder. She maneuvered through a copse of trees and then slanted left until her tires found the asphalt of East Drive, one of the main arteries running through the park. She planned to keep heading south until she reached Terrace Drive, where she would make a turn, cut across the path, and then back up West End Avenue.

Off to her right Emily could see the park's boathouse. The paddleboats and rowboats had all collected on the far bank like a flock of lost sheep. As she followed the curve of the road, leaving the building and boats behind her, Emily saw something she had never noticed in all her trips through the park; there was some kind of structure in the open grass about three hundred feet southeast of the boathouse. As Emily zipped along the final curve of the road before turning onto Terrace Drive, she caught a longer glimpse of the structure through a break in the line of trees edging the path.

What she saw made her pull back so hard on both brake levers it sent the bike into a sideways slide. The brake blocks squealed in protest as she fought to keep the bike from toppling over and spilling her and her precious cargo of supplies into the road.

Barely avoiding a nasty crash, Emily reined in the bike as if it were a headstrong horse, finally bringing it to a safe, if wobbly stop. Slipping forward off the saddle, she planted both feet firmly on the ground and stared at the sight in front of her. Rising above the tree line to her left was a towerlike structure reaching toward the sky. It was hard to make out any real details from this far away, but she felt a flutter of nervousness in her stomach as she looked at the obviously out-of-place object.

Using her feet to propel the bike forward, Emily scooted closer, heading toward the break in the tree line surrounding the open field. As she approached, Emily could see that what she was looking at was colossal and certainly not a natural part of the park vegetation. Leaving the road, she lifted the front tire of her bike up onto the grass verge of the field and headed through a natural corridor between the trees. In front of her the sun was beginning its descent toward the western horizon, its light reflecting off the still surface of the ornamental pond known as the Conservatory Water. The pond was—*had been*—a favorite hangout for model boaters from all across the city.

The sun's rays bounced and scintillated off the lake's surface, sending bursts of light through the gaps between the trees. The light was so bright Emily had to squint and shade her eyes to avoid the dazzling reflection.

She couldn't see a damn thing from where she was standing; she'd have to risk getting closer, she decided. It was probably better to do it on foot; if this developed into a situation, she would be faster on the grass using her own two feet rather than trying to pedal the bike across the field. She leaned the bike against a nearby maple tree. She was tempted to drop the backpack too, but if something unpredictable did happen she might need to get out of there as fast as she could. She did not want to risk having to leave the backpack and its precious contents behind.

A break between the trees where she stood led into the open field. Beyond that there was another line of trees and beyond those was the structure. She started through the break, cautiously heading toward the object. Emily was still two hundred feet away from the structure when the light breeze ruffling through the branches of the trees shifted in her direction, and she caught the faint but now familiar smell of ammonia.

She stopped, her head pivoting from side to side, looking for any sign that she was not alone, but she could not see anything she considered a threat. The aroma of ammonia was so faint it could be from anywhere; in fact, for all she knew, the smell might just as easily be the millions of gallons of water of the Conservatory pond slowly stagnating. Her better judgment told her to just turn around, get back on her bike, and ride away as fast as she could, but her natural curiosity got the better of her, and she decided to press on.

She was glad she hadn't left the shotgun with the bike. Her hand unconsciously reached out and caressed the black metal of the weapon slung across her chest.

Emily took a few steps closer, shading her eyes as best she could from the glare. She guessed it must have been a cloud drifting across the face of the sun for a moment that finally gave her the chance to see the object clearly. The light from the pond suddenly dimmed, her vision cleared, and the towering structure swam into breathtaking focus. As her eyes roamed over the object, Emily knew that if she had a week to stand there and stare at the sight before her, there was no way she would ever be able to understand what it was she was seeing.

It stood at least a hundred feet in height—a towering, incongruous amalgamation of red flesh. Three intertwining limbs as thick as Emily's torso twisted together and reached toward the sky. The base of the structure swept out into hundreds of interweaving duplicates of the main shaft; where they met the grass of the park Emily could see mounds of dirt kicked up like gopher holes, as the thick tendrils burrowed into the ground.

The main trunk seemed to be made of scales, large red scales that overlapped each other like armor. The structure gave Emily the impression of a piece of artwork, as though it had been specifically designed to look like a natural structure but made from the leftover bits and pieces of something unnatural. Its symmetrical appearance was ruined as Emily's eyes took in the top of the trunk; it looked unfinished, as though the designer had simply stopped midway in its creation. It was a mess of irregular angles and crenulations.

Emily began edging her way closer, her eyes fixed firmly on the imposing structure, oblivious to the low hanging branches of trees she pushed through as she moved nearer. She maneuvered around the left flank of the structure, placing the water of the pond behind her and it. From this vantage point, Emily could see a mass of translucent tendrils, each shot through with mottled spots of pink and red, growing from the base of the structure. They crept across the grass, between the thing's roots, over the concrete boat dock, and down beneath the surface of the pond.

Emily stepped down onto the concrete landing area of the boat dock and took a few careful steps nearer to the mass of tendrils. Standing just a few feet from them, she knelt and leaned in closer. Through the transparent outer skin, she could see the tendril contained some kind of clear liquid within it. It *looked* like water from the pond, but this giant plant—it was hard to categorize exactly what phylum she was looking at—must be filtering out the dirt and other crap from the lake, because the water in the tendril looked crystal clear to her, while the water in the Conservatory pond was green and brackish. Running through the center of each gelatinous tendril was a second smaller tube, as thick as Emily's thumb and filled with a darker fluid. This other liquid was a mass of different shades of red ranging from bright red to dark congealed-blood brown.

As Emily watched, the tendrils periodically expanded and then contracted, squeezing the water farther up the tendril toward the trunk, and with each pump of the water heading toward the "plant," Emily could see a smaller amount of the mottled red fluid in the inner vein pumping out toward the pond.

Emily got to her feet and followed the tendril to the lip of the concrete dock where it disappeared into the water. She looked out across the expanse of the water, shading her eyes with her hand as the sun was once again bouncing uncomfortably off the water. Toward the center of the lake Emily could just make out a thick red sludge forming on the surface, but the sun and the distance made it difficult to focus on it.

Emily turned in the direction of the structure, began walking back across the dock toward the grass verge, and froze. From the corner of her right eye, she caught something moving fast along the concrete toward her.

Tap–tap–tap–tap.

Emily's head snapped to face the source of the noise. She instantly regretted her decision.

The creature skittering across the hot concrete landing toward her was like something out of the tortured dreams of an insane-asylum inmate. The thing had eight long spider-like legs; each leg was articulated by four bulbous joints that gave the creature a lopsided, almost limping gait. The end of each leg was tipped by a scimitar-shaped claw, tempered to a point, and made the creature look as though it were standing on tiptoes. The top of each leg attached to another bulbous extrusion much like a human shoulder joint, and that joint was in turn attached to a long corkscrew-shaped body. The head was nothing but a burgundy colored bulb attached by a short neck of concentric rings that allowed the head a small degree of pivotal motion. Positioned at twelve and six o'clock on the creature's featureless head was a long fleshy stalk. At the end of each stalk was a black bulb and Emily realized with horror that she had seen that same strange append-age before. She knew that if either of those black bulbs were to open, each would contain a single eye.

Just below the bottom eye, where the creature's chin should have been, a third limb sprouted, swaying left and right as the monster scrambled over the concrete. This limb ended in a pair of serrated blades that whirled periodically like a rotary saw. At the tail end of the creature, Emily saw a wavering set of diaphanous red streamers, similar to the poisonous stinging arms of a jelly-fish but much finer. As the creature loped toward her, the stream-ers undulated and flowed in a sinusoidal rhythm that was, to her stunned mind at least, absolutely beautiful in its elegance, and the exact opposite of the rest of this repulsive monster's body.

Emily recognized that, up until that exact moment, she had not fully accepted the whole extraterrestrial virus idea Jacob had postulated in their phone call. Now, as she stood defenseless in the shadow of an otherworldly tree, as a horror on legs sped toward her, Emily realized his theory was totally and utterly true. She was staring at the proof. *This...this?* What was it exactly? She might as well call it an alien because, although it may have been born here, it surely was not from this planet.

As the creature ate up the last of the space between itself and her, a single surprising thought passed through Emily's mind: *Finally!*

She shut her eyes tight and waited for the monster to fall on her and extinguish her sad little life.

CHAPTER SIXTEEN

Tap–tap–tap–tap.

The rapid staccato beat of the creature's spike-tipped feet on the concrete grew louder as it rushed headlong toward Emily; then, just as quickly, it had passed her by.

It didn't stop! It didn't tear me to pieces!

Emily opened her eyes and twisted her body to follow the creature as it continued along the boat dock. It ignored her as though she were not even there. It just kept on running.

Run, Forrest, run! She almost yelled the movie quote aloud, and had to stifle a burst of terrified, relief-fueled laughter.

Abruptly, the creature made a ninety-degree turn. Its right legs simply stopped moving while the right side continued, *just like the tracks on a tank*, Emily thought. It moved on its new course up the grass embankment toward the alien tree. When it was within twenty feet of the main trunk, the bizarre creature's body suddenly dropped toward the ground and then it was flying upward, launched into the air by its spindly articulated legs. It landed halfway up the trunk of the huge structure. There was no reduction in the creature's forward momentum as it continued its lopsided leg-over-leg scuttle around the circumference of the tree until it reached the top of the structure.

Only then did it stop.

The highest point of the tree—at least one hundred, if not a hundred and twenty feet up by Emily's estimate—was nothing but a ragged unfinished edge, totally at odds with the natural flowing outline of the rest of the structure. It was almost as though whatever had built it had simply stopped midway through its construction.

Emily watched, her chin drooping almost to her chest, as the freakish thing began to crab-walk along the uneven lip, its eyestalks swiveling back and forth as if it was searching for something. After about a minute of scuttling along the lip, the creature reached out with its two spindly front limbs and pulled itself up into a space between two protruding crenellations? on the ragged edge. It immediately began working itself down into the space using the fine streamers of its tail like an extra set of limbs until it seemed content with the fit.

Then something even stranger happened. The creature began to melt.

At least that's what it looked like to Emily. The eye appendages went first, dripping down over the creature's body like glue. The liquid filled the few small gaps of daylight Emily had been able to make out in the spaces between the creature and the surrounding edges of the tree's upper lip. Then the legs splayed out, grasping onto the protuberances on either side of it with its wicked-looking claw tips. The spider-like creature gave a final wiggle as if it was ensuring it fit just right and then the legs melted into the structure. The tail was the last to vanish, fanning out in a final flourish before it too dissolved, vanishing into the main body of the trunk just below it.

It was all over in less than thirty seconds. The creature had added itself into the tree, become a part of it completely, as if it had never existed. In its place was one more part of the structure sprouting up against the Manhattan skyline. Emily wondered just how big this thing would actually grow. Or was it being built?

Emily decided it was not a question she was interested in hanging around and answering. Her inquisitiveness was well and truly satiated; a human mind could only cope with so much information, so much change in one sitting, she realized. She gave the alien tree growing before her a final glance, then turned on her heels and began walking as quickly as she could back to where she had parked her bicycle.

■ ■ ■

Emily readjusted the backpack. The shoulder pads had shifted as she walked back to her bike and now the webbing of the right strap was digging uncomfortably into her shoulder. The painkillers had long ago worn off, and the dull throb had slowly returned. She turned her thoughts to what she had just seen to try to take her mind off the pain.

Where the alien-thing on the dock had appeared from, she had no idea. At the time it showed up, her attention had been focused solely on the latest addition to her growing list of weirdness. It could have been wandering around the park for God knew how long, gestating from some dead park visitor. Hell, there were over 840 acres to choose from in the park alone. Or maybe it came from the city's sewer system? With more than six thousand miles of tunnels running under the city, it would seem like the perfect place for those things to congregate and move around.

How ironic was it, she thought, that in every alien invasion movie she had ever seen, every sci-fi book she had ever read, the aliens were always either intent on eating us or just misunderstood. No one ever seemed to consider the possibility they might just ignore us completely, that the survivors of the human race might be so very inconsequential to their plan.

Could it simply be that the creature had not been able to sense her presence? Emily didn't think so. When she'd stabbed the one still in its cocoon back at the paper's offices, she was sure it had seen her. It had, at the very least been aware of her, and yet, now that she thought back to that moment, it had not tried to stop her; it hadn't even fought back. It had simply tried to get away from her.

Now that she had seen what had crawled out of one of those cocoons with her own eyes, there was little doubt left that what she had witnessed over the past few days was connected, part of some unfathomable plan. None of it made any kind of sense to Emily. Her head ached from trying to wrap her brain around the implications of the events, let alone attempting to fathom any kind of structured motive to why this was happening or what the outcome would be.

The size of the assault on her planet was fantastic in its scale, she realized. Its implementation, the complete destruction of humanity and its replacement with this new life form, seemed to be as calculated and unemotional as she would be in calling a pest-control company to get rid of a colony of termites or kill off a hive of bees.

She was just an insignificant survivor.

With the backpack strap once again resting comfortably against her shoulder, Emily swung her leg over the bike and placed her butt back on the saddle.

Her heartbeat slowly returned to its regular rhythm as she began riding once more toward home. Emily pedaled as quickly as she could, following Terrace Drive in the direction of the Seventy-Second Street west-side exit, eager to get back to the apartment and put as much space between her and the park as possible. As she drew alongside the Bethesda Terrace, with its terra-cotta stonework and now silent fountain, Emily again brought her bike to a stop.

This time it was only for a few brief moments, long enough to take in the view in front of her. Just beyond the Bethesda fountain, where the Terrace met with the body of water someone in their wisdom had simply called The Lake, Emily could see that the shore was lined with more of the giant red, alien structures she had come to think of as trees. She counted twenty-three of them stretching out along the water's edge. There could even be more, she reasoned, but the ones she could see were so closely packed together it was impossible to see past the first row of them. Each one of the towering red alien monoliths was in a different stage of construction; some were far taller than the lone one she had seen earlier, with wispy leaflike additions protruding from their summits, while others had progressed little past the base.

While she watched, Emily saw movement, the blur of fast-moving limbs as more of the spider-things scuttled along the ground in the distance, heading toward these newest additions to the park's flora. There was movement around the base of the trees too; Emily saw more creatures clambering up the trunk of one of the strange, exotic plants, on their way to sacrificing themselves to the structure.

Before the rain came, all of these creatures had been New Yorkers, busy leading their lives. The lives may not have been much, but they had been theirs and they had lived them as they saw fit. Now, those lives had been snatched away from them. They had been transformed into the spider-like aliens she could see eagerly making their lopsided way to this forest, to undergo yet another metamorphosis into something even larger again, a part of some alien production line, the result ending in…well, that really was the sixty-four-thousand-dollar question, wasn't it? Ending in what?

Emily watched impassively for another few seconds, then turned and began cycling home.

She did not look that way again.

CHAPTER SEVENTEEN

By the time Emily reached the apartment complex a solid bank of gray clouds tinted by a halo of red had begun to creep menacingly across the sky from the northwest. The fine weather could not have lasted much longer, she realized. This was still New York, after all, but Emily found herself already missing the implied sense of security the previous few days of clear skies had given her. She doubted the cloud would bring any rain but it would bring a sense of heaviness to the air that would cast a torpid blanket over everything, and maybe give her a nagging headache from the change in air pressure. In the recesses of her mind, though, Emily hoped the change in weather was not an omen of darker days or darker things to come.

She was reluctant to leave the bike outside the apartment building now that it contained her vital cache of supplies. With the added weight of the full panniers and her hurt arm, the bike was just too cumbersome for her to lift, so she wheeled it up the disabled-persons' ramp and maneuvered it carefully through the door and into the foyer of the building. A small manager's office sat adjacent to the elevators; Emily could not recall it ever having been manned during the entire time she had lived in the building. It would give her extra peace of mind if she stored the bike in the tiny room, away from any potentially prying alien eyes. She wheeled the bike inside and left it resting against its kickstand.

She knew the backpack would have to come upstairs with her but it was so tempting to just leave it next to the bike in the manager's office. It would be a dumb move to leave all of her supplies in one location, but she really didn't want to have to carry that extra weight up those stairs. She had no idea what the feeding habits of Earth's newest owners were, but she didn't want to risk losing all of her supplies to some hungry bug-eyed freak that suddenly discovered it had a hankering for a can of New England clam chowder. So, the backpack and its contents would have to go with her. Besides, she still needed to pack a supply of clothes before she left and she planned to carry the lighter stuff like clothing on her back.

And, speaking of clothes, that was going to be one of the roughest parts of this journey for her. While she would never consider herself vain, she was as committed to her creature comforts as the rest of the world was...*had been*, she corrected. The thought of limited access to clean underwear, in particular, was not something she was looking forward to. Of course, Emily knew a fresh pair of panties each morning was probably going to be the least of her worries. Still, a girl had certain standards she was expected to maintain, right?

She smiled as she pushed open the door to the stairwell and began her slow, painful climb up to the seventeenth floor. As she had predicted, the trek up was even more grueling with the back pack full of canned food and supplies strapped to her back. By the time she reached her floor, Emily's knees felt as though they were ready to pop right out of their sockets. Her back didn't feel much better either. Her shoulder seemed to be improving though; it felt better than it had since she took her spill. There was still pain but she was getting more flexion back in the joint.

In her bedroom, Emily unclipped the backpack's belt from her waist and shrugged off the backpack as carefully as she could, but it still hit the floor with the sound of a dead body being dropped. She bent over at her waist and tried to touch her toes, stretching out the kink in her back. It relieved the tension there enough that she didn't think she was going to need to take any more pain pills, for a while at least. After a few more stretches, she moved to the living room to check on the sat-phone. The indicator on the battery unit showed it had managed to reach 80 percent of its capacity. She was tempted to try the phone now but, looking out the window, the clouds she had spotted earlier had crept even closer and she decided it would be best to allow the battery unit as much time as possible to charge, while the sun was still visible. The instruction manual had said the solar charger would still work under an overcast sky, but at a greatly diminished rate. But who knew when the next clear day would be, so she left the unit on its perch next to the window.

There were still a couple of hours of sunlight left, as long as the clouds didn't advance any faster than they already were, but she grabbed her flashlight anyway and placed it on the kitchen counter, then pulled the candles she had looted earlier out of the backpack. She walked around her apartment and placed one in the living room, one in the kitchen, and another in the bedroom, just to be sure; she didn't want to be caught with no light and have to fumble around in the dark. While the candles would only give off a limited amount of illumination, they would at least give her some light and allow her to save the flashlight's batteries unless she really needed them.

She walked into the bedroom and opened up her closet. Emily had always been a bit of a neat freak, bordering on obsessive but just the right side of compulsive—a trait she had picked up from her mother and one that she was glad of today. She had her wardrobe neatly arranged by season. On the right was where she kept her T-shirts, lighter blouses, jeans, and dresses. Then on the left was where she kept her sweaters, heavier blouses, jackets, dress slacks, and winter coats. Between the two sides at the far end of the closet was a set of shelving designed to hold her limited collection of shoes and boots, and below them, a set of six drawers where she kept her underwear, socks, gloves, and hats.

Layers, she knew, were the key to keeping warm while still being able to regulate her temperature and not overheat. The farther north she traveled the colder and wetter it was going to get, but it would be a bad idea to dress for that weather right now. She would need to move gradually from the lighter clothing to the cold weather gear.

She began by sorting the clothes she intended to take with her by material. Lighter cotton T-shirts and socks to help wick away moisture would act as her first layer. She pulled out all her T's and set them on the bed, laying her socks next to them. Next, she picked out a selection of wool sweaters; they would act as a great second level by trapping a layer of dead air between them and her T-shirts. That would help keep her body heat in and the cold air out. The final layer would need to act as her wind, rain, and snow barrier. For that she grabbed her two parkas. Made from tear-resistant Gore-Tex, each was filled with goose down and, best of all, stretched almost to her knees but with enough play that it wouldn't affect her ability to safely pedal her bike.

Next, she chose a pair of sneakers and a second, spare pair. They would work for her general day-to-day cycling and, as long as she wore a couple of pairs of socks, they would help when the weather got colder. She grabbed a pair of waterproof boots from the top rack; she didn't know when she'd need to go walk about or scavenge for food in the snow, so it would be a good idea to have something that was guaranteed to keep her feet dry and warm.

Finally, she pulled out her thermal socks and dug around in the back of a drawer until she found her pair of Pro X-Pert winter bike gloves. She added them to the pile, and then began planning how best to pack them.

First, she needed to empty the food from the backpack. She would pack the clothes in and then replace the food on top of them. If she ate the food from the backpack first that would give any extra room she needed for extra supplies as she traveled.

The heavy-duty winter wear could go at the bottom of the backpack she wouldn't need any of that for a while. Emily put her sweaters in next, then her boots and sneakers, before making a final layer with her T-shirts and trousers. Last of all, she repacked the supplies she had removed earlier. She rolled up her underwear, paired off her socks, and stored them in the side pouches of the pack along with her gloves.

She pulled an extra pair of jeans and a T-shirt from the closet and left them draped over a chair, ready for the morning.

Her packing complete, Emily walked back to the living room. Through the window, she could see dusk had crept up on her while she had been busy in the bedroom. The room was already beginning to disappear into shadow. She took the box of matches she'd set on the coffee table and moved from room to room lighting the candles she had placed out earlier. The candles actually gave off a decent amount of light, more than enough for her to see by. and the flickering orange of the flame gave the apartment a welcoming warm appeal.

She headed back to the living room to check on the battery pack. There was barely any daylight left now, so whatever charge was in the pack was going to have to suffice for now. The pack's LED indicator glowed green, showing it was fully charged and ready to use. Now all she needed to do was charge the actual battery of the phone. She attached the charging lead to the sat-phone's battery and flipped the rapid-charge button on the pack; the phone's battery would take about forty-five minutes to charge fully from the pack.

In the meantime, she needed to grab a bite to eat; she was famished. Emily opened the pantry and took out two cans of mixed-fruit cocktail. She pulled the lid off the first, sat down at the coffee table in the living room, and began spooning the contents into her mouth as she let her mind drift toward her plan for the morning.

Her top priority was to put as much distance as possible between herself and New York. She'd toyed with simply taking the most direct route toward her final destination but, as she thought back to her conversation with Jacob, she decided to just head directly north. If she did that she would be out of the city in a day at most. That meant—

Emily's train of thought was interrupted by the sound of something moving in the apartment above. Her hand stopped halfway to her mouth, a spoonful of fruit dripping onto the coffee table, her head cocked to the left as she listened to hear if the noise would repeat. Sure enough, there it was again, the now familiar pitter-patter of something skittering across the floor, this time in the apartment above hers.

As she listened, Emily heard the first eerie cry of one of the alien creatures rising from an apartment somewhere in the building. The call was answered by another beast on a floor below her, another added to the growing chorus, and then another. Within seconds, her apartment was echoing with the sound of a hundred alien voices, their high-pitched trilling filling her head. It sounded as though many more of the creatures had joined with this strange otherworldly choir. She guessed what she had experienced the night before was just an early batch of the freshly minted creatures, the first wave of what could tonight turn into a flood. It wasn't hard to imagine that over the past twenty-four hours the rest of the city's new occupants had been "born." Were they even technically being born or was it more of a metamorphosis? Who knew?

Emily dropped the spoon and rose slowly to her feet, all thought of food gone as the calls were joined by new, more disturbing sounds. In her mind's eye, Emily added images to the sounds she heard; she could see the creatures exploring their new world and, finding themselves trapped in mostly locked homes and apartments, following their inbuilt need to escape. The creatures, sensing the onset of night, had begun stirring in the apartments all around her, their excited scuttling back and forth punctuated by the sound of furniture pushed aside and the occasional crash of something delicate falling to the floor. Emily thought she heard something shatter, probably a vase, in the apartment next door. The creatures seemed to be whipping themselves into a frenzy.

The calls stopped as suddenly as they started.

A few moments of silence followed, punctuated only by the occasional noise of a creature moving, before that too was replaced with another, familiar sound. The sound of splintering wood buzzed through her head like an electric saw, but this was more…organic. It reminded her of a cartoon she'd seen on TV of beavers chewing through a fallen tree. The sound effects made by the rodents in the cartoon were exaggerated almost to absurdity, but the gnawing "zing" she heard echoing through the building would have fit right into the cartoon.

From the corridor outside her apartment, she heard something heavy hit the floor with a resounding thud. She rushed to the front door, and peered through the peephole. Across from her was a circular hole where the wall of the opposite apartment had been. She caught the movement of a creature that had just exited the apartment as it ran along the wall in the direction of the stairwell, its talon-tipped legs grasping at the wall as it pulled itself along the vertical surface.

Something fast and dark flitted across her vision.

Emily gasped and threw herself away from the door as her view was suddenly obscured by another of the creatures landing directly on her doorway. It paused for a second as if it could sense her watching from behind the safety of the door and then she heard it running along the wall.

Emily backed down her hallway, turned, and moved toward her bedroom but froze when she heard a commotion almost directly above her head. The creature in the upstairs apartment sounded royally pissed off. She could hear it throwing itself repeatedly against a wall as though trying to barge its way through. *It sounds as though it's trapped*, she thought.

Maybe, before he died, the owner of the apartment above hers had locked himself in the bedroom, completely unaware he would trap his transformed self after he died.

Whatever the reason, it did not sound happy.

Emily was just about to continue into the bedroom when she noticed sawdust begin to fall from the ceiling, just beyond the bedroom's threshold. The apartment suddenly filled with the weird gnawing noise as the creature trapped in the apartment above hers began chewing through its floor and her ceiling. Emily took an involuntary step back into the hall just as a large chunk of ceiling tumbled to the bedroom carpet, a contrail of dust and debris following it down.

Emily was a second away from dodging past the bedroom door and heading toward the living room when the creature dropped through the hole and bounced out into the hallway, blocking her path.

She caught herself just in time. If she had jumped she would have collided with the alien in mid-leap. She was convinced that would not have ended well for her.

The creature had pulled in its legs and culled itself up into a ball when it dropped through the hole, but now it flicked out all eight of its legs at once; they snapped into place with an almost plastic click. The alien raised itself into its normal stance and shook like a dog after a swim, sending bits of wood, plaster, and dust flying across the room. Its two eyestalks extended and the eyes popped open, focusing squarely on Emily as she backed slowly away from it. The monster's jaws vibrated in a blur of motion, rubbing together so rapidly it created a sound almost like a warning growl. It took a couple of steps toward Emily who in turn took a stumbling step backward, her only avenue of escape—other than leaving the apartment and joining this one's friends in the corridor—cut off by the creature.

Thoughts raced through her head: *Am I quick enough to run past it or jump over it?* She didn't know and wasn't willing to take a risk like that unless she absolutely had to. She had seen how agile these things could be when she watched the one climb the alien tree sprouting up in Central Park.

She continued to take small backward steps, keeping her eyes focused on the thing in her apartment but trying not to make any sudden movements that it might translate into an aggressive move on her part. The front door handle poked her in the small of her back; there was no place left to go.

"Shit," she hissed. The creature had kept pace with her as she moved but it hadn't closed the six feet or so between her and it, choosing to keep its distance…for now.

For a moment that seemed to stretch on for an eternity, the last woman left alive in New York and a creature that had, until just a few days earlier, been a living, breathing member of the human race but that was now something totally alien, stared across that six-foot divide between them. Each assessed the situation, each with its own imperative.

Then the creature sprang.

It leaped into the air, powering toward Emily. She ducked and screamed, expecting the thing to hit her and tear right through her. Instead, the spider-alien rotated sideways in midair and attached itself to the apartment wall, thrusting its feet deep into the plasterboard. It was now just three feet from her and at her head height. She could see her own distorted, fear-filled face reflected back at her from the creature's black glistening head.

The thing gave another, louder chatter, the disturbed air from its blade-like jaws washing over her as its eyestalks moved back and forth, scanning her as if it was assessing her threat potential.

But it didn't attack her.

Instead, it just clung to the wall, its obscene eyestalks continuing to move up and down but never leaving her. Twice now, Emily had been in close proximity to one of these aliens and neither of those times had it attacked. Emily knew that the thing could take her apart in a heartbeat if it so desired; it had her cornered like a proverbial rat in a trap...but it hadn't. That *had* to mean it would rather simply get past her and continue on doing whatever it had planned for its first night out on the town.

Emily began to move her left hand very slowly behind her, feeling blindly around until she found what she was looking for.

Click! The thumb latch to the door was unlocked.

She began to edge ever so slowly to her right; *easy does it*, she told herself, fighting the urge to simply sprint past the alien spider-thing sitting impatiently on her wall. She knew that idea would be a major mistake on her part. It sensed her but she didn't think it knew what to make of her and she didn't qualify as a threat to it just yet. That could all change in a second if the thing became tired of waiting around and decided to simply kill her and get on with joining its buddies, which she could still hear moving around in the building.

This is beyond surreal, her mind told her as it struggled to come to terms with the impossible situation.

When she judged she'd edged far enough, Emily slowly raised her left arm until she found the security latch, then, ever so carefully she slid it free of its receiver. The creature regarded her dispassionately, continuing to chatter at her while rocking slowly back and forth on its legs as though readying itself to launch at her at any moment. Emily could feel cold beads of sweat begin to trickle down the nape of her neck, freezing against her skin as it traced its way down her spine. She lowered her shaking hand to the door handle, pushed down until she heard the latch click, and then slowly pulled.

Inch by inch the door gradually opened, until a foot of space between the jamb and the edge of the door had been exposed.

The creature exploded forward, scuttling quickly along the wall before disappearing through the gap.

Emily suppressed a gasp of horror as one of the legs brushed against her hand as the thing shot out into the corridor, its legs gouging holes in the wall as it ran, sending puffs of powdery debris to the floor. She slammed the door shut and quickly reset the thumb lock and the security chain.

Her mind was telling her to run and find somewhere, anywhere to hide. But where was there to run to—nowhere! She *had* to press on. She forced her thoughts back to dealing with the situation.

And that was when she noticed the thin streamer of black smoke spiraling up from her open bedroom door. A cloud of smoke had already collected against the ceiling and was now moving slowly in her direction.

"Shit! Shit! Shit!" she yelled as she remembered the candle she had left burning in her bedroom. She rushed to the doorway and looked inside. On the bed one of her pillows was on fire. Small yellow tongues of flame were slowly consuming the cotton pillowcase. When the creature had dropped through the ceiling, something, either it or a piece of debris, had struck the candle, knocking it off the bedside cabinet where she had left it and onto her bed.

She rushed into the room and grabbed the edge of the pillow farthest away from the flame, trying to avoid burning her hand in the process. Flipping it over Emily threw it to the floor with the flame side down then started stomping as hard as she could until she was sure the fire was extinguished.

Goddammit, that was my favorite fucking pillow!

The room stank of burnt plastic. Emily coughed a couple of times and flipped the pillow up. It was ruined, of course. Her impromptu attempt at firefighting had also left a large scorch mark in the carpet. *There goes my security deposit.*

Emily let out a long sigh then realized with a sense of dread that now that the fire was out the only light was coming from the candles in the outer rooms. She was standing in a virtually dark room with the hole above her head where the creature had dropped through just minutes earlier. One close encounter of the weird kind was enough for her, she decided. That one was gone, but what if more of them decided to pay her a visit while she stood there in the dark? She dropped the still smoking pillow to the floor, gave it a final stomp, and then headed out of the room as quickly as her feet would carry her.

Emily picked up the flashlight, turned it on, and headed back to the bedroom, peeking her head through the doorway as she scanned the room with the flashlight, ready to run if she saw any sign of another of the creatures. The room looked empty, so she turned the flashlight toward the hole in her ceiling. It was an almost perfect circle, much like the one she had seen in the window of the crashed delivery truck and the stalled cars. Cut electrical wires dangled from the opening and she could vaguely make out some of the furniture from the apartment the creature had come from. *It's a pity the power is off*, she thought. *Chewing through those electrical wires might have fried the little son-of-a-bitch.*

She had no way of patching up the hole. It wasn't like she could call the building manager to come take a look, and there was no way in hell she was going to spend the night in the bedroom with that hole up there and the potential for more of those things to come crawling through. Besides, the place stank now.

Tentatively, she stepped back inside her bedroom, keeping her eyes on the hole, just in case another unexpected visitor decided to put in an appearance. The backpack lay where she had left it on the bed, thankfully untouched by the fire. Emily pulled it off and onto the floor, choosing to drag it rather than try to lift it. She reached out with her free hand and pulled the comforter from the bed, pulling both it and her bag of precious supplies out into the corridor before returning to close the bedroom door.

Her earlier encounter with the alien had proved these things had no idea how to deal with a closed door. They seemed quite happy to bore through it rather than simply open it, so she felt sure that she would at least get a heads-up if any more of them decided to drop by. She left the backpack in the hallway but took the comforter with her into the living room, shaking off dust and broken bits of ceiling.

Through the apartment window, Emily could see the last vestiges of daylight succumbing to the night. The light from the two candles cast flickering shadows across the walls and her still shocked mind was only too happy to turn those shadows into more of the creatures.

She dropped the comforter onto the sofa—she would spend the night there, she decided—and moved over to the table where she had left the sat-phone. The green LED indicator on the battery pack showed just three out of five of the green lights lit. It wasn't fully charged but Emily felt that would be more than enough juice to call the group in Alaska. She could finish the rest of the charge overnight. Besides, she *really* needed to hear another human voice right now.

She disconnected the battery from the charger, popped off the plastic back panel of the phone, and pushed the battery into place before reattaching the panel. The phone needed a clear line of sight of the sky to latch on to the satellite signal. There was no way she was going outside again tonight so she would just have to hope her roost by the living room window would do the trick.

She extended the antenna from the side of the phone, clicked it into place, and pressed the red power switch on the phone's keypad. The LCD display blinked the message "Searching" as it looked for a satellite signal. A minute later the phone locked onto a signal and the display changed to "Ready."

She tapped in the number Jacob had given her and waited, listening to the chirrup of his phone ringing at the research base in the Stocktons. It rang five times before it was picked up and Jacob's voice answered "Hello, Emily. We were beginning to worry about you."

■ ■ ■

Emily let out a sigh of relief, feeling some of the tension leave her body. She had secretly been harboring the thought no one would answer her call, that maybe something awful had happened in the time since she and Jacob last talked…or that she really had lost her mind and imagined the whole conversation. It was good to know she wasn't crazy.

She wanted to say something profound to transmit her relief to him but all she could manage was a weak "Well, I guess the phone works."

Jacob gave a good-humored chuckle. Then, "So how are things looking? Are you all set to leave?"

Emily considered telling him about what she had experienced since they last talked but how could she explain something so inexplicable? Best if she just skipped those details for now, so she answered with a simple "Good. I'm packed and out of here first thing tomorrow." She added, "I'm going to send you my route via e-mail, as soon as I figure out how to do that. I'm following your advice and just getting clear of the city as quickly as possible.

Once I'm out I'll identify the best route to get to you guys. Things are getting a whole lot stranger here."

Jacob sounded as though he was on the verge of asking her to elaborate on her comment but then seemed to think better of it. "Okay," he said, "that sounds like a plan." He paused for a moment, then added, "Are you sure you're safe? Do you have protection?"

Emily glanced over at the Mossberg leaning against the wall. "I'm covered," she said.

They spent the next few minutes hashing out a plan for a daily communication schedule: she would call him at 6:00 p.m. her time every evening, and if she missed her schedule's time frame someone from his group would call her. Emily knew the calls were entirely for her benefit, to give her a sense of connection and safety, something concrete for her to fix on, because both Emily and Jacob realized she was going to be truly on her own out there. At least with his calls she could hold onto the illusion of company. Emily was thankful for Jacob's kindness.

By the time Emily hung up the phone, she felt as confident as she could expect about her chances of reaching the Stocktons, given the circumstances.

Beyond her little apartment, the sounds of alien movement and their incessant calls had ebbed away to almost nothing. Emily began slowly to ease down from the intense emotional high of the day.

She knew she should get some sleep but her nerves were still buzzing. She reconnected the phone to the battery unit and checked the charge level; four of the five green LEDs were now lit. It would take a little while still for the phone to fully charge but it would definitely be ready in the morning.

She took a can of Diet Pepsi from the counter, popped the top, and downed a long swig from it as she moved around the living room back to the window. Darkness had truly descended, but the storm clouds that earlier had threatened to blot out the sky had dissipated and a fat full moon cast its glow over the city. With the lights of the city extinguished, Emily realized this was the first time she had ever been able to see the stars that, until today, had been invisible to New York's residents.

Her eyes scanned the shadowy horizon of the greatest city in the world, its towering skyscrapers and mighty financial industries now nothing more than history; a history only Emily Baxter could recall. The poignancy of the moment bit deep into her heart. Her eyes continued to roam over the shadowy rooftops and finally fell on the street below the apartment block. Emily let out a gasp of astonishment, the can of soda almost slipping from her hand.

The streets below and the rooftops of the stores lining them were nothing but a mass of shifting alien bodies. Thousands of the eight-limbed creatures jostled and pushed for position, scuttling over each other in what appeared to be two distinct streams: one heading north and the other south, moonlight glinting off their red bodies. Her limited view from the window, and the dim illumination, meant she could only see as far as a couple of blocks in either direction. Even so, she was sure she saw each of those streams bifurcate each time they reached a junction as a spur of the creatures left the main stream and headed off to whatever destination called them.

It was like watching some strange migration.

The creatures seemed to be communicating on a level imperceptible to Emily, or they were driven by a preprogrammed imperative to search and find their objective, whatever that might be.

Emily's mind immediately flew back to the giant alien trees she had witnessed being built in Central Park. Was this where this exodus was bound? If she rode through the park tomorrow, would she see even more of those treelike structures? Maybe this time they would be complete as each of these creatures below her sacrificed itself to the structure as some kind of biomechanical building block.

She looked down at the river of alien bodies streaming past her building, her eyes following others as they scuttled over the rooftops and out of buildings, leaping to join the flow of their kin. There was something strangely hypnotic about it. The ebb and flow of these creatures had a certain mathematical quality to it as they scuttled and crawled along.

Although Emily could not hear anything from her seventeenth-floor aerie, she wondered what it would sound like to stand on the sidewalk down there and listen as they clicked and clattered past on their spindly legs: terrifying, she decided. It would be terrifying, like something from the deepest depths of hell.

Emily stepped back from the window and drew the curtains together. In the solitude of her apartment, she resolved not to look out that window again until daybreak.

■ ■ ■

An hour later, Emily flicked on the flashlight and blew out the last of the candles as she stifled a long overdue yawn.

She picked up the shotgun and carried it to the sofa, laying it on the floor next to her, within easy reach if the need should arrive. She doubted it would. Each encounter with the creatures seemed to point squarely in one direction: they were nothing but drones, building blocks, if you will, for something far larger and much more complicated. If they had wanted to do her harm, well, she knew she would already be dead.

She thought she might have caught sight of some small part of the overall plan out there in the park. The creatures were adding to that structure, building something to only-they-knew what end. While she did not think these drones were any danger to her unless they were threatened, any plan created by an intelligence that could wipe out the majority of humanity and possibly most other life on this planet in a twenty-four-hour period was the purest epitome of evil to her, no matter how unfathomable that plan may be.

It was no longer what had taken place over the past few days that concerned Emily; it was what was coming next that worried her now. She had the distinct feeling she was cutting her evacuation from what was left of New York by as close a margin as imaginable, because this city no longer belonged to humanity.

New York and Earth now belonged to the aliens.

DAY SIX

CHAPTER EIGHTEEN

Outside Emily's apartment window, the dawn sky was a deep fiery red. Emily had half expected to see the streets still crawling with the alien creatures, but as she pulled the curtains apart, she could see the pavement, roads, and rooftops below her were once more deserted.

The clouds that had abandoned the sky the previous evening had returned sometime during the night with a vengeance. From horizon to horizon, the sky was quilted in a thick blanket of red-tinged roiling clouds. The red tint looked like simple refraction from the meager light of the early morning sun, but as Emily studied them more closely, she could see the clouds were actually suffused with ribbons of red, layered like strata through the cloud and along each edge. It was a beautiful yet disturbing sight, another piece of the ever-expanding jigsaw puzzle of her world's transformation from what it once was to what it was rapidly becoming.

She had spent a restless night on the sofa, her sporadic bouts of sleep punctuated by dark dreams of the creatures crawling quietly into her apartment, hundreds of them collecting around her as she slept. She woke from her nightmare when they attacked, soaked in sweat and with a strangled scream caught in her throat.

Finally she had given up on getting any more rest. Her anxiety level was through the roof and the best cure for that was to just get up and do something...*anything*. Normally that would have meant an early morning bike ride into the office or a walk along the Hudson to clear her head. Today she decided the best thing to do was simply be on her way.

She could have used a coffee to kick-start the day but she didn't feel like unpacking the portable stove, settling instead for a bottle of water she had left out the previous evening. She took a few gulps of the cool water and ran through her to-do list one final time, mentally checking off each item. When she was sure she had missed nothing, Emily picked up the shotgun from beside the sofa and walked into the hallway where she had left the backpack. She wriggled into the straps and fastened the belt around her waist, clicking the plastic clasp securely into place. She took a final moment to gaze at the apartment she had called home for the past six years. *Not exactly how I had planned to leave*, she thought. She was going to miss this little place. It had been her refuge from the outside world. Leaving it behind was going to be painful not only because of her deep emotional investment but because, when she stepped outside that door for the final time, she was also stepping away from the last remnants of her old life and all the security that came with it.

Emily Baxter, a shotgun in one hand and all that was left of her worldly possessions strapped to her back, opened the door to her apartment, stepped outside, and closed the door on her old life as she began a new journey out into the unknown.

CHAPTER NINETEEN

It was a pointless gesture but Emily automatically locked her door behind her. She knew she would never return to the place she called home; in fact, she doubted she would ever see New York again, but it just seemed like the right thing to do.

The corridor outside her apartment looked like it had been the scene of some movie-style shootout. Hundreds of punctures littered the walls and ceiling like bullet holes, the only evidence of the alien exodus she had witnessed the night before. Circular holes, the telltale signs of escaping aliens, had been chewed through doors, ceiling, and walls all along the length of the corridor; there were even a couple in the floor where the alien drones, in their frenzy to join the throng gathering outside, had simply chewed down through each consecutive floor.

Emily made sure to carefully avoid the holes in the floor as she made her way toward the stairwell for the final time. She didn't think there would be any of the creatures left in the building; the thousands she had seen last night were probably just a small portion of the newly awakened hive that had spread throughout the city while she slept. Still, she kept the shotgun ready, just in case.

Emily eased open the door to the stairwell and poked her head inside. It was dark in there, so she pulled her flashlight from the backpack's side pouch and switched it on.

The stairwell was even worse than the corridor. Huge chunks of drywall had been pulled off the walls and now hung in tatters and in dusty piles on the concrete stairs. She was glad she hadn't decided to just chance walking down without the flashlight because she could easily have tripped over the debris.

It wasn't hard to imagine the entire population of the apartment complex, potentially eight hundred or more residents, awakening from their transformation and, driven by their new alien impulses, tumbling like a waterfall down these walls and steps.

And then of course, there was the baby-thing in apartment twenty-six. So far she had only seen the strange spider-like creatures that she was sure had emerged from single pupas much like the ones she had dealt with at the *Tribune*'s offices. But what had that mess of melted flesh on the eighteenth floor transformed into? It would have been too large to form a single pupa. Could it have just been some aberration, a mutation of some sort, or could there be other, even stranger things walking the streets of New York today?

Emily didn't intend to stick around to find out.

■ ■ ■

She pushed through the doors on the ground floor and walked straight over to the security booth where she had left her bike. A quick once-over reassured her none of her precious supplies had been taken, so she wheeled the bike out of the cubby and then through the exit doors of the apartment block and onto the concrete terrace.

Overhead, the sky was a deep crimson and she squinted against the change from dark to this diffused light. The clouds seemed to have thickened into an unmoving mass of gray with an ever-growing volume of red bubbling within.

Emily swung her leg over the bike and shuffled her butt around on the seat until it was comfortable. The extra weight of the clothing in the backpack took some adjusting to. She shrugged a couple of times, wincing at the pain in her right shoulder, until the straps repositioned themselves to a more comfortable position.

Emily began pedaling.

The sun could barely force its way through the overcast sky. What little light did make it gave the streets she passed through a washed-out, black-and-white tone. The buildings on either side seemed to loom toward her as she cycled north. It wasn't hard for Emily to imagine a thousand eyes watching her from the empty windows. Strange, alien eyes that belonged to an inscrutable intelligence that regarded her as what? An insect? The proverbial fly in the ointment of their grand plan set in motion just days earlier?

If she was honest with herself, she doubted her presence had caused any more than the tiniest of blips on the radar of these things. She was a minor problem. Inconsequential. And that was fine by her.

■ ■ ■

Seventy-Second Street was as deserted as the rest of Manhattan. She took the on-ramp up to the raised section of the Henry Hudson Parkway with a head of steam, but she still had to raise her butt up off the bike's seat, her legs pumping like pistons, to maintain her momentum up the curving ramp. When she reached the top, she instinctively looked over her left shoulder to check for traffic as she merged out onto the main road, but this stretch of the freeway looked deserted on both sides of its six lanes.

In the distance, off to her left, past the concrete median and southbound lanes, Emily could just make out the New Jersey shoreline on the opposite bank of the dark sluggish Hudson. To her right, the elegant red brick offices and apartment buildings of Manhattan were quickly obscured by rows of trees lining the side of the freeway as she pedaled down the center lane, heading north.

Emily's plan was to head directly toward Albany. It was about a 145-mile ride and she estimated it would take probably two days or so for her to complete if she could keep up a decent speed. When she reached Albany, she would take either I-87 north or I-90 west, depending on how everything looked out there. She was leaning toward choosing the I-87 route though. It was a longer, more circuitous route, but it would take her through less densely populated areas and reduce her risk of contact with the aliens. It would be a slower but far safer route, she thought, in the long run.

For now, she was going to stay on the Henry Hudson Parkway until she reached 252nd Street. There she would switch over to Riverdale Avenue and follow that through Yonkers as the road transitioned over to Broadway. Eventually Broadway would intersect with I-87 just outside of Tarrytown and she could cross over the Hudson on the Tappan Zee Bridge and continue her journey north.

Riding down a deserted freeway in the middle of the day was quite possibly the strangest experience for Emily so far. It took her some time to stop glancing nervously over her shoulder, expecting some speeding vehicle to come rushing up on her, horn blaring, driver leaning from his window and screaming at her to get out of his way as he sped past her. It did not happen, of course. The only thing on this freeway was Emily and the ghosts of a million drivers.

A particularly thick blanket of gray cloud hovered on the horizon ahead of Emily. Sunlight strained to push its way through the dense cloud as best it could, but what made it through was nothing but a diffused blur that pounded Emily's eyes. She hadn't thought to grab a pair of sunglasses, but the painful glare was forcing her to stare at the bike's front tire rather than the road ahead. She had to glance up occasionally to make sure the road was still clear, squinting in the light, and then her eyes were back down again. She'd have to pick up a pair of sunglasses at some point, mentally adding them to her to-do list of items to scavenge.

The miles flowed by and Emily settled into a comfortable rhythm. While she considered herself a competent rider it had been a long time since she had ridden more than twenty miles in a single day, so she kept her speed down, pacing herself for what was going to be a very long ride.

Traveling along the parkway, it was easy to forget that beyond the tree line lay an entire city empty of all life. Human life at least. Apart from the occasional random empty vehicle stalled in the middle lane or canted awkwardly astride the median divider, there was little to draw Emily's attention to her surroundings. However, when she finally exited off the parkway, freewheeling down the looping off-ramp onto Riverdale Avenue and into the district that shared the same name, it did not take long for the gnawing feeling of isolation to return.

The streets of Riverdale were lined on both sides with beautiful, expensive-looking older homes and an occasional apartment building. Where Manhattan had seemed deserted by many of its inhabitants and workers as they fled the coming catastrophe, most of the residents of this area had apparently made it back. As she slowly pedaled along the deserted avenue, in the driveway of almost every home, Emily saw a car or a truck neatly parked, waiting for an owner who would never return.

But was she right about that? She was struck by a sudden but overwhelmingly positive thought: she had naturally jumped to the conclusion that this little suburb was as dead as Manhattan and New York, but just because she hadn't *seen* any signs of life did not mean there weren't other survivors hunkered down in their homes. Maybe they were too scared to come out? It was an expensive neighborhood, after all. Maybe, they didn't know about the creatures roaming the streets and were just waiting for rescue. With so many people making it to their homes there *had* to be survivors like her. There simply *had* to be.

Emily slowed to a stop outside a redbrick two-story with a late model Jeep Cherokee parked on the concrete driveway. She dismounted and began climbing the stone steps to the entranceway but stopped just halfway up. In the front door of the house was the all too familiar circular hole, cut, she assumed, by the transformed residents as they escaped from the locked home. Emily looked around at the other homes next door and across the street. Shading her eyes against the glare, she could see the same telltale openings in both of the neighboring homes and, she was sure, if she walked to any of the other houses, she would find more of the same evidence of this sleepy town's fate. While the tree-lined street had the appearance of life, of a lost normality, it was just as dead as the city she had left behind her.

Somewhere close by, if she took the time to search, she knew she would find more of the alien trees she had seen back in Central Park, probably tucked away in some park where kids used to play or lining the bank of a pond or lake where couples would have strolled hand in hand and watched the sunset. The alien structures would be all that remained of the residents of this town now, another piece of the inscrutable puzzle transforming what was left of Emily's world.

Emily walked back to where she had left her bike and climbed onto the saddle. Yesterday, she would probably have simply sunk to her knees and cried in despair, but that was a different Emily. Today's Emily Baxter was stronger, she told herself. Today's Emily Baxter could get past all of this. Still, a single tear escaped and trickled down her cheek. She wiped it away with a contemptuous swipe of the back of her hand. She didn't have time to shed any more tears for this dead world; she had someplace to go and she intended to get there.

■ ■ ■

She had no clue how the fire had started. Maybe it was from a lightning strike or something as simple as a candle left burning on a bedside table. Whatever the cause, about an hour after passing through the equally dead town of Irvington with its uneasy mixture of sprawling mansions and clapboard homes, Emily caught the unmistakable scent of burning wood blended with an unpleasant undertone of melted plastic.

Thanks to the local topography, it was next to impossible for her to get a good fix on where the fire was burning. Just like most of the other neighborhoods and towns that had sprung up around the northern tip of New York City, rows of trees lined every roadway, effectively limiting her view to the main thoroughfares and side streets she passed.

Emily gave a small cough and wrinkled her nose as a sudden gust delivered a particularly strong burst of fumes to her nostrils. She pulled on the bike's brakes and slowed her pace a little, stretching her neck to try to catch a glimpse of the direction of the fire through the occasional gap in the trees, but there was no sign of it, even though she knew it must be raging somewhere close by, the trees were just too densely packed together. The smell was growing stronger the farther north along the road she traveled, so she was obviously heading toward the source of the fire rather than away, which made her nervous.

As Emily passed the sweeping driveway leading up to the Lyndhurst Museum, she caught her first sight of the leading edge of the fire, revealed by a massive wall of smoke. The smoke was so gray that for the last half hour she had mistaken it for an extra layer of low-lying cloud. As she mounted a slight rise in the road, she spotted an open space between the trees large enough to give her a view past the museum building and into the distance toward where the Tappan Zee Bridge should be. But, as she looked through the break in the trees, instead of the bridge, all Emily could see was smoke billowing up from behind the main building of the Lyndhurst Museum. Adjacent to the museum, according to a sign she could barely make out, was a large hotel complex. Emily pulled the bike over to the side of the road and stared. From her vantage point, she could see wisps of smoke rising from the roof of both the museum and the hotel as embers caught by the wind landed on the unprotected buildings. It wouldn't be long before both of those structures succumbed to the fire.

"Great," she said aloud, as she watched the flames flickering in the distance. Small frail flecks of gray ash had begun to fall from the sullen sky, settling on the ground around her like snow.

Emily wasn't 100 percent sure, but it looked like the fire was between her location and the freeway she needed to take to get to the Tappan Zee Bridge, but with her limited view there was no way she could be sure. She would need to get to higher ground to see for sure.

She decided to press ahead, but less than a mile farther along the road, Emily had her answer. The way ahead was being gradually devoured by a huge wall of smoke, billowing and creeping along the road like a bank of fog. The smoke stretched skyward, obscuring all view of the bridge she knew lay somewhere beyond it.

Standing on the temporary safety provided by the wide expanse of blacktop, finally with an unobstructed view to the west, Emily could see the fire burning brightly. From behind the pall of gray smoke, a long wall of flickering orange flames stretched northeast for miles, following the outline of the Hudson River. Emily had traveled this far north only once before, so she wasn't that familiar with the area, but she was sure what she was seeing was the demise of Tarrytown and the surrounding area, as it was methodically consumed by this voracious beast made entirely of flame.

There was no way she was going to be able to continue with her original plan, she realized. Crossing the bridge or even continuing north was out of the question now, as I-87 and all other routes north were cut off by the fire or at the very least obscured by the thick smoke. She wouldn't be able to see a thing and would quickly succumb to either smoke inhalation or the fire if she stuck with her original plan and tried to travel through the smoke. There was only one way left for her to turn: she would have to head east along I-287 and then tack north when she was clear of the fire.

The fire was huge and moving fast. She estimated that it had already consumed thousands of acres. In the few minutes she had observed the fast-approaching flames, Emily had already begun to cough as the smoke had wrapped its wispy tendrils around her. The occasional falling piece of ash had now turned into a blizzard driven by a breeze that was helping to spread the flames even faster. As the smoke was pushed toward her by the fire, she chose just the wrong moment to breathe in a deep raw lungful of the hot smoky air. She choked, doubling over as the fumes seared her nose and lungs.

Emily began running, pushing her bike alongside her, then leaping into the saddle like some Wild West cowboy from a black-and-white movie. Her feet continued to pedal furiously until she was sure she had built up enough speed to outrun the approaching fire line.

Emily had no clue what lay in the direction she was heading; her plan had been to travel north and there was *no* contingency plan.

She was just going to have to wing it.

■ ■ ■

Emily only slowed her pace when she estimated she had put at least three miles between her and the leading edge of the fire, but it was hard to gauge exactly how far the fire was from her. It was moving fast and hidden behind the smoke and pushed by a breeze that was quickly transforming into a wind. If the wind grew stronger, it was going to spread the fire farther and faster, making it even more unpredictable.

She pulled the bike over to the breakdown lane, swinging it around until she could get a good look behind her. The horizon was filled with smoke; it was next to impossible to tell where its leading edge was or even how far it had spread. She needed to plot the fire's progress if she was going to be able to avoid it. The only way to do that was to get to higher ground.

Emily scanned the highway in both directions. There didn't seem to be any nearby buildings she could see, but up ahead, about another quarter mile or so, was an overpass linked to an off-ramp. That might at least give her an inkling of which direction to head. She jumped back on her bike and began riding toward the bridge over the freeway.

Emily reached the overpass, pulling to a stop near one of the bridge's concrete buttresses. It would be quicker just to climb up the grass-covered embankment to reach the bridge rather than take the curving feeder road, she decided, so she left the bike lying on its side in the grass at the base of the bridge. Emily clambered up the incline of the embankment, grabbing clumps of the sickly yellow grass to help pull her up. She was surprised at how winded she felt when she finally reached the top of the embankment, but then she had been riding for the last couple of hours without a break. It was no surprise she was feeling fatigued. She had managed to tune out the pain in her shoulder, but it too was beginning to become noticeable again, despite her best efforts to ignore it.

The bridge had four lanes for traffic. Lined with low concrete walls, each topped by a five-foot wire-mesh barricade, the bridge had been designed to stop all but the most dedicated suicide from jumping off.

Peering through the mesh back in the direction from which she had come, Emily had a better view of just how far the fire had spread. Judging from the distant flames she could see licking at the sky above the forest of trees that separated her from the blaze, the leading edge of the fire extended for several miles in a northeast direction, curving away in a wide arc of orange flame.

It looked as though it had already jumped the freeway where she had first seen it, judging by the huge plume of smoke rising from the direction of where the Lyndhurst Museum had stood.

From her vantage point on the bridge, Emily thought she could feel the wind change direction. She sucked the tip of her left index finger, ignoring the salty taste of her sweat, and raised her arm above her head. Yes, she was right; the wind *had* changed direction, for the moment anyway. It was pushing the fire away from her now, southwest, back toward Manhattan. That was the break she needed.

She looked around her for any clue that might give her an idea of where she was. At the opposite end of the bridge was a sign on the far side of the road. Emily walked closer to it until she could make out the text.

The sign read VALHALLA 2.5 MILES in large white letters.

Valhalla? Wasn't that some kind of Viking myth? Strange name for a town, but then so was Yonkers or Tenafly or any of the other hundred weird and wonderful names that had attached themselves to spots surrounding New York. But this wasn't any time to be pondering name choices. Emily looked back to the west, gauging her chances of outrunning the fire if the wind changed again and began driving it in her direction.

Just going to have to risk it, she decided. If the wind stayed on her side she could head due north and get past the worst of the fire.

She jogged back along the bridge and slid down the embankment to where she had left the bike, jumped on and pumped the pedals hard. Following the curve of the on-ramp back up to the top of the bridge, Emily began her ride toward Valhalla.

CHAPTER TWENTY

Welcome to the Hamlet of Valhalla, New York, the sign read.

Hamlet? Emily had no idea what the difference between a hamlet and a village was, but according to the weather-beaten sign on the outskirts of Valhalla, she was about to find out.

It had taken her fifteen minutes to bike the couple of miles down the double-lane road to the outskirts of the town…hamlet…whatever. The place had probably been an idyllic spot to live before the red rain, with picturesque colonial-style homes built on the side of sweeping, tree-lined hills. There couldn't have been more than a few hundred homes; maybe a couple of thousand residents had lived here, at best. It was beautiful but just like everywhere else Emily had passed through on her journey so far, the place was lifeless. *Nothing but a ghost town now*, she thought, trying to ignore the growing ache in her tired legs.

The road ahead terminated at a T-junction, guarded by an ancient redbrick firehouse that looked old enough to have been there for as long as Valhalla had existed. She hung a left at the firehouse and began heading up a gradual incline. The road led through a high-end neighborhood—if the expensive cars parked in the driveways of most of the houses were any yardstick—then past a school and a mechanic's shop. The hill topped out and began a gradual drop, winding past more beautiful but deserted homes. Emily allowed the bike to freewheel down the hill and her thoughts to drift.

She was going to need to find somewhere to rest soon. Once the fire was behind her, she was going to pull over and rest for an hour. Grab a bite to eat and maybe—

As Emily rounded a blind corner, she pulled hard on the brakes and brought the bike to a squealing stop.

"Oh!" she said.

The single syllable, half-question half-exclamation, could not begin to do justice to the incredible sight laid out before Emily, but under the circumstances, it was the best she could do.

A hundred feet or so in front of her, blocking the road completely and extending off to the left and right for several miles, was a forest—a forest unlike any that had ever existed on Earth before, composed of thousands of the same alien trees she had seen being constructed in Central Park. These were different though; these were the finished article and they were massive, reaching two hundred feet and more into the sky. Each one of the towering structures must have taken thousands of the spider-things to construct, far more, she was sure, than the couple of thousand residents that had previously occupied Valhalla.

The alien trees were packed together as densely as any earthly forest, the curling trunks stretching upward before opening into a huge canopy of featherlike leafless branches. Each branch was dotted with tubular spikes that curled outward like huge corkscrews. As Emily, mouth agape at the incredible sight, tried to take it all in, she saw a small eruption of red dust escape from the tips of one of the trees. She watched the dust slowly rise higher and higher into the air before finally melting into the low-hanging clouds.

While she continued to watch, a second tree ejected a similar cloud of the red dust high into the air. A third, fourth, and fifth tree quickly did the same, until finally the whole forest seemed to have added to the vast fog of red dust collecting above the canopy of the tree. The dust slowly rose into the air, carried skyward by warm afternoon thermals that made the dust twist and dance, before drifting off, carried by the same slow winds pushing the clouds and the stinking pall of smoke sluggishly across the sky.

It wasn't just the trees that seemed so out of place though. It was hard to make out from where she was standing, but the ground around the base of the massive treelike structures seemed different too. Where there should have been nothing but grass and hardtop road was an explosion of colorful foliage and plant life. It was difficult for her to make out from as far away as she was but it surely didn't look like it belonged in this quaint little town.

The forest reached off to her left and disappeared into the bank of smoke slowly edging ever closer to her location. The opposite end of the forest terminated at the bank of a huge lake that stretched away into the distance on her right. The only way to avoid going through the forest was to skirt around the edge of the lake and head east, and that was going to take precious hours that she didn't want to waste. Besides, she might get around to the other side of the lake and find the forest continued there too, and then still have to find a way through or risk being caught out in the open as night fell.

Trapped between the fire on one side and the vast expanse of the lake on the other, she had only two options of escape: go forward or turn around. She could turn back and try to find another way around, but she wasn't sure her legs could take having to ride for who knew how long to find a place that was safe to rest for the night.

There really was no other choice, she was going to have to find a way through the alien forest and hope she made it out before night or the fire caught up with her. Committed to her course, Emily began pedaling toward the forest.

■ ■ ■

She was right about the vegetation around the base of the forest: it was as alien as the trees themselves. Giant red fronds sprouted from bulbous spherical stems tipped with beautiful pink flowers that shined and shimmered like oil on water. Spiderweb-thin, blood-red reeds exploded in clumps, while a fine red fur that looked like creeping moss covered the ground, seeming to carpet the entire floor of the forest.

Emily kicked the bike stand down and dismounted. Dropping to one knee, she lowered her face as close as she dared to the line where the regular grass met the creeping red alien moss. On one side of the line was the moss and on the other regular grass, but running down the middle was a thin line of normal grass that was also part red moss. Emily realized that as surely as the red rain had changed the world's population into the alien drones that had built this immense forest, so too was the moss converting the grass into this new form of vegetation. As she watched, she thought she could actually see the regular blades of grass slowly submitting to the creeping growth of the moss. It was very, very slow, but it was definitely there happening right in front of her.

Her whole world, Emily realized, was being slowly but surely replaced before her eyes.

Emily stood and walked to the nearest tree. Back when she had seen that first tree in Central Park she thought it was covered in scales, but now that the three intertwining trunks were completed it was as smooth as marble and such a deep shade of red it was almost black. Some kind of a hard clear substance coated the exterior of the trunks. It gave them a veneer that glinted like obsidian. Emily gave the tree a quick rap with her knuckles; it was solid but the texture of the material felt almost like plastic beneath her fingers.

She'd seen one of the spider-aliens clamber up that first tree back in Central Park. The creature had added itself to the tree, one tiny piece of the trunk. She'd watched the thing as it melded itself into the structure. The Central Park tree had been tiny in comparison to the ones she walked through now. These were massive, and if she had to hazard a guess at just how many individual creatures it had taken to complete just one, well, it would have to be an easy thousand, probably more.

Not much light made it through the dense matrix of branches above her head so she needed to lean in closer than she was comfortable with to give the tree a more detailed examination. If she had not witnessed the alien adding itself to the tree she would never have known how they sprung up so quickly because there was no sign anywhere that Emily could see of a seam, connection, or joint. Each spider-thing had been completely absorbed into the structure.

She had no answers for the questions whirling around her head. There was obviously a far greater intelligence at work here. Anything that was able to take the entire population of a planet and turn it into tools of its own desires was unfathomably more advanced than humanity. She might just as well call it God because it seemed equally as inscrutable and unknowable as the big guy upstairs. These trees were an example of that intelligence exerting its will over who knew how far a distance. They were another step in the plan of that intelligence and she might just as well be an ant trying to understand how a computer worked. And like that ant, Emily understood that if she stepped in the wrong place she could wind up fried.

She stood up and stared deep into the forest spread out before her. The spaces between each of the trees were shrouded in the shadow cast by the thick canopy of fronds and branches above, but Emily could see far enough in to know she was going to have to push her bike most of the way through. The tentacle-like roots of the towering trees choked the ground, making it impossible for her to ride in a straight line. She would be better off on foot and carrying the bike over any obstacles where she had to.

What she *would* need to be careful of was getting lost in there. The trees all looked the same to her and stretched so far back there wasn't any visual reference point she could take a fix on to get her through and out the other side with any certainty. She was just going to have to take it slow and easy.

Grabbing her bike by the handlebars and seat, she hefted it over the first set of roots, suppressing a cry of pain as her shoulder injury reminded her it was still there, and then stepped over them herself and entered the forest.

■ ■ ■

Emily expected the air would be cool beneath the shade of the alien canopy. Instead, it was warm with a humidity level that, within minutes of her crossing into the forest, had soaked through her thin T-shirt to the point where the fabric clung with maddeningly annoying stickiness to her skin. She considered stopping and pulling out a fresh shirt from her backpack, but the idea of unloading the backpack to find the clothes she needed did not appeal to her. Besides, this place gave her the creeping heebie-jeebies. The sooner she was out of here the better.

Ten minutes into her exploration, she happened to glance back over her shoulder, and realized there really was no way to know which direction she was traveling. The sun, completely hidden by a combination of cloud, smoke, and the forest's dense sprawling canopy, was nothing but a diffused blur overhead. It would be incredibly easy to lose her bearings, wander around for hours, and never find a way out. She was confident she wasn't lost…yet. If she began to suspect otherwise, then she could always turn on the GPS unit she had attached to the bike and use that to find her way through. The only reason she had not done so already was her innate stubbornness to refuse to rely on technology unless she absolutely had to. The GPS and sat-phone were not going to work forever, so the sooner she learned to get by without them the quicker she would become self-sufficient.

Emily pushed through a particularly dense collection of brush. The thin reeds of the plant came up to her head and gave off a puff of the now familiar red dust as she parted the curtain of plants and elbowed her way through. It seemed everything in this strange new world was designed to propagate the alien presence as quickly and efficiently as possible, even down to the simple plant life.

Once through the brush, Emily found herself in a large clearing. The ground was scoured clean of any kind of plant life, earthly or otherwise, exposing the dark brown soil. The circular shaped clearing stretched for about four hundred feet from edge to edge, but in the center of the space Emily saw something unlike anything she had witnessed over the past few days.

It was a huge new structure, similar to the trees she had been walking through but with a trunk twice as thick around and stretching another thirty feet past even the highest tree she had seen. Instead of the fern-like branches of the other trees, this one held a huge cluster of milky pale orbs. Each orb was at least sixty feet in circumference and filled with a translucent pink liquid. At the center of each orb, a dark shadow was curled up within, occupying the majority of the space. As she watched, all of the shadowy silhouettes slowly rotated within their capsules, turning as though pushed by some gentle tide only they could feel.

Whatever was growing inside the orbs was huge, and, as she continued to watch, one of the shadows spasmed, twitching like a dreaming baby.

"Jesus," Emily said, taking an involuntary step backward as her eyes roamed over this latest discovery. She counted twenty of the orbs, clustered tightly together like a sprig of berries.

She was tempted to get closer, but this time her instincts told her to stay as far away from the structure as possible. She had been lucky so far in her encounter with the world's new masters, and now was not the time to push her luck. The spider-creatures she had encountered had seemed patently uninterested in confrontation, but there must be a good reason this particular tree was so obviously isolated and alone. Discretion was definitely the better part of valor here, she sensed, and decided to give the orbs as wide a berth as possible.

She began pushing the bike around the edge of the clearing. It was easier said than done because the loose earth grabbed at her sneakers and the tires of her bike, slowing her progress.

As Emily walked she began to feel a sense of unease settle over her like a dark cloud. Whatever was inside the orbs made her *very* uneasy. It felt like waves of anxiety washing over her, and Emily was sure the cause was the orbs and whatever was growing within them. Try as she might, she simply could not drag her eyes away from the cluster of strange fruit suspended from the alien tree, and the closer she got to them, the stronger her disquiet became.

By the time she had finally crossed the empty space and reached the opposite edge of the clearing, Emily's nerves were singing with anxiety. She felt ready to explode. It was a miracle she had made it this far. Her instinctual flight-or-fight gauge had quickly fixed firmly on flight soon after she spotted the orbs, and it took all of her self-control not to abandon the bike and her precious supplies and run as fast as she could away from that perplexing, terrifying stretch of open land. She felt like a little kid trapped in a haunted house. She didn't know why she was so unnerved but she knew the source of it was that bizarre cluster of things in the center of the clearing.

Finally, she reached the opposite side and pushed through the high plants growing along the border of the remainder of the forest. As soon as the clearing was behind her and obscured by the tall vegetation Emily let the bike slip to the ground, leaned one hand against the nearest trunk of a tree and vomited, violently emptying her stomach of the remainder of her breakfast onto a large clump of the red moss and her sneakers. She wiped her mouth with her hand, picked up her bike and immediately began pushing it through the forest again, her desire to place as much space between her and the clearing superseding any thought of cleaning up her shoes.

Thirty minutes later, with her panic now just a tingle in her spine, Emily spotted light breaking through the tree line about a quarter mile ahead of her. She let out a long sigh, slowing her pace a little as her fear was replaced with relief.

That was when she heard something moving through the undergrowth.

CHAPTER TWENTY-ONE

The sound of something big moving through the bushes off to her right froze Emily in midstep. Whatever was in there had effectively blocked her route out of this godforsaken place. She lowered the bike as gently to the ground as she could, trying not to make any sudden movements, then slowly reached around with her right hand to unsling the shotgun from her shoulder. She pushed the butt of the gun against her right shoulder and clasped the forestock with her left. The weight of the weapon in her hands made her feel a little more secure as she swung the barrel toward the clump of tall red plants where she last heard the sound of movement. The straps of the backpack pulled tight against her shoulders, making it awkward for her to keep the weapon steady. Her arms felt as though they wanted to spring apart as the backpack's straps dug into her shoulder muscles. Of course, that was the least of her concerns because her hands, trembling with either fear or adrenaline—she wasn't sure which—made the barrel of the Mossberg sway back and forth like a pendulum.

It's okay, she reassured herself. *You don't have to hit it, you just need to scare the fuck out of it.*

Emily sucked in a huge lungful of air and concentrated on calming her nerves. She tried to focus on relaxing her hands; they gripped the shotgun so tightly her knuckles had turned white. She spread her feet wide apart and with the front sight of the shotgun drew a bead on the spot where she thought the sound was coming from.

The rustle of movement and the sway of a tall clutch of red fronds, about ten feet to the left of where she had first noticed movement, grabbed Emily's attention. Whatever was moving through the vegetation was circling her, stalking her like a predator eyeing its prey. She swung the shotgun to point in the direction of the still swaying plants as sweat popped on her forehead, trickling down into her eyes. Immediately, her eyes began to sting.

Emily pushed the stock of the shotgun tightly into her shoulder with the hand holding the forestock, using it to support the weight of the weapon. She released the pistol grip and used her free hand to wipe the sweat from her watering eyes, then across her forehead to halt the rest of the sweat gathering there. Her hand was traveling back to the shotgun's grip when a huge shape exploded into the air from the grass, landing with a loud crash less than ten feet from her.

She staggered backward in surprise, the heel of her left foot clipping one of the roots of a tree, and she stumbled, falling flat on her back. Her arms windmilled as they flailed desperately in a vain effort to try to steady herself, but there was nothing to grab hold of and she dropped hard toward the floor of the forest. The second between her falling and hitting the ground felt like it stretched out into a minute, and in that extended moment, Emily saw the creature that stalked her.

It bore little resemblance to the alien-spider creatures she had already encountered; this thing looked more like a regular animal than an insect. It was six feet long and walked on four muscular legs. Each leg terminated in a four-toed paw tipped with wicked six-inch-long talons. Its body, covered in long spines that stretched backward from the tip of its neck, looked muscular and powerful, like a tiger. The spines were colored varying shades of red that gave the creature a striped camouflage of sorts and allowed it to blend in with the alien flora sprouting up around her. Instead of a head, there was a mass of articulated blood-red tentacles as long as her arm. Each pencil-thin tentacle moved independently and stretched out toward Emily, writhing and twisting like a pit of snakes, as though sensing the air for her body heat or smell. At the center of the mass of flailing tentacles was a long muzzle that, as Emily watched in terrified astonishment, opened wide to reveal row upon row of serrated teeth. It had no eyes that Emily could see, but the creature's "head" swung directly at her. It bobbed back and forth excitedly as it tracked her movement while she scrambled backward across the ground until she felt the backpack connect with the base of one of the tree trunks.

The creature opened its mouth wider and Emily could see a pink tongue flicking back and forth between the rows of teeth. The air was split by a sudden wavering ululation emanating from the creature. It sounded like a high-pitched growl and ended with a trilling warble.

This thing could have been stalking her the entire time she was walking through the forest, Emily realized through a mind hazy with fear. It was too small to have come from one of the red orbs she had seen growing in the clearing, so this must be something else again. Maybe it was something created to protect whatever was gestating in the orbs.

The creature moved closer to her, its head dipping low then back up again in a shoveling movement with each step it took. Emily's feet refused to move. This time, she knew she was going to die. There was no escape, nowhere to run, and even if she did manage to command her legs to move, this thing looked more than capable of running her to ground in a heartbeat.

This is it, she thought, as the creature stalked closer. *Game over. The end.*

And then she realized she still held the shotgun in her left hand. Blinded by her fear, she had forgotten the weapon, but now she grabbed hold of the pistol grip and swung the muzzle of the weapon to point directly at the advancing animal. It must have sensed her aggression because the spines covering its body vibrated loudly, giving off a threatening rattle as it dropped back on its haunches and launched itself at her, jaws wide open, tentacles striking as it soared through the air.

Emily closed her eyes and squeezed the trigger.

She heard the boom of the shot and felt the butt of the weapon buck violently back into her still recovering shoulder, sending searing pain down her arm. She heard the creature let out a grunt that turned into a squeal of pain. There was a heavy thump as the creature hit the ground.

When she finally opened her eyes, she saw the creature lying on its side at her feet. It was still alive; the round from the shotgun had caught it just above the right shoulder blade. A gaping wound leaked green fluid and the thing's right leg hung loosely at its side while the remaining three legs spasmed as the monster—and that *was* what this thing was—tried to right itself. The creature's jaws were inches from her feet, snapping angrily at her as its tentacles writhed and jerked. Emily knew that if she didn't force herself to get up and finish this thing right now, it was still more than capable of killing her even in its debilitated state.

Pulling her toes clear of the snapping jaws, Emily pushed herself to her feet, careful to stay out of range of the tentacles and teeth of the creature. She racked another round into the shotgun's chamber and aimed at the monster's head. It must have sensed its own demise because as her finger tightened on the trigger, the creature let out another of its mesmerizing ululations, only to fall silent as the shotgun blasted its head into mush.

Emily stood over the motionless body of the dead creature, her chest heaving as she sucked in huge gulps of wet air. As the boom of the shotgun blast finally faded from her ears, she heard first one, then another, and then another trilling ululation, as somewhere off in the dense undergrowth of the forest more creatures answered the call of their dead comrade.

CHAPTER TWENTY-TWO

The three alien creatures appeared within a few seconds of Emily hearing their answering calls.

She was already running toward the edge of the forest when she heard their approach as they crashed through the canopy overhead like a troop of monkeys. She risked a glance over her shoulder; two were already on the ground, closing in on the corpse of the animal Emily had killed. A third was clambering down the side of a tree trunk, the muscles in its legs bulging as it swiftly lowered its body down step by step till it almost reached the ground. It leaped the last fifteen feet and joined the two others, their tentacles playing over the body of the dead creature. As one, all three of the creatures let out one of their startling cries, then turned in her direction and began pounding after her.

"Shit," Emily hissed, and continued sprinting as fast as she could toward the edge of the forest, pushing her bike alongside her. Behind her, she heard the pounding of the aliens' feet as they chased her down like foxes after a rabbit.

A very, very slow rabbit, she thought.

If she could just make it out into the open field beyond the tree line, she was sure she would stand a chance. She just needed to get out of here and on her bike, and then she could put some space between herself and those things. She doubted they would follow her outside the perimeter of the forest…she hoped she was right.

Through the spaces between the trees, Emily could see the green of a field beyond the perimeter of the forest, and she decided to just run in a straight line for the closest gap, choosing to clamber over the tangles of tree roots where she could rather than skirting around them.

Emily's heart pounded in her ears, a counterpoint to the rapid breathing and grunts of exertion she made as she sprinted toward the opening, leaping over the outcropping roots of trees, her momentum pulling the bike over with her. Just thirty feet remained between her and freedom when one of the creatures leaped from the trunk of a tree in front of her.

These things were faster than she had given them credit for. *How the hell had one of them managed to get in front of her?* Emily's brain had time to think before she dug her heels deep into the ground and released her grip on the bike, which clattered unceremoniously away to her left. Emily hoped nothing on the bike or in the panniers was damaged as it crashed to the ground, but she would worry about that once she was out of this situation…*if* she made it out alive, that was.

In one smooth motion, Emily unslung the Mossberg from her shoulder, aimed at the creature and pulled the trigger.

Nothing happened.

"Shit! Fuck! Shit!" she hissed as she realized she hadn't racked a new round into the shotgun. She quickly rectified her mistake and pumped a shell into the chamber with a satisfying "cha-chink," aimed again at the creature in front of her, and squeezed the trigger. The shotgun blast caught it square in the neck just as it began to advance toward her, sending the head spiraling into the air trailed by a spray of green liquid. The tentacles on the beast's severed head flailed limply. It landed with a wet thump and rolled into a clump of red grass about the same time the decapitated body hit the ground.

One down, she thought, and spun around to face the remaining two attackers as she automatically ratcheted another round into the shotgun's chamber.

They were gone, disappeared back into the foliage and trees.

Emily swept the barrel of the shotgun back and forth, looking for any sign of the remaining attackers. She was soaked through with sweat and covered in dirt from her mad scramble. Red juice from the plants she had crushed as she rushed headlong through the forest smeared her clothes and skin. It stank of ammonia.

Sweat once again trickled down to sting her eyes but she resisted wiping it away, blinking rapidly and shaking her head instead to try to clear her blurred vision. She decided to leave the bike where it was for now. She couldn't risk dropping the weapon or her guard until she was absolutely sure she was clear of these creatures. If that meant leaving her bike and coming back for it later when the coast was clear, so be it.

There was a rustle in the long grass off to her left and Emily spun to face it, loosing off a shot that severed a wide swath of the grass but didn't seem to have hit anything else. She'd have to check her shots now. The shotgun only held a total of eight rounds; she'd used four already so she had only four more left in the magazine with no chance to reload; she'd left her spare ammo in one of the panniers of the bike.

Emily turned and faced back into the forest, her back to her exit as she started to edge carefully backward toward freedom while blindly feeling her way over the remaining few feet of tree trunks and uneven ground. With each tentative step she swung the barrel of the shotgun left to right to cover her retreat.

There was a sudden blur of motion in her peripheral vision and Emily instinctively dropped to the ground, just in time to avoid losing her own head to the massive paw of one of the remaining two creatures. Emily felt the hair on the top of her head fly up as claws sliced through the air where her head had been a millisecond earlier. She rolled to her right and brought the weapon up to where she thought the creature should be but it was already gone, leaping off the ground to land on the trunk of a nearby tree. It stopped for a second and stared at Emily, spines vibrating in anger and its mouth wide open in a vicious snarl. As she brought the shotgun to bear on the alien, it began climbing in swift graceful leaps up the tree trunk. Emily tracked it with the shotgun as it used its claws to pull itself up the tree before finally disappearing into the dense canopy, well out of range of her weapon. The feathery branches shook as it leaped from tree to tree above her head. It seemed to be heading toward the edge of the forest as if it knew that direction was her only escape route.

The bastard's trying to cut me off.

The second creature melted into view from behind a tree to her right. Leaping over twisting roots it ran between her and the path she had already come, blocking any chance she had to retreat into the forest. The creature's tentacles undulated and the spines on its body vibrated angrily, but it seemed to understand the shotgun represented almost certain death if it got within range. It slinked back and forth as Emily tried to get a bead on it but it moved too quickly for her to risk another missed shot.

She began backing away toward the edge of the forest. The creature on the ground in front of her matched her pace but kept its distance, never stopping its evasive dance. With each backward step she took, Emily risked taking her eyes off the alien for a second to glance up and over her shoulder, searching the canopy, ground, and trees for any sign of the second monster that had moved to block her exit from the forest.

Each step took her closer to freedom and she began mentally counting down the remaining distance between her and the edge of the forest. She could feel the air begin to cool the closer she got to freedom, stirred by a light breeze seeping in from outside, but it didn't slow the continuous river of perspiration that coated her body like early morning dew.

Emily had managed to count down to the final seven feet when she heard the creature dropping from the canopy above her. At the same time, she saw the second creature on the ground drop back on its haunches and begin to launch itself into the air toward her in a beautifully synchronized joint attack. The next few seconds stretched out into a dreamy slow-motion movie played out frame by frame. She observed everything from a distance, disconnected from the reality of the situation as her sympathetic nervous system took control of her body and forced her conscious mind into the passenger seat.

Emily felt herself drop to the ground and roll over onto her back, positioning her body to face the direction of the creature falling toward her from above. The shotgun traversed an agonizingly slow arc toward the creature as it hit the ground with a grunt just a few feet from her prone body, its muscles tensing as it raised one of its paws, the talons catching the sunlight that filtered through the tree line just a few feet away. The thing's spines rustled in anticipation of the kill and she watched the tentacles flicker excitedly back and forth toward her like snakes readying to strike. Its jaws opened wide and she could smell the fetid breath from way down in its stomach as it washed over her. And that was where she aimed the shotgun; she heard the boom echoing through the strange alien trees and watched as the buckshot tore through the mouth, obliterating the tentacles into a fine red mist and exiting through the back of the creature's skull. Globs of whatever amounted to a brain went spinning into the air behind it. The alien fell dead at her feet, its pink tongue lolling from what was left of its mouth as the dead creature's legs gave a final few kicks before becoming still.

Good shot. Good shot, her distant self cheered, as she flipped herself over onto her front and began to push herself up to her feet. *Now there's just one last one to—*

The thought was pounded from her mind as the third creature landed on her back, its weight smashing her down into the ground and forcing the air from her lungs. Emily heard herself scream in pain as its claws found their way under the backpack and sank into her flesh just below her right shoulder. The force of the impact sent the shotgun spinning from her hands.

Her ears filled with the sound of shredding and ripping. She was sure it was the thing slicing the skin from her body, but then she realized with relief that it was her backpack tearing as the creature tried to get through it to her.

Emily began thrashing as hard as she could, but she was pinned firmly to the ground by the monster's one paw while the other relentlessly tore at her backpack. The thing was just too strong and heavy for her to stand a chance of turning over to face the creature, not that it would do any good if she could because the shotgun now lay just outside of her reach. It was just a matter of time before the monster slashed its way through the layers of the backpack and snapped her spine or decided to take a bite from her throat. As if it sensed her thoughts, the monster dipped its head toward Emily's face and she felt the wet slathering of its tentacles brush over her skin, probing into her mouth, nostrils and ears. She screamed in terror as it brought its mouth down to her eye level and opened wide, giving Emily a perfect view of the black rows of teeth lining its mouth. Emily felt the tongue, rough and scaly, against her face as it tasted her, savoring its moment of glory before it delivered the final coup de grâce.

It wasn't so bad, she thought from the solitude of her inner mind. The pain was a distant distraction, the weight of the creature on top of her more disconcerting to her as she was finding it harder and harder to breathe. Darkness was already starting to close in around the periphery of her vision as her oxygen-starved brain slowly began to shut down.

Through her blurred vision, Emily could see something advancing rapidly toward her from the direction of the field beyond the forest. The shape was just a silhouette of motion, backlit by the afternoon sun as it darted swiftly between the trees, leaping over the roots. It was another of the creatures, she supposed, come to join in the kill.

The shadow vaulted over a particularly large root, using it as a springboard to launch itself through the air toward her. She closed her eyes and waited for the end to come.

Instead, the weight of the creature suddenly lifted from her as she felt rather than heard something heavy collide with the creature on her back, knocking it away from her and tearing its claws from the backpack and her shoulder. The relief was instant and she sucked in a huge gasp of air. The blackness began to recede and pain flooded in its place as she found herself once again in the driving seat of her own body.

"Oh, good God," she moaned, through teeth gritted so tightly in pain she could feel the enamel beginning to buckle.

The dirt was cool against her cheek and she was tempted to simply lay there, close her eyes again and sleep, but she couldn't do that, not if she wanted to live.

And she *did* want to live.

So, instead, she rolled over onto her back, ignoring the pain in her shoulder and ribs, and turned her head in the direction she thought her attacker had been knocked.

The creature was still there, crouched low as it sidestepped around the trunk of a tree, its lipless mouth bared in a snarl, tentacles quivering, muscles tensed and ready to leap. But the beast's anger was no longer focused on Emily. Its attention was squarely on the thing that had saved her.

The dog, a male, was almost as large as the alien creature it now faced down. Its dense light-gray fur was shot through with stripes of darker gray and its broad chest was a tabard of white stretching from its throat under its belly back to its muscled haunches. The dog's head was also gray, broken only by a mask of white fur around his eyes that stretched down his muzzle to his jet-black nose, while a thick gray tail curled proudly in a question mark above his back.

He was the most beautiful thing Emily had ever seen.

Emily recognized the breed as an Alaskan malamute. Her uncle had owned two on his farm when she was child. It looked kind of like a husky but it was bigger and far stronger. Originally bred as sled dogs, malamutes were incredibly powerful and highly intelligent. Where it had come from and how it had survived the red rain, Emily had no idea, but she owed this dog her life and she'd be damned if she was simply going to lie there and let him take on the alien bastard on his own.

The dog was crouched low to the ground between Emily and the alien, his lips pulled back in a silent snarl as he eyed the creature while it continued to circle around, unsure of how to deal with the dog.

While the malamute and the alien faced off against each other, Emily sat up and rolled over onto her knees. She had to find the shotgun. It had fallen somewhere nearby, but in the struggle that followed, the alien must have knocked it away because it wasn't where she had last seen it. Flipping back onto her butt, Emily scanned the other direction and spotted the stock of the shotgun protruding from beneath the root of a tree. She willed her shaking legs to stand but they just would not obey. The best she could do was to get on all fours and crawl toward the weapon.

The alien must have figured out what she was going for because it let out an ear-piercing shriek, leaping toward her.

The dog leaped too. Emily saw his jaws open wide, and his white fangs flashed as he collided in midair with the alien, sinking his teeth deep into where the throat would have been if the thing had had a neck. The momentum of the dog bowled the creature over and the two entangled animals rolled off into the underbrush, both snarling at the other as they tried to land a killing bite.

It was now or never, Emily decided, and she pushed herself to her feet, ignoring the tingling pain that ran from her shoulders all the way down into her legs. Limping the final few feet to where the shotgun lay, she pulled it from between the tree's roots. She quickly checked to make sure the barrel was clear of any debris, then racked another round into the chamber, ejecting the spent shell. She turned back toward where the two animals were fighting in time to see the alien erupt from the underbrush, closely followed by the dog. The malamute snapped ferociously at the monster's hindquarters as they both raced toward her, the dog's ears flat against his head, white froth coating his muzzle and flying from his mouth as he pounded after her attacker.

Emily drew a bead on the rapidly advancing monster and eased her finger onto the trigger...then released the pressure. If she fired now she risked hitting the dog following so closely behind the charging alien, and she would be damned if she was going to be the one who risked killing what very well may be the last specimen of humanity's best friend. Instead, as the advancing monster ate up the final few feet between its quarry, Emily breathed in what felt like the deepest breath of her life but in reality must have been the shortest intake of air she ever made and then yelled...

"Down, boy. Get down."

The malamute instantly obeyed, dropping to the ground and forcing the flat of its jaw tight against the earth while tucking its tail around its flank. It only took a second for her to issue her command and the dog to obey, but that was all she needed to ensure sufficient space between the dog and the charging monster. The creature's butt-ugly face seemed to take up her entire vision as she squeezed the trigger on the Mossberg. It disappeared in a spray of green gore, as the twelve-gauge buckshot obliterated it. Momentum carried the body of the alien past Emily and she felt the spray of green arterial blood splash over her as the dead body sailed past and crashed into the undergrowth behind her.

The dog was still lying where she had commanded it to stop. Its mouth was open as it panted hard, its tongue lolling between its front canines. Its left flank was smeared with dirt and stained with red blood, but the dog's eyes were bright and clear and fixed directly on her as she limped her way over to it.

A wave of gratitude washed through her as she noticed the dog's tail begin gently swooshing back and forth, sending a small cloud of dusty soil into the air. Emily knelt down on one knee, using the butt of the shotgun shoved into the ground to help steady her.

"Come here, boy," she called quietly. The dog immediately jumped to its feet and ran to the woman he had just saved, ramming his head under her arm and almost bowling her over while his tail swished back and forth with joy. Emily threw her arms around the dog and pulled him to her, burying her face in the thick ruff of fur around his neck.

Oh! He smells so damn good.

She pulled back and planted a kiss on his muzzle. The malamute responded by covering her face in wet slobber as he licked at her, bouncing back and forth excitedly.

"I'm happy to see you too, boy," she said between a fit of giggles.

A blue dirt-stained leather collar hung around the dog's neck and she heard the telltale jangle of identity tags lost somewhere in the mass of fur. "Keep still for a second, would you, you big oaf." She laughed as she felt around until she found the metal tag. She tugged on the collar until she was able to read the information engraved on it.

"Thor?" she said, reading the name aloud. At the sound of his name the dog's tail wagged even faster, sending a cool waft of air across Emily's face. Someone had obviously taken living in Valhalla to heart, naming him after the Norse god of thunder.

She took the dog's head in both hands and stared deep into his brown eyes. "Hello, Thor," she said. "Thank you for saving my life. Now, what do you say we blow this joint?"

Judging by the dog's single excited bark, he was as ready to leave as she was.

CHAPTER TWENTY-THREE

Emily limped back to where she had dropped her bike. Thor followed obediently by her side, stopping only to sniff at the dead aliens and occasionally to nibble at the wound on his side.

"We'll get both of us fixed up as soon as we're out of here," Emily told the dog. He glanced up at her, his tail wagged in understanding.

Other than a few scratches to the paint work, there didn't appear to be any damage to the bike, the panniers, or their contents from what Emily could tell by her quick inspection. The backpack was another matter though. She unlocked the belt buckle and let the backpack slip to the ground, wincing as the strap rubbed across her wounded shoulder. She was going to have to deal with that injury but not now, not here. The chance that there were more of those creatures roaming the forest outweighed her chance of contracting an infection right now. So, it would have to wait. Besides, the first thing she needed to do was secure her supplies so she and her new companion could go find somewhere safe to lay up for the night. Then she could treat their wounds, eat, and hopefully get some rest.

Emily gave Thor a pat on the head as he sat down next to her, watching intently while she inspected the damaged backpack. The back pouches were sliced clean through and were now useless, hanging limply from the main body of the backpack. They had been empty, so she hadn't lost anything. The creature's claws had however punctured through the pack's reinforced material and into the clothing stored inside. She could make out tufts of white thermal wadding sticking out from the ragged puncture holes and slits. That could only mean her cold weather gear was damaged. Better her clothing than her skin. She shuddered as her imagination summoned up an image of what she would have looked like if she *hadn't* been wearing the backpack. She forced the bloody image from her mind.

There was no way she was going to stay here a moment longer than necessary, and no way was she going to start unpacking her kit now. She would double-check the contents when she could. At least the backpack was still serviceable. She would have to perform some cosmetic surgery on it at some point, just to shore up the damage and make certain it remained waterproof.

There was one thing she *was* going to do though.

She unzipped the pouch where she had stored her extra shells for the shotgun—mercifully untouched by the creature's frenzied attack— and pulled out enough to refill the magazine. She slid them one after the other into the loading port of the shotgun until it was full, and then added a final round into the main chamber.

Emily slung the backpack back onto her shoulders, fastened up her belt, picked the bike up from the ground, and walked the short distance to the break in the forest.

She kept the shotgun in her hands…just in case.

■ ■ ■

Stepping out of the forest and into the familiar green of a field full of normal grass immediately helped lift Emily's spirits. That feeling quickly evaporated though as she spotted the fire still raging off to the west. The fire line looked to have advanced several miles closer to where she was now.

Good, she thought. *With any luck, the fire will rip through that demented forest and kill every last thing in it.*

While thoughts of the forest's potential destruction were all very satisfying, Emily knew she still needed to put some distance between her, the fire, and any other beasts that might decide she and Thor would make a nice bedtime snack, and she needed to do it as quickly as possible. Ahead of her was a wooden fence bordering the farthest edge of the field. Beyond the fence, Emily could see a red stop sign, which meant there was a road. It was as good a direction to head for as any other, so she began pushing the bike toward it.

The fence had definitely seen better days. The occasional fleck of white was all that remained of the original paint job; the aged wood was rotten and flaky after exposure to the elements for many years. In several places Emily saw that wooden struts were missing, leaving a gap large enough to lift her bike through. Thor easily jumped over it.

The dog sat patiently next to Emily as she stopped to look up the road. She had no idea what might lie up there, but it was at least heading in the right direction, one that would take her away from both the fire and the forest. "Well, what do you think?" Emily asked, glancing at the dog. "Want to tag along with me?"

Thor's tail fanned the dusty surface of the road.

"Okay," said Emily, a smile crossing her face despite the pain of her wounds and the aching in her muscles. "I guess we should get going." She swung her leg over the bike and, once she was comfortable, began pedaling up the road. Thor trotted alongside the bike, easily keeping pace, his lolling tongue lolling from first one side of his open mouth and then the other, as his claws clicked against the road's surface.

Three miles farther up the winding road, Emily saw the first signs of civilization: a small cluster of houses off to the right.

She pulled the bike over to the side of the road and looked back in the direction she had just ridden from. The fire was a good five or six miles distant now, and judging by the direction the smoke was blowing, it was heading away from her at last. She hadn't put as much distance from it as she would have liked, but there was no way she could go on any longer. Exhausted, and with the rush of adrenaline finally beginning to wear off, the pain in Emily's shoulder and her ribs was making itself known. She had to stop and it had to be soon.

This would have to do.

She chose a gray clapboard two-story with a chimney. A chimney meant a fireplace, which meant warmth, light, and heat to cook with. She pulled up outside the house and dismounted, wheeling her bike around the side of the building. She left the bike behind a large privet hedge, hiding it from any prying eyes, no matter how unlikely that scenario might be. She had no idea whether there were any other survivors close by, or how they might react if they found a stranger in their town. She would sleep better knowing her bike was safe until she had a chance to scout out the area.

The door to the house was ajar. She prodded it open with the barrel of the shotgun and leaned inside. "Hello? Is anyone home?"

she called out. Emily already knew there would be no reply but it didn't feel right simply walking into someone's home without at least announcing her presence. It would also alert anything else that might have taken up residence in the days since the red rain that it had company. Between the Mossberg and Thor, Emily felt confident she could take care of potential threats from any alien lodger that might have taken up residence in the owner's absence. As she had predicted, there was no reply. The place was empty.

Thor didn't seem anxious as he followed her into the house, which was a good sign since the two of them were truly alone, but she still did a quick sweep of every room, just to make sure. The last thing she needed after the kind of day she'd had was any surprises.

There were no signs anything untoward had happened in the home. There wasn't even any remnant of the alien cocoons, which, coupled with the open door and the empty garage she found while searching the house, meant the owners had probably left in a hurry.

Only to die somewhere out there in their car.

The living room had a large fireplace with three neatly chopped logs waiting in the grate. A coalscuttle full of extra wood sat nearby. There was enough wood to last them through the night, she estimated. Emily left her backpack leaning against the back of the sofa closest to the fireplace, and after a few minutes searching the kitchen cupboards she found a packet of firelighters and a box of extra-long matches in a drawer next to the sink. Within minutes, she had a fire lit and giving off more than enough light to fight back the rapidly approaching shadows escorting in the evening. The small room would warm up quickly, and as long as she kept the fire stoked and fed, it should stay toasty all night long.

Her stomach had been complaining to her since she exited the forest, and now it was screaming for food. Her head and body ached from the beating she had taken, and the lack of food was not helping, but before she could prepare something to eat, she had to deal with the wounds the creature had inflicted on both her and her new companion.

Thor had curled up in front of the fireplace, already asleep, but he raised his head when he heard Emily's grunt of pain as she stripped off her grimy T-shirt. "It's okay, boy," she said, reassuring the dog as best as she could. Removing her jeans proved more difficult—and painful—than the T-shirt. She made the mistake of trying to take them off as she normally would and had to bite her lip to stifle a scream as she felt a shooting pain stab at her ribs. God, she hoped none of them were broken.

Two more painful attempts and several cuss words later and Emily was convinced there was no way she was going to get the jeans off without a little ingenuity. Finally, she had to resort to lying flat on the floor and pushing on the waist band of the jeans until they were over her butt, then wriggling slowly out of them using the carpet for traction. By the time she had finished she was even more exhausted and lay there panting until she recovered.

She looked over at Thor sound asleep next to her on the rug. "A lot of good you are," she whispered. The dog opened one eye, gave a half-hearted wag of his tail before letting out a contented hiss of breath as he settled down again.

Emily had spotted a full-length mirror hanging on the wall in the hallway when she entered. It was too far from the light of the fire for her to see very well, so she lifted it from its hook then carried it back into the living room, resting it on the cushions of the couch. She angled her body until she could see her back as clearly as possible and twisted her head over her right shoulder until she could make out the four puncture marks just below her right shoulder blade. They didn't look as bad or as deep as they felt, she decided with some relief. Blood had already congealed in the wounds but the skin around the edges of each puncture was puffy and had turned an angry-looking red. The punctures were directly below the curve of her shoulder blade, so every time she moved her arm the bone and muscle would agitate the wound, which hurt like a son of a bitch. She'd been lucky this time; the wounds weren't life threatening, as long as they weren't already infected.

Emily examined the rest of her body in the mirror. Scratches and dried blood—both hers and that of the monsters she had killed—covered her hands and face. Just below her left breast was a nasty-looking bruise that covered the flat of her abdomen and extended around her side and onto her back. Emily gently probed around the area checking each rib. Nothing was broken, thank God, but it was going to be sore as hell for a while.

She was tempted to use some of her precious water to clean off; she felt like she hadn't showered in months. Instead, she reverted to her supply of wet wipes, spending the next ten minutes gently wiping away the grime and blood, first from her feet, then making her way up her legs and finally her remaining upper half. By the time she was finished she looked almost presentable…she smelled strongly of lemons, but she certainly passed for human again.

Emily had unpacked the first-aid kit from the backpack already. She had a tube of antiseptic cream and some clean gauze ready and waiting. She cleaned the wounds with a couple of iodine-soaked pads, making sure she pulled out any bits of dirt that had collected in the wound. She twisted the top off the tube of antiseptic cream and applied the pungent smelling cream to her wounds, stretching to reach the farthest hole with the tips of her fingers. The remaining cuts and scratches received similar treatment.

By the time she finished Emily was beginning to feel a little better. No way was she going to win a beauty pageant anytime soon, but at least she was clean and patched up. The gauze she had intended to cover her injuries wasn't going to work though, because she had no way to reach back there and accurately position it to cover all the wounds—so instead, she opted to simply put on a clean T-shirt.

Emily looked down at Thor. The dog was still fast asleep on the rug in front of the fireplace, as though saving a random stranger's life from alien invaders was something he did every day. She walked over as quietly as she could and knelt down next to the dog. He didn't open his eyes when she started stroking him along his spine, but his tail beat a gentle rhythm against the hearth of the fireplace and he stretched all four legs out and gave a rumble of contentment.

"Have I told you what a good boy you are?" she whispered in one cocked ear. His tail beat a little faster as he graciously accepted the praise, but his eyes still stayed closed. She ran her hands down his side and over his flank, searching for the wound she had seen him nibbling at earlier. Her fingers ran across the cut an inch or two below his ribs. She probed around the area as gently as possible; the only indication of discomfort the dog gave was a slowing of his tail wagging. She parted the fur to one side and leaned in to examine the dog's wound. It looked nasty: a six-inch-long tear that, if it had gone any deeper, would probably have taken stitches to fix properly. She unscrewed the antiseptic tube and applied some of the cream to her fingers, then, as gently as she could, Emily spread the cream over her new friend's wound, working it in past the fur until she was sure the entirety of the cut was covered.

Thor gave a low whimper.

"Stings, I know," she said, "but it's for your own good." The dog's tail thumped the floor with renewed vigor. "Okay, big boy," she said when she was finished and confident it was the only wound the dog had received during the fight. "How about I fix us some dinner? You hungry, boy?"

The mention of food seemed to get Thor's attention because he instantly flipped over onto his front, fixed his eyes on her, and let out a half-yawn half-whine that clearly conveyed that he thought food was a really, really good idea.

"Okay, let's go see what we can find to eat."

Emily pushed herself to her feet, wincing at the pain in her shoulder as the T-shirt rubbed against the cuts on her back. "I think I have something you may like," she cooed to the dog padding alongside her while she walked over to where she had left the backpack.

Her poor backpack looked like it had been through a shredder. Several pouches had split open and slashes crisscrossed the back of it where the creature had attacked her. She would deal with that later. What was more important was getting some food inside them both.

Emily untied the top flap of the pack and rooted around inside until she found what she was looking for. She pulled out the bag of jerky strips.

"Perfect," she said. Thor was now sitting obediently next to her staring at the bag in Emily's hand. She tore the top strip from the bag and instantly smelled the astoundingly delicious aroma of the dried meat. Her stomach began doing cartwheels. Thor began drooling.

She fed the dog several pieces at a time. He devoured them without even bothering to chew, gulping down six pieces before

Emily had even finished one. "Jeez!" she said, laughing as she handed him more of the jerky. "When was the last time you ate anything?"

That was a good question. There didn't seem to be any food source around the area for the dog. She hadn't seen any rabbits or squirrels. In fact, when she thought about it, she hadn't seen *any* other life at all. Not even so much as a bee or moth since the red rain first fell.

"Okay! Okay! Just slow down."

They shared the packet of jerky between them, but it was obvious by the time Emily showed Thor the empty bag that neither of them were satiated. "I've got an idea," she said, checking through the backpack again.

"This should do the trick," she said, pulling four square cans of corned beef from the pack, which she then took into the kitchen.

She placed the cans on the counter and popped open the first. Thor sat obediently next to her, but he did not take his eyes from the food for one second. In one of the kitchen cabinets she found two soup bowls. She mashed the entire contents of one of the tins of beef and fat into smaller pieces, breaking the meat apart until it became a soft mush, and placed it in one of the bowls. The other bowl she filled with water and added a large glass for her.

"There you go," she said and placed the two bowls on the floor next to the dog.

Thor looked at the food then back to Emily then back at the food again. He gave a small whine of frustration. Emily looked at him, confused for a moment before she understood what was wrong: this was a well-trained dog. He was starving but he wasn't going to touch the food until he was told he could. Like a soldier, he stood obediently waiting for the go-ahead from his new mistress.

"Eat, you silly dog," she said and patted him on the head.

The dog must have been a magician in another life because he made the food disappear in a second. Ignoring the water, Thor stared at the now empty food bowl. He sat back down and looked up at Emily, who had managed barely make a dent in her own dinner in the time it had taken him to devour his in its entirety.

"Wow," she said, impressed. "Okay. You get one more can, doggy. I don't want you being sick." She picked up the bowl, opened a second can for the dog, and placed it back on the floor. It took just a nod from Emily before he began eating, this time at a slightly more leisurely pace.

Apparently satisfied with his dinner, Thor took a few deep gulps of water, then cleaned the final few morsels of meat from the bowl with his tongue before curling up at Emily's feet, letting out a contented sigh and closing his eyes once again.

Emily finished her own meal and washed it down with a few swigs of water from her bottle. Her shoulder hurt sufficiently that she decided it warranted a painkiller, which she swallowed with a few more gulps of water. Walking over to the fireplace, she warmed her hands in front of the orange flames as they danced in the hearth.

She smothered a yawn with her hand and realized how incredibly exhausted she was. It was definitely time for sleep.

There was a perfectly serviceable bed in the master bedroom on the second floor, but Emily didn't feel comfortable sleeping in someone else's bed. Besides, sleeping next to the light and warmth of the fireplace was far more appealing. She pulled her flashlight from the backpack and climbed the stairs, after telling Thor to stay put.

In the linen closet on the second-floor landing Emily found a spare pillow and a thick blanket. She took them both downstairs, throwing them on the sofa, then pushed the sofa closer to the fire but not so close that it might singe.

Emily climbed into her makeshift nest while Thor slowly circled twice around the rug and then curled up with his head resting on one paw between her and the fire, his eyes never leaving his new mistress until they finally closed in sleep.

Emily Baxter lay silently on the sofa, watching flames dance in the fireplace, basking in the warmth of the fire and the presence of her new friend.

Within minutes, her eyes closed and she too was asleep.

■ ■ ■

Emily awoke momentarily in the middle of the night to the sound of Thor whimpering. The fire was still burning brightly enough she could see the dog lying next to the fireplace, sound asleep but obviously dreaming. His legs were jerking uncontrollably, his chest rising and falling in short, rapid bursts, his jaws drawn back in a muffled growl as his head moved up and down as if he was running from something.

"Shhhhhhhh," Emily whispered. "It's okay, boy. You're safe now. I promise I won't let anything happen to you. I'm right here."

The sound of her voice seemed to soothe the dog. Emily could see the tension leave his body, and his breathing become slow and deep again. "Good boy," she whispered.

Her final thought, as she allowed herself to succumb to sleep again, was that she hoped she could follow through with that promise.

DAY SEVEN

CHAPTER TWENTY-FOUR

A thin veil of mist greeted Emily as she examined the world outside the next morning. At least, she had taken it for mist at first, but when she opened the door to let an insistent Thor out to do his morning business, she caught the unmistakable scent of the fire.

It wasn't mist—it was smoke!

During the night, the wind had apparently changed yet again and the fire had caught up with her. Although she could not see any sign of the main fire, judging by the amount of smoke slowly creeping through the trees and past the house, it was a lot closer than she was comfortable with. Emily had hoped to stay another day in the house while she recovered from her battle but that didn't look like was an option now. The best thing for her to do was continue north and put as many miles behind her as she could.

"Well, boy. What do you think?" she asked the malamute as he returned from watering the nearby hedge. Thor regarded her with his soft eyes, wagging his tail enthusiastically. Emily took it he agreed with her.

But, before she did anything else, they both needed to eat. For breakfast Emily opened the final can of corned beef and fed it to Thor. She was going to have to track down some real dog food for him soon. Feeding him human food would only upset his stomach and weaken him. The idea of adding a huge bag of kibble to her pack was not an option so she would have to either pick up a supply of canned food or a smaller bag of dried food every couple of days. It was going to be a hassle but it was the very least she could do for the mutt after his brave actions the day before.

A couple of energy bars satisfied her own hunger, but Emily decided she could afford the extra twenty minutes it would take to boil a mug's worth of water in a pot over the fireplace. Adding the water to a couple of teaspoonfuls of instant coffee, Emily took a few minutes to gather her thoughts and savor the coffee's aroma as the warmth of the hot liquid filled her stomach.

Last night she had been too depleted to even think about calling Jacob and his crew in the Stocktons. She knew they would be concerned about her, so she would need to reach out to them before she left.

The phone! Emily hadn't even thought to check whether the phone had been damaged in the fight. She rushed over to the backpack and pulled the satellite phone from where she had stored it. It looked intact but these things were delicate pieces of technology. A bump in the wrong place could easily break it and then what would she do? She extended the antenna and switched the phone on. After a painfully long moment, the phone gave a beep informing her it was booting up.

Emily let out a sigh of relief as the phone's display informed her it was ready to make a call. The battery was 96 percent charged; she would give herself an extra hour later in the day to set up the solar charger and replenish the unit. Emily pressed the redial button. She waited patiently while the phone established a connection with the satellite and for the sound of the phone ringing somewhere on that remote island in northern Alaska.

The sat-phone picked up on the second ring. "Emily?" Jacob's voice sounded tired but she could hear concern laced through his voice. His obvious anxiety over her well-being gave Emily's heart a surprising emotional tug and she found herself smiling at his concern for her safety.

"I'm here, Jacob," she said. "I'm okay."

She spent the next twenty-five minutes talking to Jacob about the events of the previous day. When she explained about the forest and her attackers, he accepted her story without reservation, apparently more fascinated by her description of the creatures than the mortal peril she had been in.

"Fascinating! Absolutely fascinating," he said, before sheepishly adding, "Are you all right?"

Before answering, Emily gave her shoulder a gentle rotation and had to suppress a hiss as she felt pain tear through the injured muscles. "All fine," she replied. "Nothing more than a scratch."

She must have sounded convincing because, for the next ten minutes, Jacob fired question after question at her about the creatures that had attacked her and the strange globes she had seen in the clearing. However, when she mentioned the approaching fire, concern returned to his voice.

"Em, you need to get out of there as quickly as possible. Uncontrolled fires can spread faster than you can ride and in unexpected directions. You don't want to get cut off."

Emily wondered how a scientist who lived in one of the coldest climates on Earth knew anything about brush fires. But he was right, of course, so she reassured Jacob she would be out of there in the next half hour. He relaxed a little but insisted she cut the phone call short and reconnect with him again that evening, after she reached her next stop-off point.

"Be safe, Emily Baxter," had been his parting words to her as he hung up from the call.

"Easier said than done these days," she told Thor.

- - -

Emily climbed the stairs to the second floor of the house and found a west-facing window in one of the spare bedrooms. She tried to ignore the pink-colored wallpaper and the dolls stacked on one shelf, and a forgotten teddy bear propped against a pillow on the child-sized bed.

From the window, Emily could see out across the edge of town and back in the direction she had traveled the previous day. Rolling waves of battleship-gray smoke covered most of the area, pushed along by a light breeze toward whatever this town was called. At the farthest edge—Emily estimated that to be about three miles or so—she could see a partition of flame moving within the smoky shroud.

The wind was gradually pushing the fire closer to the house and she expected the quaint home, along with the surrounding neighborhood she had taken shelter in to be little more than ashes by this same time tomorrow morning. For now though, she was in no immediate danger. As long as she kept her word to Jacob and left soon she felt confident she could quickly outdistance the fire.

Emily made her way back down the stairs and readied the backpack, repacking the few things she had used the previous night. A quick reconnoiter of the kitchen cupboards turned up two more cans of soup, a can of green peas, and a jar of hearts of palm. Emily added them to her stock. She also decided to keep the blanket she had found. She rolled it up and tied it off with a piece of string she found in a drawer before securing the blanket to the bottom of the backpack using the two loops there.

"Okay, doggy," she said to Thor, as she gingerly pulled the backpack up onto her shoulders and gave one final look around the living room to make sure she hadn't forgotten anything. "Let's go."

Once outside, Emily could see the smoke had already grown thicker. It collected in the street and seemed to cling to the air, refusing to move. Emily coughed as she inhaled the smoke and Thor gave a couple of snorts, then sneezed loudly, shaking his head and spraying drool in all directions. She pulled the bike from the hedge where she had left it, wiping a sheen of dew from the seat; the last thing she needed to start her day was a soggy butt. The bike's metal frame was cold against her hands.

Emily wheeled the bike down to the main road, mounted, and began pedaling along the small side street until she hit the main road. Making a right at the junction, Emily began riding away from town, north, toward her future.

EPILOGUE

Emily and Thor crested the rise of the hill.

In front of them, the freeway lay clear and empty, stretching out toward the horizon. Behind them, several miles distant now, Emily could see the town they had left behind, almost entirely hidden within a swirling bank of smoke. Beyond that, she could see the fire stretching away into the distance, a glowing arc of flame consuming everything in its path, alien and earthly alike. It did not discern between either.

Emily looked down at her dog and then back to the open expanse of blacktop leading north into the distance. "Well, boy, are we ready to do this?" Thor gave a loud bark and began padding his way forward along the road.

"Talkative mutt, aren't you."

Emily set off after the dog. Whatever lay before them was in the future and right now, in this moment, as strange as it sounded even to her ears, Emily couldn't have been any happier.

The past, where the old Emily lived—well, that was gone, swept away forever. The future was unknown, nothing more than potential and full of unpredictability. There were very few certainties left. Emily found that oddly comforting.

The one truth she could clearly see was this was no longer *her* world. It belonged instead to the invaders who had wiped humanity from the planet in a single day. She, and all the survivors left on this rock they called home, were now the aliens.

And it was going to be up to her and whoever was still left alive out there to try to take it back.

FOLLOW THE ADVENTURES OF

Emily Baxter in book two of the series, EXTINCTION POINT: EXODUS, coming 2013. Join my mailing list at www.DisturbedUniverse.com to receive early notification of its release.

ACKNOWLEDGMENTS

I'd like to say a very quick thank-you to a couple of people who helped make this book a reality.

First, I'd like to say an extra big thank-you to the members of the Goodreads' Apocalypse Whenever group (especially Gertie, the group moderator), who were kind enough to tell me what they really wanted in a post-apocalyptic novel. Hopefully, I've delivered.

I know she's heard it a thousand times before, but I really could not have written this book without the help and support of my wife, Karen. You are my inspiration, sweetheart. Thank you for all that you have done.

And, of course, I would also like to thank *you*, the reader, for taking a chance on an unknown author and buying my book. It is truly appreciated.

ABOUT THE AUTHOR

Photograph © Paul Jones, 2011

A native of Cardiff, Wales, Paul Antony Jones now resides near Las Vegas, Nevada, with his wife. He has worked as a newspaper reporter and commercial copywriter, but his passion is penning fiction. A self-described science geek, he's a voracious reader of scientific periodicals, as well as a fan of things mysterious, unknown, and on the fringe. That fascination inspired *Extinction Point*, his first novel in a proposed series following heroine Emily Baxter's journey into the bizarre new alien world our earth has become. The first sequel, *Extinction Point: Exodus* will be available soon.